In Red and Gold

by

Samuel Merwin

Double 9
BOOKS

In Red and Gold
by Samuel Merwin

ISBN: 978-93-65787-15-3

Published by

DOUBLE 9 BOOKS

2/13-B, Ansari Road
Daryaganj, New Delhi – 110002
info@double9books.com
www.double9books.com
Tel. 011-40042856

ABOUT THE AUTHOR

Samuel Merwin was an American dramatist and author. Merwin was born on October 6, 1874, in Evanston, Illinois, to Ella B. and Orlando H. Merwin. His father was the postmaster in Evanston. Merwin and Edna Earl Fleshiem got married in 1901. The marriage had two sons, Samuel Kimball Merwin, Jr. and Banister Merwin, as well as an adoptive son named John Merwin. After graduating from Northwestern University, he served as Success magazine's associate editor and later editor from 1905 to 1911. In 1907, the magazine sent him to China to examine the opium trade. He died of a stroke while dining at The Player's Club in Manhattan on October 17, 1936.

CONTENTS

CHAPTER I
FELLOW VOYAGERS

ON a night in October, 1911, the river steamer *Yen Hsin* lay alongside the godown, or warehouse, of the Chinese Navigation Company at Shanghai. Her black hull bulked large in the darkness that was spotted with inadequate electric lights. Her white cabins, above, lighted here and there, loomed high and ghostly, extending as far as the eye could easily see from the narrow wharf beneath. Swarming continuously across the gangplanks, chanting rhythmically to keep the quick shuffling step, crews of coolies carried heavy boxes and bales swung from bamboo poles.

During the evening the white passengers were coming aboard by ones and twos and finding their cabins, all of which were forward on the promenade deck, grouped about the enclosed area that was to be at once their dining-room and "social hall." Here, within a narrow space, bounded by strips of outer deck and a partition wall, these few casual passengers were to be caught, willy-nilly, in a sort of passing comradeship. For the greater part of this deck, amidships and aft, was screened off for the use of traveling Chinese officials, and the two lower decks would be crowded with lower class natives and freight. And, not unnaturally, in the minds of nearly all the white folk, as they settled for the night, arose questions as to the others aboard. For strange beings of many nations dig a footing of sorts on the China Coast, and odd contrasts occur when any few are thrown together by a careless fate.... And so, thinking variously in their separate cabins of the meeting to come, at breakfast about the single long table, and of the days of voyaging into the heart of oldest China, these passengers, one by one, fell asleep; while through open shutters floated quaint odors and sounds from the tangle of sampans and slipper-boats that always line the curving bund and occasional shouts and songs from late revelers passing along the boulevard beyond the rows of trees.

It was well after midnight when the *Yen Hsin* drew in her lines and swung off into the narrow channel of the Whangpoo. Drifting sampans, without lights, scurried out of her path. With an American captain on the strip of promenade deck, forward, that served for a bridge, a yellow pilot, and Scotch engineers below decks, she slipped down with the tide, past the roofed-over opium hulks that were anchored out there, past the dimly outlined stone buildings of the British and American quarter, on into the broader Wusung. Here a great German mail liner lay at anchor, lighted from stem to stem. Farther down lay three American cruisers; and below these a junk, drifting dimly by with ribbed sails flapping and without the sign of a light, built high astern, like the ghost of a medieval trader.

"There's his lights now!" Thus the captain to a huge figure of a man who stood, stooping a little, beside him, peering out at the river. And the captain, a stocky little man with hands in the pockets of a heavy jacket, added—"The dirty devil!"

Indeed, a small green light showed now on the junk's quarter; and then she was gone astern.

After a silence, the captain said: "You may as well turn in."

"Perhaps I will," replied the other. "Though I get a good deal more sleep than I need on the river. And very little exercise."

"That's the devil of this life, of course. Look a' me—I'm fat!" The captain spoke in a rough, faintly blustering tone, perhaps in a nervous response to the well-modulated voice of his mate, "Must make even more difference to you—the way you've lived. And at that, after all, you ain't a slave to the river."

"No.... in a sense, I'm not." The mate fell silent.

There were, of course, vast differences in the degrees of misfortune among the flotsam and jetsam of the coast. Captain Benjamin, now, had a native wife and five or six half-caste children tucked away somewhere in the Chinese city of Shanghai.

"We've gut quite a bunch aboard this trip," offered the captain.

"Indeed?"

"One or two well-known people. There's our American millionaire, Dawley Kane. Took four outside cabins. His son's with him, and a secretary, and a Japanese that's been up with him before. Wonder if it's a pleasure trip—or if it means that the Kane interests are getting hold up the river. It might, at that. They bought the Cantey line, you know, in nineteen eight. Then there's Tex Connor, and his old sidekick the Manila Kid, and a couple of women schoolteachers from home, and six or eight others—customs men and casuals. And Dixie Carmichael—she's aboard. Quite a bunch! And His Nibs gets on tomorrow at Nanking."

"Kang, you mean?"

"The same. There's a story that he's ordered up to Peking. They were talking about it yesterday at the office."

"Do you think he's in trouble?"

"Can't say. But if you ask me, it don't look like such a good time to be easy on these agitators, now does it? And they tell me he's been letting 'em off, right and left."

The mate stood musing, holding to the rail. "It's a problem," he replied, after a little, rather absently.

"The funny thing is—he ain't going on through. Not this trip, anyhow. We're ordered to put him off at his old place, this side of Huang Chau. Have to use the boats. You might give them a look-see."

"They've gossiped about Kang before this at Shanghai."

"Shanghai," cried the captain, with nervous irrelevancy, "is full of information about China—and it's all wrong!" He added then, "Seen young Black lately?"

The mate moved his head in the negative.

"Consul-general sent him down from Hankow, after old Chang stopped that native paper of his. I ran into him yesterday, over to the bank. He says the revolution's going to break before summer."

The mate made no reply to this. Every trip the captain talked in this manner. His one deep fear was that the outbreak might take place while he was far up the river.

It had been supposed by all experienced observers of the Chinese scene, that the Manchu Dynasty would not long survive the famous old empress dowager, the vigorous and imperious little woman who was known throughout a rational and tolerant empire, not without a degree of affection, as "the Old Buddha." She had at the time of the present narrative been dead two years and more; the daily life of the infant emperor was in the control of a new empress dowager, that Lung Yu who was notoriously overriding the regent and dictating such policies of government as she chose in the intervals between protracted periods of palace revelry.

The one really powerful personage in Peking that year was the chief eunuch, Chang Yuan-fu, a former actor, notoriously the empress's personal favorite, who catered to her pleasures, robbed the imperial treasury of vast sums, wreaked ugly vengeance on critical censors, and publicly insulted dukes of the royal house.

All this was familiar. The Manchu strain had dwindled out; and while an empress pleased her jaded appetites by having an actor cut with the lash in her presence for an indifferent performance, all South China, from Canton to the Yangtze, seethed with the steadily increasing ferment of revolution. Conspirators ranged the river and the coast. At secret meetings in Singapore, Tokio, San Francisco and New York, new and bloody history was planned. The oldest and hugest of empires was like a vast crater that steamed and bubbled faintly here and there as hot vital forces accumulated beneath.

The mate, pondering the incalculable problem, finally spoke: "I suppose, if this revolt should bring serious trouble to Kang, it might affect you and me as well."

The captain flared up, the blustering note rising higher in his voice. "But somebody'll have to run the boats, won't they?"

"If they run at all."

His impersonal tone seemed to irritate further the captain's troubled spirit. "If they run at all, eh? It's all right for you—you can go it alone—you haven't got children on your mind, young ones!"

The big man was silent again. A great hand gripped a stanchion tightly as he gazed out at the dark expanse of water. The captain, glancing around at him, looking a second time at that hand, turned away, with a little sound.

"I will say good night," remarked the mate abruptly, and left his chief to his uncertain thoughts.

The steamer moved deliberately out into the wide estuary of the Yangtze, which is at this point like a sea. Squatting at the edge of the deck, outside the rail, the pilot spoke musically to the Chinese quartermaster. Slowly, a little at a time, as she plowed the ruffling water, the steamer swung off to the northwest to begin her long journey up the mighty river to Hankow where the passengers would change for the smaller Ichang steamer, or for the express to Peking over the still novel trunk railway. And if, as happened not infrequently, the *Yen Hsin* should break down or stick in the mud, the Peking passengers would wait a week about the round stove in the old Astor House at Hankow for the next express.

A mighty river indeed, is the Yangtze. During half the year battle-ships of reasonably deep draught may reach Hankow. In the heyday of the sailing trade clippers out of New York and blunt lime-juicers out of Liverpool were any day sights from the bund there. Through a busy and not seldom bloody century the merchants of a clamorous outside world have roved the great river (where yellow merchants of the Middle Kingdom, in sampan, barge and junk, roved fifty centuries before them) with rich cargoes of tea (in leaden chests that bore historic ideographs on the enclosing matting)—with hides and horns and coal from Hupeh and furs and musk from far-away Szechuen, with soya beans and rice and bristles and nutgalls and spices and sesamum, with varnish and tung oil and vegetable tallow, with cotton, ramie, rape and hemp, with copper, quicksilver, slate, lead and antimony, with porcelains and silk. Along this river that to-day divides an empire into two vast and populous domains a thousand thousand fortunes have been gained and lost, rebellions and wars have raged, famines have blighted whole peoples. Forts, pagodas and palaces have lined its banks. The gilded barges of emperors have drifted idly on its broad bosom. Exquisite painted beauties have found mirrors in its neighboring canals. Its waters drain to-day the dusty red plain where Lady Ch'en, the Helen, of China, rocked a throne and died.

The morning sun rode high. Soft-footed cabin stewards in blue robes removed the long red tablecloth and laid a white. By ones and twos the passengers appeared from their cabins or from the breezy deck and took their seats, eying one another with guarded curiosity as they bowed a morning greeting.

Miss Andrews, of Indianapolis, stepped out from her cabin through a narrow corridor, and then, at sight of the table, stopped short, while her color rose slightly. Miss Andrews was slender, a year or so under thirty, and, in a colorless way, pretty. Shy and sensitive, the scene before her was one her mind's eye had failed to picture; the seats about the long table were half filled, and entirely with men. She saw, in that one quick look, the face of a young German between those of two Englishmen. A remarkably thin man in a check suit looked up and for an instant fixed furtive eyes on hers. Just beyond him sat a big man, with a round wooden face and one glass eye; he turned his head with his eyes to look at her. A quiet man of fifty-odd, with gray hair, a nearly white mustache that was cropped close, and the expression of quiet satisfaction that only wealth and settled authority can give, was putting a spoonful of condensed milk into his coffee. Next to him sat a young man—very young, certainly not much more than twenty or twenty-one—perhaps his son (the aquiline nose and slightly receding but wide and full forehead were the same)—rubbing out a cigarette on his butter plate. He had been smoking before breakfast. She remembered these two now; they had been at the Astor House in Shanghai; they were the Kanes, of New York, the famous Kanes. They called the son, "Rocky"—Rocky Kane.

Unable to take in more, Miss Andrews stepped back a little way into the corridor, deciding to wait for her traveling companion, Miss Means, of

South Bend. She could hardly go out there alone and sit down with all those men.

But just then a door opened and closed; and across the way, coming directly, easily, out into the diningroom, Miss Andrews beheld the surprising figure of a slim girl—or a girl she appeared at first glance—of nineteen or twenty, wearing a blue, middy blouse and short blue shirt. Her black hair was drawn loosely together at the neck and tied with a bow of black ribbon. Her somewhat pale face, with its thin line of a mouth, straight nose, curving black eyebrows and oddly pale eyes, was in some measure attractive. She took her seat at the table without hesitation, acknowledging the reserved greetings of various of the men with a slight inclination of the head.

It seemed to Miss Andrews that she might now go on in there. But the thought that some of these men had surely noticed her confusion was disconcerting; and so it was a relief to hear Miss Means pattering on behind her. For that firmly thin little woman had fought life to a standstill and now, except in the moments of prim severity that came unaccountably into possession of her thoughts, found it dryly amusing. They took their seats, these two little ladies, Miss Means laying her copy of *Things Chinese* beside her coffee cup; and Miss Andrews tried to bow her casual good mornings as the curious girl in the middy blouse had done. The girl, by the way, seemed a very little older at close view.

Miss Andrews stole glimpses, too, at young Mr. Rocky Kane. He was a handsome boy, with thick chestnut hair from which he had not wholly succeeded in brushing the curl, but she was not sure that she liked the flush on his cheeks, or the nervous brightness of the eyes, or the expression about the mouth. There had been stories floating about the hotel in Shanghai. He plainly lacked discipline. But she saw that he might easily fascinate a certain sort of woman.

A door opened, and in from the deck came an extraordinarily tall man, stooping as he entered. On his cap, in gilt, was lettered, "1st Mate." He took the seat opposite Mr. Kane, senior, next to the head of the table. It seemed to Miss Andrews that she had never seen so tall a man; he must have stood six feet five or six inches. He was solid, broad of shoulder, a magnificent specimen of manhood. And though the hair was thin on top of his head, and his grave quiet face exhibited the deep lines of middle age, he moved with almost the springy-step of a boy. If others at the table were difficult to place on the scale of life, this mate was the most difficult of all. With that strong reflective face, and the bearing of one who knows only good manners (though he said nothing at all after his first courteously spoken, "Good morning!") he could not have been other than a gentleman—Miss

Andrews felt that—an American gentleman! Yet his position.... mate of a river steamer in China....!

The atmosphere about the table was constrained throughout the meal. The Chinese stewards padded softly about. The one-eyed man stared around the table without the slightest expression on his impassive face. The girl in the middy blouse kept her head over her plate. Miss Andrews once caught Rocky Kane glancing at her with an expression nearly as furtive as that of the thin man in the check suit. It was after this small incident that young Kane began helping her to this and that; and, when they rose, followed her out to her deck chair and insisted on tucking her up in her robe.

"These fall breezes are pretty sharp on the river," he said. "But say, maybe it isn't hot in summer."

"I suppose it is," murmured Miss Andrews.

"I've been out here a couple of times with the pater. You'll find the river interesting. Oh, not down here"—he indicated the wide expanse of muddy water and the low-lying, distant shore—"but beyond Chinkiang and Nanking, where it's narrower. Lots of quaint sights. The ports are really fascinating. We stop a lot, you know. At Wuhu the water beggars come out in tubs."

"In tubs!" breathed Miss Andrews.

Miss Means joined them then, book under arm; and met his offer to tuck her up with a crisply pointed, "No, thank you!"

He soon drifted away.

Said Miss Andrews: "Weren't you a little hard on him, Gerty?"

"My dear," replied Miss Means severely—her Puritan vein strongly uppermost—"that young man won't do. Not at all. I saw him myself, one night at the Astor House, going into one of those private dining-rooms with a woman who—well, her character, or lack of it, was unmistakable!... Right there in the hotel.... under his father's eyes. That's what too much money will do to a young man, if you ask me!"

"Oh....!" breathed Miss Andrews, looking out with startled eyes at the gulls.

It was mid-afternoon when Captain Benjamin remarked to his first mate: "Tex Connor's got down to work, Mr. Duane. Better try to stop it, if you don't mind. They're in young Kane's cabin—sixteen."

Number sixteen was the last cabin aft in the port side, next the canvas screen that separated upper class white from upper class yellow. The wooden shutters had been drawn over the windows and the light turned on within. Cigarette smoke drifted thickly out.

They were slow to open. Doane heard the not unfamiliar voice of the Manila Kid advising against it. He had to knock repeatedly. They were crowded together in the narrow space between berth and couch, a board across their knees—Connor twisting his head to fix his one eye on the intruder, the Kid, in his check suit, a German of the customs and Rocky Kane. There were cards, chips and a heap of money in American and English notes and gold.

"What is it?" cried Kane. "What do you want?"

"You'd better stop this," said the mate quietly.

"Oh, come, we're just having a friendly game! What right have you to break into a private room, anyway?"

The mate, stooping within the doorway, took the boy in with thoughtful eyes, but did not reply directly.

Connor, with another look upward, picked up the cards, and with the uncanny mental quickness of a practised *croupier* redistributed the heap of money to its original owners, and squeezed out without a word, the mate moving aside for him. The German left sulkily. The Kid snapped his fingers in disgust, and followed.

Doane was moving away when the Kid caught his elbow. He asked: "Did Benjamin send you around?"

Doane inclined his head.

"Running things with a pretty high hand, you and him!"

"Keep away from that boy," was the quiet reply.

The thin man looked up at the grave strong face above the massive shoulders; hesitated; walked away. The mate was again about to leave when young Kane spoke. He was in the doorway now, leaning there, hands in pockets, his eyes blazing with indignation and injured pride.

"Those men were my guests!" he cried.

"I'm sorry, Mr. Kane, to disturb your private affairs, but—"

"Why did you do it, then?"

"The captain will not allow Tex Connor to play cards on this boat. At least, not without a fair warning."

The boy's face pictured the confusion in his mind, as he wavered from anger through surprise into youthful curiosity.

"Oh...." he murmured. "Oh.... so that's Tex Connor."

"Yes. And Jim Watson with him. He was cashiered from the army in the Philippines. He is generally known now, along the coast, as the Manila Kid."

"So that's Tex Connor!.... He managed the North End Sporting in London, three years ago."

"Very likely. I believe he is known in London and Paris."

"He's a professional gambler, then?"

"I am not undertaking to characterize him. But if you would accept a word of advice—"

"I haven't asked for it, that I'm aware of." An instant after he had said this, the boy's face changed. He looked up at the immense frame of the man before him, and into the grave face. The warm color came into his own. "Oh, I'm sorry!" he cried. "I needn't have said that." But confusion still lay behind that immature face. The very presence of this big man affected him to a degree wholly out of keeping with the fellow's station in life, as he saw it. But he needn't have been rude. "Look here, are you going to say anything to my father?"

"Certainly not."

"Will the captain?"

"You will have to ask him yourself. Though you could hardly expect to keep it from him long, at this rate."

"Well—he's so busy! He shuts himself up all day with Braker, his secretary. The chap with the big spectacles. You see"—Kane laughed self-consciously; a naively boyish quality in him, kept him talking more eagerly than he knew—"the pater's reached the stage when he feels he ought to put himself right before the world. I guess he's been a great old pirate, the pater—you know, wrecking railroads and grabbing banks and going into combinations. Though it's just what all the others have done. From what I've heard about some of them—friends of ours, too!—you have to, nowadays, in business. No place for little men or soft men. It's a two-fisted game. This fellow spent a couple of years writing the pater's autobiography:—seems funny, doesn't it!—and they're going over it together on this trip. That's why Braker came along; there's no time at home. The original plan was to have Braker tutor me. That was when I broke out of college. But, lord!...."

"You'll excuse me now," said the mate.

Meantime the Manila Kid had sidled up to the captain.

"Say, Cap," he observed cautiously, "wha'd you come down on Tex like that for?"

"Oh, come," replied the captain testily, not turning, "don't bother me!"

"But what you expect us to do all this time on the river—play jackstraws?"

"I don't care what you do! Some trips they get up deck games."

"Deck games!" The Kid sniffed.

"You'll find plenty to read in the library"

"Read!...."

"Then I guess you'll just have to stand it."

For some time they stood side by side without speaking; the captain eying the river, the Kid moodily observing water buffalo bathing near the bank.

"Tex has got that Chinese heavyweight of his aboard—down below."

"Oh—that Tom Sung?"

"Yep. Knocked out Bull Kennedy in three rounds at the Shanghai Sporting. Got some matches for him up at Peking and Tientsin. Taking him over to Japan after that. There's an American marine that's cleaned up three ships'." He was silent for a space; then added: "I suppose, now, if we was to arrange a little boxing entertainment, you wouldn't stand for that either, eh?"

"Oh, that's all right. Take the social hall if the ladies don't object. But who would you put up against him?"

"Well—if we could find a young fellow on board, Tex could tell Tom to go light."

"You might ask Mr. Doane. He complains he ain't getting exercise enough."

"He's pretty old—still, I'd hate to go up against him myself.... Say, you ask him, Cap!"

"I'll think it over. He's a little.... I'll tell you now he wouldn't stand for your making a show of it. If he did it, it 'ud just be for exercise."

"Oh, that's all right!"

Miss Means awoke with a start. It was the second morning out, at sunrise. The engines were still, but from without an extraordinary hubbub rent the air. Drums were beating, reed instruments wailing in weird dissonance, and innumerable voices chattering and shouting. A sudden crackling suggested fire-crackers in quantity. Miss means raised herself on one elbow, and saw her roommate peeping out over the blind.

"What is it?" she asked.

"It looks very much like the real China we've read about," replied Miss Andrews, raising her voice above the din. "It's certainly very different from Shanghai."

The steamer lay alongside a landing hulk at the foot of broad steps. Warehouses crowded the bank and the bund above, some of Western construction; but the crowded scene on hulk and steps and bund, and among the matting-roofed sampans, hundreds of which were crowded against the bank, was wholly Oriental. From every convenient mast and pole pennants and banners spread their dragons on the fresh early breeze. A temporary *pen-low*, or archway, at the top of the steps was gay with fresh paint and streamers. In the air above were scores of kites, designed and painted to represent dragons and birds of prey, which the owners were maneuvering in mimic aerial warfare; swooping and darting and diving. As Miss Means looked, one huge painted bird fell in shreds to a neighboring roof, and the swarming assemblage cheered ecstatically.

Soldiers were marching in good-humored disorder down the bund, in the inevitable faded blue with blue turbans wound about their heads. It appeared as if not another person could force his way down on the hulk without crowding at least one of its occupants into the water, yet on they came; and so far as our two little ladies could see none fell. Fully two hundred of the soldiers there were, with short rifles and bayonets. Amid great confusion they formed a lane down the steps and across to the gangway.

Next came a large, bright-colored sedan chair slung on cross-poles, with eight bearers and with groups of silk-clad mandarins walking before and behind. Farther back, swaying along, were eight or ten more chairs, each with but four bearers and each tightly closed, waiting in line as the chair of the great one was set carefully down on the hulk and opened by the attending officials.

Deliberately, smilingly, the great one stepped out. He was a man of seventy or older, with a drooping gray mustache and narrow chin beard of gray that contrasted oddly with the black queue. His robe was black with a square bit of embroidery in rich color on the breast. Above his hat of office a huge round ruby stood high on a gold mount, and a peacock feather slanted down behind it.

Bowing to right and left, he ascended the gangplank, the mandarins following. There were fifteen of these, each with a round button on his plumed hat—those in the van of red coral, the others of sapphire and lapis lazuli, rock crystal, white stone and gold.

One by one the lesser chairs were brought out on the hulk and opened. From the first stepped a stout woman of mature years, richly clad in heavily embroidered silks, with loops of pearls about her neck and shoulders, and with painted face under the elaborately built-up head-dress. Other women of various' ages followed, less conspicuously clad. From the last chair appeared a young woman, slim and graceful even in enveloping silks, her face, like the others, a mask of white paint and rouge, with lips carmined into a perfect cupid's bow. And with her, clutching her hand, was a little girl of six or seven, who laughed merrily upward at the great steamer as she trotted along.

Blue-clad servants followed, a hundred or more, and swarming cackling women with unpainted faces and flapping black trousers, and porters— long lines of porters—with boxes and bales and bundles swung from the inevitable bamboo poles.

At last they were all aboard, and the steamer moved out.

"Who were all those women, in the chairs, do you suppose?" asked Miss Andrews.

"His wives, probably."

"Oh....!"

"Or concubines."

Miss Andrews was silent. She could still see the waving crowd on the wharf, and the banners and kites.

"He must be at least a prince, with all that retinue."

Miss Andrews, thinking rapidly of Aladdin and Marco Polo, of wives and concubines and strange barbarous ways, brought herself to say in a nearly matter-of-fact voice: "But those women all had natural feet. I don't understand."

Miss Means reached for her *Things Chinese*; looked up "Feet,"

"Women,"

"Dress," and other headings; finally found an answer, through a happy inspiration, under "Manchus."

"That's it!" she explained; and read: "'The Manchus do not bind the feet of their women.'"

"Well!" Thus Miss Andrews, after a long moment with more than a hint of emotional stir in her usually quiet voice: "We certainly have a remarkable assortment of fellow passengers. That curious silent girl in the middy blouse.... traveling alone..."

"Remarkable, and not altogether edifying," observed the practical Miss Means.

CHAPTER II
BETWEEN THE WORLDS

TOWARD noon Miss Means and Miss Andrews were in their chairs on deck, when a gay little outburst of laughter caught their attention, and around the canvas screen came running the child they had seen on the wharf at Nanking. A sober Chinese servant (Miss Means and Miss Andrews were not to know that he was a eunuch) followed at a more dignified pace.

The child was dressed in a quilted robe of bright flowered silk, the skirt flaring like a bed about the ankles, the sleeves extending down over the hands. Her shoes were high, of black cloth with paper soles. Over the robe she wore a golden yellow vest, shortsleeved, trimmed with ribbon and fastened with gilt buttons. Over her head and shoulders was a hood of fox skin worn with the fur inside, tied with ribbons under the chin, and decorated, on the top of the head, with the eyes, nose and ears of a fox. As she scampered along the deck she lowered her head and charged at the big first mate. He smiled, caught her shoulders, spun her about, and set her free again; then, nodding pleasantly to the eunuch, he passed on.

Before the two ladies he paused to say: "We are coming into T'aiping, the city that gave a name to China's most terrible rebellion. If you care to step around to the other side, you'll see something of the quaint life along the river."

"He seems very nice—the mate," remarked Miss Andrews. "I find myself wondering who he may have been. He is certainly a gentleman."

"I understand," replied Miss Means coolly, "that one doesn't ask that question on the China Coast." They found the old river port drab and dilapidated, yet rich in the color of teeming human life. The river, as usual, was crowded with small craft. Nearly a score of these were awaiting the steamer, each evidently housing an entire family under its little arch of matting, and each extending bamboo poles with baskets at the ends. As the steamer came to a stop, a long row of these baskets appeared at the rail, while cries and songs arose from the water.

The little Manchu girl had found a friend in Mr. Rocky Kane. He was holding her on the rail and supplying her with brass cash which she dropped gaily into the baskets. The eunuch stood smiling by. After tiffin the child appeared again and sought her new friend. She would sit on his knee and pry open his mouth to see where the strange sounds came from. And his cigarettes delighted her.

It was the Manila Kid himself who asked Miss Means and Miss Andrews if they would mind a bit of a boxing: match in the social hall. They promptly withdrew to their cabin, after Miss Means had uttered a bewildered but dignified: "Not in the least! Don't think of us!"

Shortly after dinner the cabin stewards stretched a rope around four pillars, just forward of the dining table. The men lighted cigarettes and cigars, and moved up with quickening interest. Tex Connor, who had disappeared directly after the coffee, brought in his budding champion, a large grinning yellow man in a bathrobe. The second mate, and two of the engineers found seats about the improvised rings. Then an outer door opened, and the great mandarin appeared, bowing and smiling courteously with hands clasped before his breast. The fifteen lesser mandarins followed, all rich color and rustling silk.

The young officers sprang to their feel and arranged chairs for the party. The great man seated himself, and his attendants grouped themselves behind him.

Into this expectant atmosphere came the mate, in knickerbockers and a sweater, stooping under the lintel of the door, then straightening up and stopping short. His eyes quickly took in the crowded little picture— the gray-bearded mandarin in the ringside chair, backed with a mass of Oriental color; that other personage, Dawley Kane, directly opposite, with the aquiline nose, the guardedly keen eyes and the quite humorless face, as truly a mandarin among the whites as was calm old Kang among the yellows; the flushed eager face of Rocky Kane; the other whites, all smoking, all watching him sharply, all impatient for the show. He frowned; then, as the mandarin smiled, came gravely forward, bent under the rope and addressed him briefly in Chinese.

The mandarin, frankly pleased at hearing his own tongue, rose to reply. Each clasped his own hands and bowed low, with the observance of a long-hardened etiquette so dear to the Oriental heart.

"How about a little bet?" whispered Rocky Kane to Tex Connor. "I wouldn't mind taking the big fellow."

"What odds'll you give?" replied the impassive one.

"Odds nothing! Your man's a trained fighter, and he must be twenty years younger."

"But this man Doane's an old athlete. He's boxed, off and on, all his life. And he's kept in condition. Look at his weight, and his reach."

"What's the distance?"

"Oh—six two-minute rounds."

"Who'll referee?"

"Well—one of the Englishmen."

But the Englishmen were not at hand. A friendly bout between yellow and white overstepped their code. One of the customs men, an Australian, accepted the responsibility, however.

"I'll lay you a thousand, even," said Rocky Kane.

"Make it two thousand."

"I'll give you two thousand, even," said Dawley Kane quietly.

"Taken! Three thousand, altogether—gold."

The mate, turning away from the mandarin, caught this; stood motionless looking at them, his brows drawing together.

"Gentlemen," he finally remarked, "I came here with the understanding that it was to be only a little private exercise. I had no objection, of course, to your looking on, some of you, but this...."

"Oh, come!" said Connor. "It's just for points. Tom's not going to fight you."

Young Kane, gripping the rope nervously with both hands, cried: "You wouldn't quit!"

The mate looked down at these men. "No," he replied, in the same gravely quiet manner, "I shall go on with it. I do this"—he made the point firmly, with a dignity that in some degree, for the moment, overawed the younger men—"I do it because his excellency has paid us the honor of coming here in this democratic way. He tells me that he is fond of boxing. I shall try to entertain him." And he drew the sweater over his head, and caught the gloves that the Kid tossed him.

The elder Kane shrewdly took him in. The authority of the man was not to be questioned. Without so much as raising his voice he had dominated the strange little gathering. Physically he was a delight to the eye; anywhere In the forties, his hair thin to the verge of baldness, his strong sober face deeply lined, yet with shoulders, arms and chest that spoke of great muscular power and a waist without a trace of the added girth that middle age usually brings; of sound English stock, doubtless; the sort that in the older land would ride to hounds at eighty.

Dawley Kane looked, then, at the Chinese heavyweight. This man, though not quite a match in size for the giant before him, appeared every inch the athlete. Kane understood the East too well to find him at all surprising; he had seen the strapping northern men of Yuan Shi K'ai's new army; he knew that the trained runners of the Imperial Government were expected, on occasion, to cover their hundred miles in a day; in a word, that the curious common American notion of the Chinese physique was based on an occasional glimpse of a tropical laundryman. And he settled back in his comfortable chair confident of a run for his money. The occasion promised, indeed, excellent entertainment.

The mate, still with that slight frown, glanced about. Not one of the crowded eager faces about the ropes exhibited the slightest interest in himself as a human being. He was but the mate of a river steamer; a man who had not kept up with his generation (the reason didn't matter)—an individual of no standing.... He put up his hands.

Tom Sung fell into a crouch. With his left shoulder advanced, his chin tucked away behind it, he moved in close and darted quick but hard blows to the stomach and heart. Duane stepped backward, and edged around him, feeling him out, studying his hands and arms, his balance, his footwork. It early became clear that he was a thoroughgoing professional, who meant to go in and make a fight of it.... Doane, sparring lightly, considered this. Conner, of course, had no sportsmanship.

Tom's left hand shot up through Doane's guard, landing clean on his face with a sharp thud; followed up with a remarkably quick right swing that the mate, by sidestepping, succeeded only in turning into a glancing blow. And then, as Doane ducked a left thrust, he uppercut with all his strength. The blow landed on Doane's forearms with a force that shook him from head to foot.

A sound of breath sharply indrawn came from the spectators, to most of whom it must have appeared that the blow had gone home. Doane, slipping away and mopping the sweat from eyes and forehead, heard the sound; and for an instant saw them, all leaning forward, tense, eager for a knockout, the one possible final thrill.

The yellow man was at him again, landing left, right and left on his stomach, and butting a shaven head with real force against his chin. For an instant stars danced about his eyes. Elbows had followed the head, roughing at his face. Doane, quickly recovering, leaped back and dropped his hands.

In Red and Gold | 23

"What is this?" he called sharply to Connor, whose round expressionless face with its one cool light eye and thin little mouth looked at him without response. "Head? Elbows? Is your man going to box, or not?"

The eyes that turned in surprise about the ringside were not friendly. These men cared nothing for his little difficulties; their blood was up. They wanted what the Americans among them would term "action" and "results."

Tom was tearing at him again. So it was, after all, to be a fight. No preliminary understandings mattered. He felt a profound disgust, as by main strength he stopped rush after rush, making full use of his greater reach to pin Tom's arms and hurl him back; a disgust however, that was changing gradually to anger. He had known, all his life, the peculiar joy that comes to a man of great strength and activity in any thorough test of his power.

The customs man called time.

Rocky Kane—flushed, excited, looking like a boy—felt in his pockets for cigarettes; found none; and slipped hurriedly out to the deck.

There a silken rustle stopped him short.

A slim figure, enveloped in an embroidered gown, was moving back from a cabin window. The light from within fell—during a brief second—full on an oval face that was brightly painted, red and white, beneath glossy black hair. The nose was straight, and not wide. The eyes, slanted only a little, looked brightly out from under penciled brows. She was moving swiftly toward the canvas screen; but he, more swiftly, leaped before her, stared at her; laughed softly in sheer delighted surprise. Then, with a quick glance about the deck, breathing out he knew not what terms of crude compliment he reached for her; pursued her to the rail; caught her.

"You little beauty!" he was whispering now. "You wonder! You darling! You're just too good to be true!" Beside himself, laughing again, he bent over to kiss her. But she wrenched an arm free, fought him off, and leaned, breathless, against the rail.

"Little yellow tiger, eh?" he cried softly. "Well, I'm a big white tiger!"

She said in English: "This is amazing!"

He stood frozen until she had disappeared behind the canvas screen. Then he staggered back; stumbled against a deck chair; turning, found the strange thin girl of the middy blouse stretched out there comfortably in her rug.

She said, with a cool ease: "It's so pleasant out here this evening, I really haven't felt like going in."

With a muttered something—he knew not what—he rushed off to his cabin; then rushed back into the social hall.

The customs man called time for the second round.

As Doane advanced to the center of the ring, Tom rushed, as before, head down. Doane uppercut him; then threw him back, forestalling a clinch. The next two or three rushes he met in the same determined but negative way; hitting a few blows but for the most part pushing him off. The sweat kept running into his eyes as he exerted nearly his full strength. And Tom Sung's shoulders and arms glistened a bright yellow under the electric lights.

Rocky Kane, lighting a cigarette and tossing the blazing match away, called loudly: "Oh, hit him! For God's sake, do something! Don't be afraid of a Chink!"

Doane glanced over at him. Tom rushed. Doane felt again the crash of solid body blows delivered with all the force of more than two hundred pounds of well-trained muscle behind them. Again he winced and retreated. He knew well that he could endure only a certain amount of this punishment.... Suddenly Tom struck with the sharpest impact yet. Again that hard head butted his chin; an elbow and the heel of a glove roughed his face.... Doane summoned all his strength to push him off. Then he stepped deliberately forward.

At last the primitive vigor in this giant was aroused. His eyes blazed. There was no manner of pleasure in hurting a fellow man of any color; but since the particular man was asking for it, insisting on it, there was no longer a choice. The fellow had clearly been trained to this foul sort of work. That would be Connor's way, to take every advantage, place a large side bet and then make certain of winning. There was, of course, no more control of boxing out here on the coast than of gambling or other vice.

When Tom next came forward, Doane, paying not the slightest heed to his own defense, exchanged blows with him; planted a right swing that raised a welt on the yellow cheek. A moment later he landed another on the same spot.

At the sound of these blows the men about the ringside straightened up with electric excitement. Then again the long muscular right arm swung, and the tightly gloved fist crashed through Tom's guard with a force that knocked him nearly off his balance. Doane promptly brought him back with a left hook that sounded to the now nearly frantic spectators as if it must have broken the cheek-bone.

Tom crouched, covered and backed away.

"Have you had enough?" Doane asked. As there was no reply, he repeated the question in Chinese.

Tom, instead of answering, tried another rush, floundering wildly, swinging his arms.

Doane stepped firmly forward, swinging up a terrific body blow that caught the big Chinaman at the pit of the stomach, lifted his feet clear of the floor and dropped him heavily in a sitting position, from which he rolled slowly over on his side.

"What are you trying to do?" cried the Manila Kid, above the babel of excited voices, as he rushed in there and revived his fellow champion. "What are you trying to do—kill 'im?"

The mate stripped off his wet gloves and tossed them to the floor. "Teach your man to box fairly," he replied, "or some one else will." With which he stepped out of the ring, drew on his sweater and, with a courteous bow to the mandarin, went out on deck. There, after depositing with the purser the winnings paid over by a surly Connor, Dawley Kane found him.

"Well!" cried the hitherto calm financier, "you put up a remarkable fight."

Doane looked down at him, unable to reply. He was still breathing hard; his thoughts were traveling strange paths. He heard the man saying other things; asking, at length, about the mandarin.

"He is Kang Yu," Doane replied now, civilly enough, "Viceroy of Nanking."

"No! Really? Why, he was in America!"

"He toured the world. He has been minister at Paris, Berlin, London, I believe. He is a great statesman—certainly the greatest out here since Li Hung Chang."

"No—how extremely interesting!"

"He is ruler of fifty million souls, or more." The mate had found his voice. He was speaking a thought quickly, with a very little heat, as if eager to convince the great man of America of the standing and worth of this great man of China. "He has his own army and his own mint. He controls railroads, arsenals, mills and mines. Incidentally, he is president of this line."

"The Chinese Navigation Company? Really! You are acquainted with him yourself?"

"No. But he is a commanding figure hereabouts. And of course, I—at present I'm an employee of the Merchants' Line."

"Oh, yes! Yes, of course! You seem to speak Chinese."

"Yes"—the mate's voice was dry now—"I speak Chinese."

A shuffling sound reached their ears. Both turned. The viceroy had come out of the cabin and was advancing toward them, followed by all his mandarins. Before them he paused, and again exchanged with the mate the charming Eastern greeting. In Chinese he said—and the language that needs only a resonant, cultured voice to exhibit its really great dignity and beauty, rolled like music from his tongue: "It will give me great pleasure, sir, if you will be my guest to-morrow at twelve."

The mate replied, with a grave smile and a bow: "It is a privilege. I am your servant."

They bowed again, with hands to breast. And all the mandarins bowed. Then they moved away in stately silence to their quarters aft.

Kane spoke now: "How very curious! Very curious!"

Doane said nothing to this.

"They really appear to have charm, these upper class people. It's a pity they are so poorly adapted to the modern struggle."

Doane looked down at him, then away. As a man acquainted with the East he knew the futility of discussing it with a Western mind; above all with the mind of a successful business man, to whom activity, drive, energy, were very religion.

His own thoughts were ranging swiftly back over two thousand years, to the strong civilization of the Han Dynasty, when disciplined Chinese armies kept open the overland route to Bactria and Parthia, that the silks and porcelains and pearls might travel safely to waiting Roman hands; to the later, richer, riper centuries of Tang and Sung, after Rome fell, when Chinese civilization stood alone, a majestic fabric in an otherwise crumbled and chaotic world—when certain of the noblest landscapes and portraits ever painted were finding expression, when philosophers held high dreams of building conflicting dogma into a single structure of comprehensive and serene faith. The Chinese alone, down the uncounted centuries, had held their racial integrity, their very language. Surely, at some mystical but seismic turning of the racial tide, they would rise again among the nations.

This giant, standing there in sweater and knickerbockers, bareheaded, gazing out at the dark river, was not sentimentalizing. He knew well enough the present problems. But he saw them with half-Eastern eyes; he saw America too, with half-Eastern eyes—and so he could not talk at all to the very able man beside him who saw the West and the world with wholly Western eyes. No, it was futile. Even when the great New Yorker, who had just won two thousand dollars, gold, spoke with wholly unexpected kindness, the gulf between their two minds remained unfathomable.

"I want you to forgive me, sir—I do not even know your name, you see—but, frankly, you interest me. You are altogether too much of a man for the work you are doing here. That is clear. I would be glad to have you tell me what the trouble is. Perhaps I could help you."

This from the man who held General Railways in the hollow of his hand, and Universal Hydro-Electric, and Consolidated Shipping, and the Kane, Wilmarth and Cantey banks, a chain that reached literally from sea to sea across the great young country that worshiped the shell of political freedom as insistently as the Chinese worshiped their ancestors, yet gave over the newly vital governing power of finance into wholly irresponsible private hands.

The situation, grotesque in its beginning, seemed now incredible to Doane. He drew a hand across his brow; then spoke, with compelling courtesy but with also a dismissive power that the other felt: "You are very kind, Mr. Kane. At some other time I shall be glad to talk with you. But my hours are rather exacting, and I am tired."

"Naturally. You have given a wonderful exhibition of what a man of character can do with his body. I wish I had you for a physical trainer. And I wish the example might start my boy to thinking more wholesomely... Good night!" And he extended a friendly hand.

Mr. Kane's boy presented himself on the following morning as an acute problem. He was about the deck, shortly after breakfast, playing with the Manchu child. Then, after eleven, Captain Benjamin handed his mate a note that had been scribbled in pencil on a leaf torn from a pocket note-book and folded over. It was addressed:

"To the Chinese Lady who spoke English last night." And the content was as follows: "I shouldn't have been rude, but I must see you again. Can't you slip around the canvas this evening, late? I'll be watching for you." There was no signature.

"Make it out?" asked the captain. "Old Kang sent it up to me—asks us to speak to the young man. But how'm I to know which young man it is?"

"Do you know how it was sent?"

"Yes. The little princess took it back."'

"It won't be hard to find the man."

"You know?"

"I think so."

"Well, just put him wise, will you?"

"I'll speak to him."

"Wait a minute! You thinking of young Kane?"

The mate inclined his head.

"Well—you know who he is, don't you? Who they are?"

Doane bowed again.

"Better use a little tact."

Doane walked back along the deck to cabin sixteen. A fresh breeze blew sharply here; the chairs had all been moved across to the other side where the sunlight lay warm on the planking. Within the social hall the second engineer—a wistful, shy young Scot—had brought his battered talking machine to the dining table and was grinding out a comic song. Two or three of the men were in there, listening, smoking, and sipping highballs; Doane saw them as he passed the door. Through the open but shuttered window of cabin number twelve came the clicking of a typewriter and men's voices, that would be Mr. Kane, discussing his "autobiography" with its author.

Before number sixteen, Doane paused; sniffed the air. A curious odor was floating out through these shutters, an odor that he knew. He sniffed again; then abruptly knocked at the door.

A drowsy voice answered! "What is it? What do you want?"

"I must see you at once," said Doane.

There was a silence; then odd sounds—a faint rattling of glass, a scraping, cupboard doors opening and closing. Finally the door opened a few inches. There was Rocky Kane, hair tousled, coat, collar and tie removed, and shirt open at the neck. Doane looked sharply at his eyes; the pupils were abnormally small. And the odor was stronger now and of a slightly choking tendency.

"What are you looking at me like that for?" cried young Kane, shrinking back a little way.

"I think," said Doane, "you had better let me come in and talk with you."

"What right have you got saying things like that? What do you mean?"

"I have really said nothing as yet."

Kane, seeming bewildered, allowed the door to swing inward and himself stepped back. The big mate came stooping within.

"Your note has been returned," he said shortly; and gave him the paper.

Kane accepted it, stared down at it, then sank back on the couch.

"What's this to you!" he managed to cry. "What right.... what do you mean, saying I wrote this?"

"Because you did. You sent it back by the little girl."

"Well, what if I did! What right—"

"I am here at the request of his excellency, the viceroy of Nanking. You have been annoying his daughter. The fact that she chooses, while in her father's household, to wear the Manchu dress, does not justify you in treating her otherwise than as a lady. Perhaps I can't expect you to understand that his exellency is one of the greatest statesmen alive to-day. Nor that this young lady was educated in America, knows the capitals of Europe better, doubtless, than yourself, and is a princess by birth. She went to school in England and to college in Massachusetts. Take my advice, and try no more of this sort of thing."

The boy was staring at him now, wholly bewildered. "Well," he began stumblingly, "perhaps I have been a little on the loose. But what of it! A fellow has to have some fun, doesn't he?"

The mate's eyes were taking in keenly the crowded little room.

"Well," cried Kane petulantly, "that's all, isn't it? I understand! I'll let her alone!"

"You don't feel that an apology might be due?"

"Apologize? To that girl?"

"To her father."

"Apologize—to a Chink?"

The word grated strangely on Doane's nerves. Suddenly the boy cried out: "Well—that's all? There's nothing more you want to say? What are you—what are you looking like that for?"

The sober deep-set eyes of the mate were resting on the high dresser at the head of the berths. There, tucked away behind the water caraffe, was a small lamp with a base of cloisonné work in blue and gold and a small, half globular chimney of soot-blackened glass.

"What are you looking at? What do you mean?"

The boy writhed under the steady gaze of this huge man, who rested a big hand on the upper berth and gazed gravely down at him; writhed, tossed out a protesting arm, got to his feet and stood with a weak effort at defiance.

"Now I suppose you'll go to my father!" he cried. "Well, go ahead! Do it! I don't care. I'm of age—my money's my own. He can't hurt me. And he knows I'm on to him. Don't think I don't know some of the things he's done—he and his crowd. Ah, we're not saints, we Kanes! We're good fellows—we've got pep, we succeed—but we're not saints."

"How long have you been smoking opium?" asked the mate.

"I don't smoke it! I mean I never did. Not until Shanghai. And you needn't think the pater hasn't hit the pipe a bit himself. I never saw a lamp until he took me to the big Hong dinner at Shanghai last month. They had 'em there. And it wasn't all they had, either—"

"If you are telling me the truth," said the mate.

—"I am. I tell you I am."

"—Then you should have no difficulty in stopping. It would take a few weeks to form the habit. You can't smoke another pipe on this boat."

"But what right—good lord, if the pater would drag me out here, away from all my friends.... you think I'm a rotter, don't you!"

"My opinion is not in question. I must ask you to give me, now, whatever opium you have."

Slowly, moodily, evidently dwelling in a confusion of sulky resentful thoughts, the boy knelt at the cupboard and got out a small card-board box.

The mate opened it, and found several shells of opium within. He promptly pitched it out over the rail.

"This is all?" he asked.

"Well—look in there yourself!"

But the mate was looking at the suit-case, and at the trunk beneath the lower berth.

"You give me your word that you have no more?"

"That's—all," said the boy.

The mate considered this answer; decided to accept it; turned to go. But the boy caught at his sleeve.

"You do think I'm a rotter!" he cried. "Well, maybe I am. Maybe I'm spoiled. But what's a fellow to do? My father's a machine—that's what he is—a ruthless machine. My mother divorced him ten years ago. She married that English captain—got the money out of father for them to live on, and now she's divorced him. Where do I get off? I know I'm overstrung, nervous. I've always had everything I want. Do you wonder that I've begun to look for something new? Perhaps I'm going to hell. I know you think so. I can see it in your eyes. But who cares!"

Doane stood a long time at the rail, thinking. The ship's clock in the social hall struck eight bells. Faintly his outer ear caught it. It was time to join his excellency.

CHAPTER III
MISS HUI FEI

THE luncheon table of his excellency was simply set, with two chairs of carven blackwood, behind a high painted screen of six panels. It was at this screen that the first mate (left by a smiling attendant) gazed with a frown of incredulity. Cap in hand, he stepped back and studied the painting, a landscape representing a range of mountains rising above mist in great rock-masses, chasms where tortured trees clung, towering, lagged peaks, all partly obscured by the softly luminous vapor—a scene of power and beauty. Much of the brighter color had faded into the prevailing tones of old ivory yellow shading into some thing near Rembrandt brown; though the original, reds and blues still held vividly in the lower right foreground, where were pictured very small, exquisite in detail yet of as trifling importance in the majestic scheme of the painting as are man and his works in all sober Chinese thought when considered in relation to the grim majesty of nature, a little friendly cluster of houses, men at work, children at play, domestic animals, a stream with a water buffalo, a bridge, a wayfarer riding a donkey, and cultivated fields. The ideographic signature was in rich old gold, inscribed with unerring decorative instinct on a flat rock surface.

The mate bent low and looked closely at the brush-work; then stepped around an end panel and examined the texture of the silk.

"Ah!"—it was a musical deep voice, speaking in the mandarin tongue—"you admire my screen, Griggsby Doane." The name was pronounced in English.

His excellency wore a short jacket of pale yellow over a skirt of blue, both embroidered in large circles of lotus flowers around centers of conventional good-fortune designs, in which the swastika was a leading motive. His bared head was shaved only at the sides, as the top had long been bald. He looked gentle and kind as he stood leaning on his cane and extending a wrinkled hand; smiling in the fashion of forthright friendship. The thin little gray beard, the unobtrusively courteous eyes, the calm manner, all gave him an appearance of simplicity that made it momentarily difficult to think of him as the great negotiator of the tangled problems of statesmanship involved in the expansion of Japan, the man who very nearly convinced Europe of American good faith during the agitated discussion and correspondence that arose out of the "Open Door" proposals of John Hay, a man known among the observant and informed in London, Paris and Washington as a great statesman and a greater gentleman.

"I thought at first"—thus the mate, touched by the fine honor done him (an honor that would, he quickly felt, demand tact on the bridge)—"that it was a genuine Kuo Hsi."

"No. A copy."

"So I see. A Ming copy—at least the silk appears to be Ming—the heavy single strand, closely woven. And the seals date very closely. If it were woven of double strands, even in the warp alone, I should not hesitate to call it a genuine Northern Sung."

"You observe closely, Griggsby Doane. It is supposed that Ch'uan Shih made this copy." His smile was now less one of kindness and courtesy than, of genuine pleasure. "You shall see the original."

"You have that also, Your Excellency?"

"In my home at Huang Chau."

"I have never seen a genuine panting of Kuo Hsi. It would be a great privilege. I have read some of the sayings attributed to him, as taken down by his son. One I recall—'If the artist, without realizing his ideal, paints landscapes with a careless heart, it is like throwing earth upon a deity, or casting impurities into the clean wind.'"

"Yes," added his excellency, almost eagerly, "and this—'To have in landscape the opportunity of seeing water and peaks, of hearing the cry of monkeys and the song of birds, without going from the room.'" Servants appeared bearing covered dishes. His excellency placed the mate in the seat commanding the wider view of the river. A clear broth was served, followed by stewed shell fish with cassia mushrooms, steamed sharks' fins set red with crabmeat and ham, roast duck stuffed with young pine needles, and preserved pomegranates, carambolas and plums, followed by small cups of rice wine.

The conversation lingered with the great Sung painters, passing naturally then to the conflict during the eleventh and twelfth centuries between the free vitality of Buddhist thought and the deadening formalism of the Confucian tradition.

And Doane's thoughts, as he listened or quietly spoke, dwelt on the attainments and character of this great man who was so simple and so friendly. His excellency had spoken his own full name, Griggsby Doane, which would mean that the wide-reaching, instantly responsive facilities for gathering information that may be set at work by the glance of a viceroy's eye or a movement of his jeweled finger had been brought into play within the twenty-four hours.

"My heart is there in the Sung Dynasty," his excellency said. "I never look upon the old canals of Hang Chow or the ruins of stone-walled lotus gardens by the Si-hu without sadness. And Kai-feng-fu to-day wrings my heart."

"Truly," mused Doane, "it was in the days of Tang and Sung that the soul of China so nearly found its freedom."

"You indeed understand, Griggsby Doane!" The two English words stood out with odd emphasis in the musical flow of cultured Chinese speech. "Had that spirit endured, China would to-day, I like to think, have Korea and Manchuria and Mongolia and Sin Kiang. China would not to-day wear a piteous smile on the lips, turning the head to hide tears of shame, while the Russians absorb our northern frontiers and the French draw tribute from Annam and Yunnan, while the English control this great valley of the Yangtze, while the Germans drive their mailed fist into Shantung, and the Japanese send their spies throughout all our land and stand insolently at the very gate of the Forbidden City. I could not, perhaps, speak my heart freely to one of my own countrymen, but to you I can say, Confucian scholar though they may term me, that since what you call the thirteenth century there has been a gradual paralysis of the will in China, a softening of the political brain.... You will permit an old man this latitude? I have served China without thought of self during nearly fifty years. To the Old Buddha I was ever a loyal servant. If toward the new emperor and the empress dowager I find it impossible to feel so deeply, my heart is yet devoted to the throne and to my people. If while sent abroad in service of my country it has been given me to see much of merit in Western ways, it is not that I have become a revolutionist, a traitor to the government of my ancestors."

There was a light in the kindly eyes; a strong ring in the deep voice. He went on:

"No, I am not a traitor. It is not that. It is that my country has suffered, is now prostrate, with a long sickness. She must be helped; but she must as well help herself. She is like one who has lain too long abed. She must think, arise, act. With my poor eyes I can see no other hope for her. Even though I myself may suffer, I can not, in truth to my own faith, punish those who, loving China as deeply as I myself love her, yet feel that they must goad her until she awakens from her pitiful sleep of more than six centuries.... Nor am I a republican. China is not like your country. In an imperial throne I must believe. Yet, she must listen to all, study all, draw from all. Freedom of thought there must be. We must not longer worship books and the dead. We must learn to look about us and on before."

Their chairs were drawn about to the window's. Slowly the wide river slipped off astern.

"But you, Griggsby Doane, why are you here? This is not the life for which you so laboriously and so worthily prepared yourself. I knew of you over in T'ainan-fu. You were a true servant of your faith. After the dreadful year of the Boxers you returned to your task. And during the trouble in nineteen hundred and seven, the fighting with the Great Eye Society in Hansi, you conducted yourself with bravery. I was at Sian-fu that year, and was well informed. Yet you gave up the church mission."

The mate's eyes were fixed gloomily on the long vista of the river. For a moment it seemed as if he would speak; and the viceroy, seeing his lips part, leaned a little way forward; but then the lips were closed tightly and the great head bent deliberately forward.

"I knew," continued his excellency, "when the Asiatic Company of New York was negotiating with me the contract for rebuilding the banks of the Grand Canal in Kiang-su that you had gone from T'ainan, and that you had, as well, left the church. You had even gone from China."

"That was in nineteen nine," said Doane, in the somber voice of one who thinks moodily aloud. "I was in America then."

"Yes, it was in your year nineteen nine. For a time those negotiations hung, I recall, on the question of the means to be employed in dealing with local resentments. The trouble over the Ho Shan Company in Hansi, of which you knew so much and which you met with such noble courage, had taught us all to move with caution."

"My position in that Hansi trouble has not been clearly understood, Your Excellency. I was there only, a short time, and was ill at that."

The viceroy smiled, kindly, wisely. "You went alone and on foot from T'ainan-fu to So T'ung in the face of a Looker attack, and yourself settled that tragic business. You then walked, without even a night's rest, the fifty-five *li* from T''ainan to Hung Chan. There, at the city gate, you were attacked and severely wounded, and crawled to the house of a Christian native. But while still weak and in a fever you walked the three hundred *li* to Ping Yang and made your way through the Looker army into Monsieur Pourmont''s compound...."

He pronounced the two words "Monsieur Pour-mont" in French. What a remarkable old man he was—mentally all alive, sensitive as a youth to the quick currents of life! The accuracy of his information, like his memory, was surprising. Though to the Westerner, every normal Chinese memory is that. Merely learning the language needs or builds a memory....

Most surprising was that so deep attention had been given to Doane's own small case. The fact bewildered; was slow in coming home. For Kang was a great man; his proper preoccupations were many; that he was a poet, and had early aspired to the laureateship, was commonly known—indeed, Doane had somewhere his own translation of Kang's *Ode to the Rich Earth*, from the scroll in the author's calligraphy owned by Pao Ting Chuan at T'ainan-fu. As an amateur in the art of his own land of fine taste and sound historical background he was known everywhere; his collection of early paintings, porcelains, jades and jewels being admittedly one of the most valuable remaining in China. And he was reputed to be the richest individual not of the royal blood (excepting perhaps Yuan Shi K'ai).

A contrast, not untinged with a passing bitterness, arose in Doane's mind. Here before him quietly sat this so-called yellow man who was more competent than perhaps any other to select his own art treasures and write his own poems and state papers; whose journals, known to exist, must inevitably, if not lost in a war-torn land, take their place as a part of China's history; a man who was at once manufacturer, financier, and statesman, on whom for a decade a weakening throne had leaned. While in the cabin forward was a great white man as truly representative of the new civilization as was Kang of the old; yet who hired men of special knowledge to select the art treasures that would be left, one day, in his name and as a monument to his culture, who even employed a trained writer to pen the work that he proposed unblushingly to call his "autobiography." For such a man as Dawley Kane, whatever his manners, Doane felt now, knew only the power of money. Through that alone his genius functioned; the rest was a lie. On the one hand was culture, on the other—something else. The thought bit into his brain.

But his excellency had not finished:

"And there, my dear Griggsby Doane, while still suffering from your wound, you learned that those in Monsieur Pourmont's compound were cut off from communication with their nationals at Peking. You at once volunteered to go again, alone, through the Looker lines to the railhead with messages, and successfully did so.... Do you wonder, my dear young friend, that knowing this, and more, of your honesty and personal force from my one-time assistant, Pao Ting Chuan, of T'ainan-fu, I pressed strongly on the gentlemen from New York who represented the Asiatic Company my desire that they secure you to act as their resident director? And do you wonder that I regretted your refusal so to act?"

This statement came to Doane as a surprise.

"They offered me a position, yes," he said, pondering on the inexplicable ways in which the currents of life meet and cross. "But they told me nothing of your interest."

His excellency smiled. "It might have raised your price. They would think of that. The sharpest trading, Griggsby Doane, is not done in the Orient. That I have learned from a long lifetime of struggling against the aggressions of white nations. During the discussion of the concerted loan to China—you recall it?—they talked of lending us a hundred million dollars, gold. To read your New York papers was to think that we were almost to be given the money. It seemed really a philanthropy. But do you know what their left hands were doing while their right hands waved in a fine gesture of aid to the struggling China? These were the terms. First they subtracted a large commission—that for the bankers themselves; then, what with stipulations of various sorts as to the uses to which the money—or the credit—was to be put, mostly in purchases of railway and war material from their own hongs at further huge profits to themselves, they whittled it down until the actual money to be expended under our own direction, amounted to about fifteen millions. And with that went immense new concessions—really the signing away of an empire—and new foreign supervision of our internal affairs. For all these privileges we were to pay an annual interest and later repay the full amount, one hundred millions. It was quite unbearable." He sighed. "But what is poor old China to do?"

Doane nodded gravely. "I felt all that—the sort of thing—when I talked with representatives of the Asiatic Company. Not that I blamed them, of course. It is a point of view much larger than any of them; they are but part of a great tendency. I couldn't go into it."

"Why not?" The viceroy's keen eyes dropped to the slightly faded blue uniform, then rested again on the strong face.

"The past few years—I will pass over the details—have been—well, not altogether happy for me. I have been puzzled. All the rich years of my younger manhood were given to the mission work. But I had to leave the church. At first I felt a joy in simple hard work—I am very strong—but hard work alone could not satisfy my thoughts."

"No.... No."

"For a time I believed that the solution of my personal problem lay in taking the plunge into commercial life. I had come to feel, out there, that business was, after all, the natural expression of man's active nature in our time."

"Yes. Doubtless it is."

"It was in that state of mind that I returned home—to the States. But it proved impossible. I am not a trader. It was too late. My character, such as it was and is, had been formed and hardened in another mold. I talked with old friends, but only to discover that we had between us no common tongue of the spirit. Perhaps if I had entered business early, as they did, I, too, would have found my early ideals being warped gradually around to the prevailing point of view."

"The point stands out, though," said the viceroy, "that you did not enter business. You chose a more difficult course, and one which leaves you, in ripe middle age, without the means to direct your life effectively and in comfort."

"Yes," mused Doane, though without bitterness. "I feel that, of course. And it is hard, very hard, to lose one's country. Yet...."

His voice dropped. He sat, elbow on crossed knees, staring at the ever-changing river. When he spoke again, the bitter undertone was no longer in his voice. He was gentler, but puzzled; a man who has suffered a loss that he can not understand.

"All my traditions," he said, "my memories of America, were of simple friendly communities, a land of earnest religion, of political freedom. In my thoughts as a younger man certain great figures stood out—Washington, Lincoln, Charles Sumner, Wendell Philips, Philips Brooks and—yes, Henry Ward Beecher. I had deeply felt Emerson, Longfellow, Lowell and Whittier. The Declaration of Independence could still fire my blood. And it was such a land of simple faith that I tried for so many years, however ineffectually, to represent here in China. To be sure, disquieting thoughts came—church disunity, the spectacle of unbridled license among so many of my fellow countrymen in the coast ports, the methods of certain of our great corporations in pushing their wares in among your people. But even when I found it necessary to leave the church, I still believed deeply in my country."

He paused to control a slight unsteadiness of voice; then went on:

"May I ask if you, Your Excellency, after your long visits in Europe, have not come home to meet with something the same difficulty, to find yourself looking at your own people with the eyes of a stranger, receiving such an impression as only a stranger can receive?"

"Indeed, yes!" cried the viceroy softly, with deep feeling. "It is the most difficult moment, I have sometimes felt, in a man's life. It is the summit of loneliness, for there is no man among his friends who can share his view, and there is none who would not misunderstand and censure him. And yet, a country, a people, like a city, does present to the alien eye, a complete impression, it exhibits clearly outlined characteristics that can be observed in no other way. Even the alien lose that clear, true impression on very short acquaintance. He then becomes, like all the others, a part of the picture he has once seen."

"It is so, Your Excellency. My country, in that first, startled, clear glance, affected me—I may as well use the word—unpleasantly. It was utterly different from anything I had known, a trader's paradise, a place of unbelievable confusion, of an activity that bewildered, rushing to what end I could not understand."

He was speaking now not only in the Chinese language but in the idiom as well, generalizing rhetorically as the Chinese do. It was almost as if the words came from a Chinese mind.

They were silent for a time Then the viceroy asked, in his gently abrupt way: "Why did you leave the church?"

"Because I sinned."

"Against the church?"

"That, and my own faith."

"Were you asked to leave?"

"No."

"They knew of your sin?"

"I told them."

"Yet they would have kept you?"

"Yes. My own feeling was that my superior temporized."

"He knew your value."

"I can not say as to that. But he wished me to marry again. I couldn't do that—not in the spirit intended. Not as I felt."

"We are different, Griggsby Doane, you and I. I am a Manchu, you an American. The customs of our two lands are very different. What would seem a sin to you, might not seem so to me. Yet I, too, have a conscience to which I must answer. I believe I understand you. It is, I see, because of your conscience that you sit before me now, on this boat and in this uniform, a man, as your great Edward Everett Hale has phrased it, without a country."

He paused, and filled again the little pipe-bowl, studied it absently as his wrinkled fingers worked the tobacco. His nails were trimmed short, like those of a white man. Doane thought, swiftly, of the man's dramatic past, sent out as he had been to become a citizen of the world by a nation that would in very necessity fail to understand the resulting changes in his outlook. There was his daughter; she would be almost an American, after four years of college life. And she, now, would be a problem indeed! What could he hope to make of her life in this Asia where woman, like labor in his own country, was a commodity. It would be absorbingly interesting, were it possible, to peep into that smooth-running old brain and glimpse the problems there. They were gossiping about him. His stately figure was to-day the center about which coiled the life and death intrigue of Chinese officialdom and over which hung suspended the silken power of an Oriental throne.... Doane's personal problem shrank into nothing—a flitting memory of a little outbreak of egotism—as he studied the old face on which the revealing hand of Age had inscribed wisdom, kindliness and shrewdness.

Soft footfalls sounded; then, after a moment, a sharper sound that Doane assumed, with a slight quickening of the imagination, to be the high wooden clogs of a Manchu lady, until he realized that no clogs could move so lightly; no, these were little Western shoes.

A young woman appeared, slender and comely, dressed in a tailored suit that could have come only front New York, and smiling with shy eagerness. She was of good height (like the Manchus of the old stock), the face nearly oval, quite unpainted and softly pretty, with a broad forehead that curved prettily back under the parted hair, arched eyebrows, eyes more nearly straight than slanting (that opened a thought less widely than those of Western people), and with a quaint, wholly charming friendliness in her smile.

He felt her sense of freedom; and knew as she tried to take his huge hand in her own small one that she carried her Western ways, as her own people would phrase it, with a proud heart. She was of those aliens who would be happily American, eager to show her kinship with the great land of fine free traditions.

And holding the small hand, looking down at her, Doane found his perhaps overstrained nerves responding warmly to her fine youth and health. He reflected, in that swift way of his wide-ranging mind, on the amazing change in Chinese official life that made it even remotely possible for the viceroy to present his daughter with a heart as proud as hers. The change had come about during the term of Doane's own residence.... America, then, was not alone in changing. It was a shaking, puzzled and puzzling world.

"This," his excellency was saying, "is my daughter, Hui Fei."

"I am very pleas' to meet you," said Hui Fei.

They sat then. The girl became at once, as in America, the center of the talk. Though of the heedlessness not uncommonly found among American girls she had none. She was prettily, sensitively, deferential to her father. Somewhere back of the bright surface brain from which came the quick eager talk and the friendly smile, deep in her nature, lay the sense of reverence for those riper in years and in authority that was the deepest strain in her race. She dwelt on things almost utterly American: the brightness of New York—she said she liked it best in October, when the shops were gay; the approaching Yale-Harvard football game, a motoring tour through the White Mountains, happy summers at the seashore.

Doane watched her, speaking only at intervals, wondering if there might not be, behind her gentle enthusiasm, some deeper understanding of her present situation. He could not surely make out. She had humor, and when he asked if it did not seem strange to step abruptly back into the old life, she spoke laughingly of her many little mistakes in etiquette. Her English he found charming. She was continually slipping back into it from the Mandarin tongue she tried to use, and as continually, with great gaiety, reaching back into Chinese for the equivalent phrase. She had so nearly conquered the usual difficulty with the l's and r's as to confuse them only when she spoke hurriedly. At these times, too, she would leave off final consonants. The long *e* became then, a short *i*. Doane even smiled, with an inner sense of pleasure, at her pretty emphasis when she once converted *people* into *pipple*. She was, unmistakably, a young woman of charm and personality. Despite the quaintness of her speech, she was accustomed to thinking in the new tongue. Her command of it was excellent; better than would commonly be found in America. All of which, of course, intensified the problem.

His excellency sat back, smoked comfortably, and looked on her with frankly indulgent pride.

A servant came with a message; bowing low. The viceroy excused himself, leaving his daughter and Doane together. Doane asked himself, during the pause that followed his departure, what the observant attendants beyond the screen would be thinking. The situation, from any familiar Chinese point of view, was unthinkable. Yet here he sat; and there, her brows drawn together (he saw now) in sober thought, sat delightful Miss Hui Fei.

She said, in a low voice, while looking out at the river: "Mr. Doane, no matter what you may think—I mus' see you. This evening. You mus' tell me where. It mus' not be known to any one. There are spies here."

Doane glanced up; then, too, looked away. There could be no question now of the girl's deeper feeling. She was determined. Her tune was honest and forthright, with the unthinking courage of youth. It would be her father, of course...

But his mind had gone blank. He knew not what to think or say.

"Please!" she murmured. "There is no one else. You must help us. Tell me—father will be coming back."

And then Griggsby Doane heard his own voice saying quietly: "The boat deck is the only place. You will find a sort of ladder near the stern. If you can—"

"I will go up there."

"It will be only just after midnight that I could arrange to be there."

His excellency returned then. And Doane took his leave. He had been but a few moments in his own cabin when two actors of his excellency's suite appeared, each with a lacquered tray, on one of which was a small chest of tea, wrapped in red paper lettered in gold and bearing the seal stamp of the private estate of Kang Yu, on the other an object of more than a foot in height carefully wound about with cotton cloth.

Doane dismissed the lictors with a Mexican dollar each and unwrapped the larger object, which the servant had placed with great care on his berth. It proved to be a *pi*, a disk of carven jade, in color a perfect specimen of the pure greenish-white tint that is so highly prized by Chinese collectors. The diameter was hardly less than ten inches, and the actual width of the stone from the circular inner opening to the outer rim about four inches. It stood on edge set in a pedestal of blackwood, the carving of which was of unusual delicacy. The pedestal was, naturally, modern, but Doane, with a mounting pulse, studied the designs cut into the stone itself. That cutting had been done not later than the Han Dynasty, certainly within two hundred years of the birth of Christ.

CHAPTER IV
INTRIGUE

THE *Yen Hsin* would arrive at Kiu Kiang by mid-afternoon.

Half an hour earlier. Doane, on the lower deck, came upon a group of his excellency's soldiers—brown deep chested men, picturesque in their loose blue trousers bound in above the ankles and their blue turbans and gray cartridge belts—conversing excitedly in whispers behind the stack of coffins near the stern. At sight of him they broke up and slipped away.

A moment later, passing forward along the corridor beside the engine room, he heard his name: "Mr. Doane! If you please!" This in English.

He turned. Just within the doorway of one of the low-priced cabins stood a pedler he had observed about the lower decks; a thin Chinese with an overbred head that was shaped, beneath the cap, like a skull without flesh upon it; the eyes concealed behind smoked glasses.

"May I have a word with you, Mr. Doane?"

The mate considered; then, stooping, entered the tiny cabin. The pedler closed the door; quietly shot the bolt; then removed his cap and the queue with it, exposing a full head of stubbly black hair, trimmed, as is said, pompadour. The glasses came off next; discovering wide alert eyes. And now, without the cap, the head, despite the hair and the seriously intellectual face, looked, balanced on its thin neck, more than ever like a skull.

"You will not know of me, Mr. Doane. I am Sun Shi-pi of Shanghai. I was attached, as interpreter, to the yamen of the tao-tai. I left his service some months ago to join the republican revolutionary party. I was arrested shortly after that at Nanking and condemned to death, but his excellency, the viceroy—"

"Kang?"

"Yes. He is on this boat. He released me on condition that I go to Japan. I kept my word—to that extent; I went to Japan—but I could not keep my word in spirit. My life is consecrated to the cause of the Chinese Republic. Nothing else matters. I returned to Shanghai, and was made commander there of the 'Dare-to-dies.' You did not know of such an organization? You will, then, before the winter is gone. We shall be heard from. There are other such companies—at Canton, at Wuchang—at Nanking—at every center."

Doane seated himself on the narrow couch and studied the quietly eager young man.

"You speak English with remarkable ease," he said.

"Oh, yes. I studied at Chicago University. And at Tokio University I took post-graduate work."

"And you are frank."

"I can trust you. You are known to us, Mr. Doane. Wu Ting Fang trusts you—and Sun Yat Sen, our leader, he knows and trusts you."

"I did know Sun Yat Sen, when he was a medical student."

"He knows you well. He has mentioned your name to us. That is why I am speaking to you. America is with us. We can trust Americans."

Doane's mind was ranging swiftly about the situation. "You are running a risk," he said.

Sun Shi-pi shrugged his shoulders. "I shall hardly survive the revolution. That is not expected among the 'Dare-to-dies.'"

"If his excellency's soldiers find you here they will kill you now."

"The officers would, of course. Many of the soldiers are with us. Anyway, it doesn't matter."

"What is your errand?"

"I will tell you. The revolution, as you doubtless know, is fully planned."

"I've assumed so. There has been so much talk. And then, of course, the outbreak in Szechuen."

"That was premature. It was the plan to strike in the spring. This fighting in Szechuen has caused much confusion. Sun Yat Sen is in America. He is going to England, and can hardly reach China within two months. He will bring money enough for all our needs. He is the organizer, the directing genius of the new republic. But the Szechuen outbreak has set all the young hotheads afire."

"I am told that the throne has sent Tuan Fang out there to put down the disturbance. But we have had no news lately."

"That is because the wires are cut. Tuan Fang will never come back. We will pay five thousand taels, cash, to the bearer of his head, and ask no questions. We must exterminate the Manchus. It has finally come down to that. It is the only way out. But we must pull together. Did you know that the Wu Chang republicans plan to strike at once?"

"No."

"I have been sent there to tell them to wait. That is our gravest danger now. If we pull together we shall win. If our emotions run away with our judgment—"

"The throne will defeat your forces piecemeal and destroy your morale."

"Exactly. My one fear is that I may not reach Wu Chang in time. But"—with a careless gesture—"that is as it may be. I will tell you now why I spoke to you. We need you. Our organization is incomplete as yet, naturally. One matter of the greatest importance is that our spirit be understood from the first by foreign countries. There is an enormous task—diplomatic publicity, you might call it—which you, Mr. Doane, are peculiarly fitted to undertake You know both China and the West. You are a philosopher of mature judgment. You would work in association with Doctor Wu Ting Fang at our Shanghai offices. There will be money. Will you consider this?"

"It is a wholly new thought," Doane replied slowly. "I should have to give it very serious consideration."

"But you are in sympathy with our aims?"

"In a general way, certainly. Even though I may not share your optimism."

"On your return to Shanghai would you be willing to call at once on Doctor Wu and discuss the matter?"

"Yes.... Yes, I will do that. I must leave you now. We are nearly at Kiu Kiang."

Sun, glancing out the window, raised his hand. Doane looked; two small German cruisers, the kaiser's flag at the taff, were steaming up-stream.

"They know," murmured Sun, with meaning. "I wish to God I could find their means of information. They *all* know. From the Japanese in particular nothing seems to be hidden. Two or three of your American warships are already up there. And the English, naturally, in force."

"They must be on hand to protect the foreign colony at Hankow. The Szechuen trouble would justify such a move."

But Sun shook his head. "They know," he repeated. Then he clasped Doane's hand. "However.... that is a detail. It is now war. You will find events marching fast—faster, I fear, than we republicans wish. Good-by now. You will call on Doctor Wu."

The steamer moved slowly in toward the landing hulk. Doane, from the boat deck, by the after bell pull, gazed across at the park-like foreign bund, with its embankment of masonry and its trees. Behind lay, compactly, the walled city. Everything looked as it had always looked—the curious crowd along the railing, the water carriers passing down and up the steps, the eager shouting swarm of water beggars. Below, the coolies swung out from the hulk, ready to make their usual breakneck leap over green water to the approaching steamer. Now—they were jumping. The passengers were leaning out from the promenade deck to watch and applaud.... Doane's thoughts, as he went mechanically through his familiar duties, wandered off inland, past the battlements and towers of the ancient city to the thousands of other ancient cities and villages and farmsteads beyond; and he wondered if the scores of millions of lethargic minds in all those centers of population could really be awakened from their sleep of six hundred years and stirred into action.

Could a republic, he asked himself, possibly mean anything real to those minds? The habit of mere endurance, of bare existence, was so deep-seated, the struggle to live so intense, the opportunity so slight. Sun Shi-pi and his kind were a semi-Western product. They were, when all was said and done, an exotic breed. They were the ardent, adventurous young; and they were the few. There had always been a throne in China, always extortionate mandarins, always a popular acceptance of conditions.

The lines were out now. And suddenly a blue-clad soldier climbed over the rail, below, balanced along the stern hawser, leaped to the hulk, and was about to disappear among the coolies there when a rifle-shot cracked and he fell. He seemed to fall, if anything, slightly before the shot. Another soldier, following close, was caught by a second shot as he was balancing on the hawser, and spun headlong into the water where the propeller still churned.

A few moments later, when Doane moved among the passengers, it became clear that they knew nothing of the casual tragedy astern. They were all pressing ashore for a walk in the native city, eager to buy the worked silver that is traditionally sold there. The slim girl in the middy blouse had apparently captured young Rocky Kane; they strolled off across the bund together. But Dawley Kane remained aboard, stretched out comfortably in a deck chair, listening thoughtfully to the stocky little Japanese, one Kato, who was by now generally known to be his *alter ego* in the matter of buying objects of Oriental art.

None of these folk knew or cared about China. Excepting this Kato. Him Doane was continually encountering below decks, chatting smilingly in Chinese with the good-natured soldiers. His work along the river, doubtless, ranged over a wider field than his present employer would ever learn. It would be interesting, now, to know what he was saying, talking so rapidly and always, of course, smiling.... The rest of this upper-deck white man's existence Doane dismissed from his mind as he went about his work. It was all too familiar. Though later he thought of Rocky Kane. The boy, wild though he might be, had attractive qualities. It was not pleasant to see that girl get her hands on him. Just one more evil influence.

He thought, at this juncture, of the—the word came—appalling change in himself. That he, once a fervid missionary, could stand back like a sophisticated European, and let the wandering and vicious and broken human creatures about him go their various ways, as might be, was disturbing, was even saddening. Something apparently had died in him. Sun had called him a philosopher. The Oriental, of course, even the blazing revolutionist, admired this passive quality, this fatalistic acceptance of the fact. He sighed. To be a philosopher was, then, to be emotionally dead. The church had been taken out of his life, leaving—nothing. A mate on a river steamer, in China. Life had gone quite topsy-turvey. Even the amazing courtesy of his excellency—it was that, when you considered— and this profound compliment from the revolutionary junta seemed but incidents. Too many promises had smiled at Doane, these years of his spiritual Odyssey—smiled and faded to nothing—to permit an easy hope of anything new and beautiful. He was beginning to believe that a man can not build and live two lives. And he had built and lived one.

Captain Benjamin found him; a dogged little captain with dull fright in his eyes. "It's happened," he said, trying desperately to attain an offhand manner. "Company wire. They're fighting at Wu Chang. What do you know about that!"

Doane was silent. It was extraordinarily difficult, here by this calm old city, on a sunny afternoon, to believe that it was, as Sun had put it, war.

"We're to tie up," the captain went on, "until further orders. The foreign concessions at Hankow were safe enough this noon, but with an artillery battle just across the river, and an imperial army moving down from the north over the railway, they stand a lot of show, they do."

"I wonder if they'll send us on."

"What difference will it make?" The captain's voice was rising. "You know as well as I do that they'll be fighting at Nanking before we could get back there. Here, too, for that matter. I tell you the whole river'll be ablaze by to-morrow. This bloody old river! And us on a Manchu-owned boat! A lot o' chance we stand."

The sight-seers strolled across the shady bund, passed a stone residence or two and a warehouse, and made their way through the tunneled gateway in the massive city wall. Little Miss Andrews was escorted by young Mr. Braker. Miss Means walked with one of the customs men. Two or three others of the men wandered on ahead. Rocky Kane and the thin girl in the middy blouse brought up the rear.

As they entered the crowded city within the wall a babel of sound assailed their ears—the beating of drums and gongs, clanging cymbals, a musket shot or two, fire-crackers; and underlying these, rising even above them, never slackening, a continuous roar of voices. The teachers paused in alarm, but the customs man smilingly assured them that in a busy Chinese city the noise was to be taken for granted.

Nearly every shop along the way was open to the street, and at each opening men swarmed—bargaining, chaffering, quarreling. The only women to be seen were those in black trousers on a wheelbarrow that pushed briskly through the crowds, the barrow man shouting musically as he shuffled along. Beggars wailed from the niches between the buildings. Dogs snarled and barked—hundreds of dogs, fighting over scraps of offal among the hundreds of nearly naked children.

A mandarin came through in a chair of green lacquer and rich gold ornament, supercilious, fat, carried by four bearers and followed by imposing officials who wore robes of black and red and hats with red plumes. As the street was a scant ten feet in width and the crowds must flatten against the walls to make way the roar grew louder and higher in pitch.

There were shops with nothing but oils in huge jars of earthenware or in wicker baskets lined with stout paper. There were tea shops with high pyramids of the familiar red-and-gold parcels, and other pyramids of the brick tea that is carried on camel back to Russia. There were the shops of the idol makers, and others where were displayed the carven animals and the houses and carts and implements that are burned in ancestor worship, and the tinsel shoes. There were shops where remarkably large coffins were piled in square heaps, some of glistening lacquer with the ideograph characters carven or embossed in new gold. There were varnishers, lacquerers, tobacconists; open eating houses in which could be seen rows of pans set into brickwork. There were displays of bean cakes, melon seeds and curious drugs.

Two Manchu soldiers sauntered by, in uniforms of red and faded blue; fans stuck in their belts and painted paper umbrellas folded in their hands. One bore a hooded falcon on his wrist.

Miss Andrews sniffed the penetrating odor of all China, that was spiced just here with smells of garlic cooking and frying fish and pork and strong oil? and—like the perfume of a dainty lady amid the complex odors of a French theater—an unexpected whiff of burning incense. She looked up between the high walls, on which hung, close together, the long elaborate signs of the tradesmen, black and green and red with gold, always the gold. Across the narrow opening from roof to roof, extended a bamboo framework over which was drawn coarse yellow matting or blue cotton cloths; and through these the sunbeams, diffused, glowed in a warm twilight, with here and there a chance ray slanting down with dazzling brightness on a golden sign character.

"It's all rather terrifying," murmured Miss Andrews, at Braker's ear, "but it's beautiful—wonderful! I never dreamed of China being so human and real."

"And to think," said he eagerly, "that it has always been like this, and always will be. It was just so in the days of Abraham and Isaac. The one people in the world that doesn't change. It's their whole philosophy—passive non-resistance, peace. And-do you know, I'm beginning to wonder if they aren't right about it. For here they are, you know. Greece is dead. Rome's dead. And Assyria, and Egypt. But here they are. It's their philosophy that's done it, I suppose. Almost be worth while to come out here and live a while, when our part of the world gets too upset. Just for a sense of stability— somewhere."

These two young persons, dreaming of stability while the earth prepared to rock beneath their feet!

Rocky Kane and the slim girl had dropped out of sight, lingering at this shop and that. The party later found them at a silversmith's counter. They had bought a heap of the silver dragon-boxes and cigarette cases; and then devised a fresh little idea in gambling, weighing ten Chinese dollars against other ten in the balanced scales, the heavier lot winning.

Young Kane had got through his clothing, somehow, there in the street, to his money belt, for he held it now carelessly rolled in one hand. He was flushed, laughing softly. He and the thin girl were getting on.

"Come along, you two," remarked the customs man. "We stop only two hours here."

The young couple, gathering up their purchases and the heaps of silver dollars, slowly followed.

"That was great!" exclaimed Rocky Kane. The thin girl, he had decided, was a good fellow. She was always quiet, discreet, attractive. In her curiously unobtrusive way she seemed to know everything. The face was cold in appearance. Yet she was distinctly friendly. Made you feel that nothing you might say could disturb or shock her. He wondered what could be going on behind those pale quiet eyes, behind the thin lips. The men had remarked on the fact that she was traveling alone. She was a provocative person—the curiously youthful costume; the black hair gathered at the neck and tied, girlishly, with a bow—really an exciting person. The way she had taken that little scene out on deck with the gorgeous Chinese girl—Rocky knew nothing of the distinctions between the Asiatic peoples—who spoke English; quite as a matter of course. Though she took everything that way. This little gambling, for instance. She loved it—was quick at it.

"I'm wondering about you," he said, as they wandered along. "Wondering—you know—why you're traveling this way. Have you got folks up the river?"

"Oh, no," she replied—never in his life had he known such self-control; there wasn't even color in her voice, just that easy quiet way, that sense of giving out no vitality whatever. "Oh, no. I have some business at Hankow and Peking."

That was all she said. The subject was closed. And yet, she hadn't minded his asking. She was still friendly; he felt that. His feelings rose. He giggled softly.

"Lord!" he said, "if only the pater wasn't along!"

"Does he hold you down?"

"Does he? Brought me out here to discipline me. Trying to make me go back to college—make a grind of me.... I was just thinking—here's a nice girl to play with, and plenty of fun around, and not a thing to drink. He gave me fits at Shanghai because I took a few drinks."

"You have the other stuff," said she. He turned nervously; stared at her. But she remained as calmly unresponsive as ever. Merely explained: "I smelt it, outside your cabin. You ought to be careful—shut your window tight when you smoke it."

He held his breath a moment; then realized, with an uprush of feeling warmer than any he had felt before, that he had her sympathy. She would never tell, never in the world. That big mate might, but she wouldn't.

She added this: "I can give you a drink. Wait until things settle down on the boat and come to my cabin—number four. Just be sure there's no one in the corridor. And don't knock. The door will be ajar. Step right in. Do you like saké?"

"Do I—say, you're great! You're wonderful. I never knew a girl like you!"

She took this little outbreak, as she had taken all his others, without even a smile. It was, he felt, as if they had always known each other. They understood—perfectly.

If he had been told, then, that this girl had been during two or three vivid years one of the most conspicuous underworld characters along the coast—that coast where the underworld was still, at the time of our narrative, openly part of what small white world there was out here—a gambler and blackmailer of what would very nearly have to be called attainment—he would have found belief impossible, would have defended her with the blind impulsiveness of youth.

It was said that the steamer would not proceed at the scheduled hour, might be delayed until night. Disgruntled white passengers settled down, in berth and deck chair, to make the best of it. There was, it came vaguely to light, a little trouble up the river, an outbreak of some sort.

Rocky Kane, a flush below his temples, slipped stealthily along the corridor. At number four he paused; glanced nervously about; then, grinning, pushed open the door and softly closed it behind him.

The strange thin Miss Carmichael was combing out her black hair. With a confused little laugh he extended his arms. But she shook her head.

"Sit down and be sensible," she said. "Here's the saké."

She produced a bottle and poured a small drink into a large glass. He gulped it down.

"Aren't you drinking with me?" he asked.

"I never take anything."

"You're a funny girl. How'd you come to have this?"

"It was given to me. You'd better slip along. I can't ask you to stay."

"But when am I going to see you, for a good visit?"

"Oh, there'll be chances enough. Here we are."

"That's so. Looks as if we'd stay here a while, too. There's a battle on, you know, up at Wu Chang and Hankow. Big row. We get all the news from Kato. He's that Japanese that father has with him. The revolutionists have captured Wu Chang, and are getting ready to cross over. The imperial army's being rushed down to defend Hankow. Regular doings. Shells were falling in the foreign concessions this morning. Kato's got all the news there is. It's a question whether we'll go on at all. You see the Manchus own this boat, and the republicans would certainly get after us. There are enough foreign warships up there to protect us, of course.... How about another drink?"

"Better not. Your father will notice it."

"He won't know where I got it." Rocky chuckled. He felt himself an adventurous and quite manly old devil—here in the mysterious girl's cabin, watching her as she smoothed and tied her flowing hair, and sipping the potent liquor from Japan. "It's funny nothing seems to surprise you. Did you know they were fighting up there?"

"No."

"Wouldn't you be a little frightened if we were to steam right into a battle?"

"I shouldn't enjoy it particularly."

"Aren't you even interested? Is there anything you're interested in?"

"Certainly—I have my interests. You must go—really.... No, be quiet! Some one will hear! We can visit to-night—out on deck."

"But you're—I don't understand! Here we are—like this—and you shoo me out. I don't even know your first name."

"My name is Dixie—but I don't want you to call me that."

"Why not? We're friends, aren't we—"

"Of course, but they'd hear you."

"Oh!"

"Wait—I'll look before you go.... It's all clear now."

They visited long after dinner. He was brimming with later advices from the center of trouble up the river. Mostly she listened, studying him with a mind that was keener and quicker and shrewder in its sordid wisdom than he would perhaps ever understand.

Everything that Kato had told his father and himself he passed eagerly on to her. He was a man indeed now; making an enormous impression; possessor of inside information of a vital sort—the viceroy's priceless collection of jewels, jades, porcelains and historic paintings, which Kato was advising his father to pick up for a song while red revolution raged about the old Manchu, the dramatic plans of the republicans, their emblems and a pass-word (Kato knew everything)—"Shui-li"—"union is strength";

the small meeting below decks ending in the death of two soldiers. He dramatized this last as he related it.

The girl, lying still in her chair, listened as if but casually interested, while her mind gathered and related to one another the probable facts beneath his words. She was considering his dominant quality of ungoverned hot-blooded youth. Of discretion he clearly enough had none; which fact, viewed from her standpoint, was both important and dangerous. For the information he so volubly conveyed she had immediate use. That was settled, however cloudy the details. But this further question as to the advisability of holding the boy personally to herself she was still weighing. Two courses of action lay before her, each leading to a possible rich prize. If the two could be combined, well and good; she would pursue both. But it was not easy to sense out a possible combination. The obvious first thought was to go whole-heartedly after the larger of the prizes and as whole-heartedly forget the other. As usual in all such choices, however, the lesser prize was the easier to secure. Perhaps, even, by working—the word "working" was her own—with great rapidity she might make—again her word—a killing with this wild youth in time to discard him and pursue the still richer prize.

Because he was, at least, the bird in hand, she submitted passively when his fingers found hers under the steamer rug. Twilight was thickening into night now on the river. And they were in a dim corner. He was, she saw, at the point of almost utter disorganization. He was sensitive, emotional, quite spoiled. It was almost too easy to do what she might choose with him. It would be amusing to tantalize him, if there were time; watch him struggle in the net of his own nervously unripe emotions, perhaps shake him down (we are yet again dropping into her phraseology) without the surrender of a *quid pro quo*. That would please her sense of cool sharp power. But he might in that event, like the young naval officer down at Hong Kong, shoot himself; which wouldn't do. No, nothing in that!

This other larger matter, now, was a problem indeed; really, as yet, only a haze in her sensitive, strangely gifted mind. It put to the test at once her imagination, her instinct for dangerous enterprise, her skill at organizing the sluggish minds of others. It would mean dangerous and intense activity.

She asked, in a careless manner, where the viceroy kept his treasures; and fixed in her mind the place he named—Huang Chau.

The fool was squeezing her fingers now; unquestionably building in his ungoverned brain an extravagant image of herself; an image wrapped in veils of somewhat tarnished but certainly boyish innocence, sentimentalized, curiously less interesting than the complicated wickedness and intrigue of actual human life as it presented itself to her.

When he tried to kiss her she left him. But lingered to listen to his proposal that she should follow him to his own cabin; smiled enigmatically in the dusk beneath the deck light; humming lightly, pleasingly, she moved away; turned to watch him bolting for his room.

She strolled around the deck then. Apparently none other was sitting out. The teachers and the young men were spending the evening, she knew, with Dawley Kane at the consulate. Rocky had got out of that. Tex Connor was in his cabin; reading, doubtless, with his one good eye. For rough as he might be, this gambler and promoter of boxing and wrestling reveled secretly in love stories. He read them by the hundred, the old-fashioned paper-covered romances and tales of adventure. A pretty able man. Tex; useful in certain sorts of undertakings; certainly useful now; but with that curious romantic strain—a weakness, she felt. And a difficult man, strong, arrogant, leaning on crude power and threats where she leaned on delicately adjusted intrigue. Had Tex known better how to cover his various trails he would be in New York or London now, not out here on the coast picking up small change. Approaching him would be a bit of a problem; for a year or so their ways, hers and his, had lain far apart. It was not known, here on the boat, that they were so much as casually acquainted. They bowed at the dining table; nothing more.

The Manila Kid was in the social hall, rummaging through the shelf of battered and scratched records above the taking machine. A quaint spirit, the Kid; weak, oddly useless, gloomily devoted to music of a simple sort, quite without enterprise. But.... by this time the delicate steel machinery of her mind was functioning clearly.... he would serve now, if only as a means of solving that first little problem of interesting Tex.

She paused in the doorway; caught his furtive eye, and with a slight beckoning movement of her head, moved back into the comparative darkness. Slowly—thick-headedly of course—he came out.

"Jim," she said, "I'm wondering if you and Tex wouldn't like to pick up a little money."

"What do you think we are?" he replied in a guarded sulky voice. "Tex dropped three thousand at that fight. There's no talking to him. He's rough—that's what he is."

"Jim—" she considered the man before her deliberately; his lank spineless figure, his characterless, hatchet face: "Jim, send Tex to me."

"Why should I, Dix? Answer me that."

"Don't act up, Jim. I've never handed you anything that wasn't more than coming to you. I know all about you, Jim. Everything! I'm not talking—

but I know. This is a big proposition I've got in mind, and you'll get your share, if you come in and stick with me? How about half a million in jewels?"

"I don't know's Tex would care to go in for anything like that. If it's a yegg job—"

"I'm not a yegg," she replied crisply. "Ask Tex to slip around here. I don't want to talk on that side of the deck."

"I suppose you wouldn't like young Kane to know what you are—er?"

"That sort of talk won't get you anywhere, Jim."

"Well—I've got eyes, you know."

"Better learn how to use them. You hurry around to Tex's cabin. We may have to move quickly." Sulkily the Kid went; and shortly returned.

"Well"—this after a silence—"what did he say? Is he coming?"

"He wants you to go around there—to his stateroom."

"I won't do that. He's got to come here."

This decision lightened somewhat the gloom on the Kid's saturnine countenance. He went again, more briskly.

The girl slipped into her own cabin and consulted a folding map of China she had there. Huang Chau—she measured roughly from the scale with her thumb—would be seventy or eighty miles up-stream from Kiu Kiang here, perhaps thirty-five down-stream from Hankow.

Tex was chewing a cigar by the rail. At her step his round impassive face turned toward her.

She said, "Hello, Tex!"

He replied, his one eye fixed on her: "Well, what is this job?"

"Listen, Tex—are you game for a big one?"

"What is it?"

"The revolution's broken out at Hankow—or across at Wu Chang—"

"Yes, I know!"

"There's going to be another big battle near Hankow. The republicans are moving over. Sure to be a mix-up."

"Oh yes!"

"There'll be loot—"

"Oh, that!"

"Wait! I know where there's a collection of jewels—diamonds, pearls, rubies, emeralds—all kinds."

"Do you know how to get it?"

"Yes. It's a big thing. We'd be selling stones for years in America and Europe, Will you go in with me, fifty-fifty?"

"What's the risk?"

"Not much—with things so confused. Looks to me like one of those chances that just happens once in a hundred years. Take some imagination and nerve."

"Where is this stuff?"

"I'll tell you when we get there. You'll have to trust me about that. I've never lied to you, and you have lied to me."

"But—"

"Listen! Here's the idea. There's a lot of nervous soldiers on this boat that wouldn't mind a little loot on their own. Here's your boxer—what's his name?"

"Tom Sung." Connor's eye never left her face; and she, on her part, never flinched.

"To those soldiers he's the biggest man on earth. He wouldn't mind a little clean-up either. Oh, there's enough, Tex—plenty! You see what I'm getting at. With your Tom for a leader you can pick up a few of those soldiers, enough to get away clean—"

"But they're shooting 'em!"

"They shot two. They'd have trouble shooting forty. Make Tom do the work—right now, to-night, while we're lying up here. They'll follow him; and you won't have to stand back of him if he's caught. He'll just be one of the rebels then. Get this right, Tex! It's a real chance. You'll never get another like it. With the soldiers we can get a launch—hire it, even, if you want to play safe—and go right up there and get the stuff. Nobody'll ever know it wasn't just a case of soldiers on the loose."

"How're you going to get away? They'd know we weren't here, wouldn't they?"

"Don't try to tell me we couldn't slip out of China, if we had to. This isn't England or America. I don't believe we'd even have to. Just a case of playing it right—using your head."

"Where is this place?"

"It's there, and I'll take you to it."

"You'll have to tell me."

Quietly she moved her head in the negative. He would hardly know that the viceroy was not going on through to Hankow and Peking; she had the information herself only from Rocky Kane. Nor would he know, by any chance, the situation of his excellency's ancestral home. For Tex was not what they termed a "sinologue"; he knew white men and women and yellow servants, the steamers and railways, the gambling clubs and race tracks; little else. There was then, little reason why he should think of the viceroy at all.

"It's anything from a million or two up, Tex," she said coolly. "And my information comes straight. I'll prove it by taking the chance with you."

He shook his head; half turned. "Where is it?" She smiled.

He left her abruptly then. And coolly she watched him go. It would take a little time for Tex's imagination to rise to it; and until the last moment he would try to bluff her down. It was just poker; they had played that game before, she and Tex. Once he had robbed her. But not this time—not, as she phrased it, if she saw him first.

The Kid came edging out of the social hall. "Will he do it?" he whispered hoarsely.

"He says he won't," replied Dixie.

"Say—that's tough! I didn't think Tex would overlook a thing like that. What's the matter?" Dixie now considered this curiously useless man. Or useless he had always seemed to her. Now she was not so sure. "He makes it a condition that I tell him where the stuff is."

"Well—Dix, you'd tell him that, wouldn't you?" The Kid was whining. "If you really knew yourself."

"Of course I won't tell him, Jim. Not yet."

His eyes sank before hers. He fumbled in a pocket; produced a tiny wrist watch of platinum. "Look here. Dix," he remarked clumsily, "things ain't always been's pleasant as they might be between you and I, but I was wondering if you wouldn't put this on, for old times' sake, like."

She took the gift, weighed in in her hand. "Thank you, Jim," she replied. "That's awfully nice of you. Though perhaps I'd better not wear it here on the boat."

"I suppose young Kane might ask questions, eh?"

"Nothing like that. I'll wear it. Here—you snap the catch, Jim."

"I—I might wish it on, Dix, like the kids do."

"All right. Have you wished?"

"Sure, Say, Dix, you won't mind the little place where the initials got scratched off inside the back cover. Nobody'll see that."

"Surely not," said Dixie.

At a little after midnight Griggsby Doane mounted to the boat deck and walked quietly aft past the funnels and the engine room ventilators. A half moon threw shadows along the bund and among the landing hulks and the moored silent sampans, lorchas, junks. The mile-wide river shimmered in a million ripples.

A slight figure rose from a skylight.

Hui Fei wore the black jacket and trousers of the lower class Chinese women below decks. Her head was uncovered, and her hair waved prettily down across the wide forehead. She should have oiled it flat, of course, to complete her disguise; this careless arrangement was charming in the moonlight but was neither Manchu nor Chinese.

Doane found himself holding her small hand and looking gravely down at her. He even slowly shook his head. "You must tell me quickly what you have to say, Miss Hui. As soon as possible you must go back. This is very unsafe."

"Oh, yes," she said. "It will not be long. It is ver' har' to say. But I am so alone. There is no one to tell me what I mus' do."

She plunged bravely into her story. Her information had come from one or another of her maids. And she had overheard gossip among the mandarins. The throne had sent her father the silken cord. She could not discover why. To be sure they called him a secondary devil, meaning one who sympathised with the foreigners. The reactionary Manchus at Peking, reveling and plotting within the sacred walls of the Forbidden City, remembered nothing, it appeared, of the recent past. The eunuchs, always the stormy petrels of China's darkest days, were again in power at the palace; the great empress dowager, she whom all China termed, half-affectionately, "the Old Buddha," had given them their head, and now this new young empress with all the arrogance of the Old Buddha and none of her genius for power or her profound experience, was running wild. And as a consequence, Kang Yu, the statesman who more than any other was equipped to counsel her wisely during this stormy time, was returning to the home of his ancestors to die by his own hand. It would be said at the

Forbidden City that a gracious empress dowager had "permitted" him to go.... Doane's disturbed thoughts darted back over the bloodstained recent history of Manchu officialdom. The Old Buddha had "permitted" Ch'i Ying, late Manchu Viceroy of Canton, to slay himself; and had graciously extended the same privilege to others after the Boxer trouble of the year 1900, among them an acquaintance of Doane's, Chao Shu-ch'iao. Others she had decapitated—Yuan Ch'ang, Li Shan, Controller of the Household, and Hsu Ching, President of the Board of War. She killed, too, Hsu Ching-Ch'eng, who, like Kang, had held the post of minister in more than one of the capitals of Europe. The only known charge against this Hsu was that he had come to admire foreign customs.

In her narrative the girl spoke only English. Her voice was deep in quality, without heaviness; musical, like most voices among the better-to-do in the Middle Kingdom, Chinese and Manchu alike. And, colored now with deep emotion, it had an appealing quality to which Doane found a response—difficult, at the moment, to repress—among his own emotions. He sensed, too, with a pleasure that was, in his lonely life, stirring, the naiveté of her Western feeling. Standing here in simple native costume, in the heart of old China, gazing wistfully out over the tangled hundreds of sleeping junks and sampans, this girl, freshly out of a Massachusetts college, was pleading against hope that her father might be spared the final jealous vengeance of the mightiest remaining Oriental throne.

The China that Doane had so long known, that had, indeed, for better or worse, been woven into the fiber of his being, was turning suddenly incredible. He stared, more intently than he knew, straight down at the slim little figure—for beside his own huge frame this tall girl appeared as hardly more than a child—at the unadorned face that was softly girlish, at the Mack hair waving down over the pale forehead, glistening in the moonlight.

"They mean to confisca'"—she left off, in her eagerness to explain, the final *te*—"all his property. Tell me, Mister Duane, can they do that—all his property?"

He reflected. There would be vast areas of tea-lands and rice lands, almost innumerable shares in these new corporations, the famous collections of jades, paintings, carvings and jewels. Finally he inclined his head.

"I'm afraid they could. It would be an outrageous act, but the government now, I'm sorry to say, is in outrageous hands. If the empress is determined, as apparently she is, there are ways enough of getting at all his possessions. Even through the banks." His heart was full, his voice tender;

but he could not deceive her. He added a question: "Does his excellency, your father, know all this?"

She nodded. "I have tol' him. But I can no' make him see it like me. Oh, we are so differen'. I am, you see, an American girl. I am free here," she laid a pretty hand on her breast. "When I try to think of all these dreadful things—of these wicked eunuchs an' the empress who is like thousan' of years ago—blin', childish!—an' the people who can no' yet see it differen'—I get bewilder'. You un'erstan'. You are an American, too. I can speak with you. That is well, because there isn' anybody else I can speak with. An' my father admires you. If you will only speak with him—if you will only help me make him think differen'!"

Doane wondered what he could do, what she imagined he could do, without influence or money. He quite forgot, in this matter of influence alone, the significance of the viceroy's courtesy, as of Sun Shi-pi's appeal to him. For a little too long he had been a beaten man. It was becoming dangerously near a habit so to consider himself. And now, to make active clear thinking impossible, emotion flooded his brain. Gently he asked her what she would have him do.

"My father will no' listen when I speak, He is ver' kind, ver' generous. He has made me an American girl. That is one of the things they say is wrong. Even for tha' they attack his good name. But when I ask Him no' to do this, no' to die so wrongly, he speaks to me like an ol' Manchu of long ago."

"He is between the worlds," mused Doane, aloud.

"Yes, it is that. An' I, perhaps, am between the worl's."

"And I."

"But he mus' no' do it! It is so simple! The throne will no' live. Not one year more. I know that. They are fighting now at Wu Chang."

Doane inclined his head. "I know that, Miss Hui, but the revolution has not yet gone so far that success is sure."

"But it is sure. The people will everywhere rise. I know it—here!"

"That is my hope, too. But to stir this great land means so much in effort and education. You have changed, yes. Your father has changed. Sun Yat Sen was educated in a medical school and has lived in America and England; he has changed. But all China—I do not want to dash your hopes, dear Miss Hui, but I fear China is not nearly so far along as you and I would wish."

"Then—even so—mus' my father die because a wicked empress has no brains? It is no' right. Listen, please! If you, Mis'er Doane, would jus' try to persua' my father! He will listen to you. Oh, if you woul' stay with us, an' help us. We coul' take some money, some jewels, an' escape down the river—to Shanghai—to Japan, or even America. My father mus' no' die like this. There will be a few servan's we can trus'. You speak to my father, sir, an' he will listen. I know that. He says you have the mind of the ol' philosopher—of Lao-tze himself. He said that. An' you have the Western strength that he admires. An' he says you un'erstan' China. Oh, will you speak to him?"

Doane stared out into the luminous night. This response in his breast to her eager youth frightened him now. He had felt of late that life mattered little; certainly not his own. But youth, and hope, and faith—they mattered.

He took her small hand in his own. His heart was beating high. It was going to be hard now, to control his voice. He was, then, after all the years, the struggles, the beatings, incurably romantic....

Stirred yet by the vibrant pulse of youth that in some men and women never dies. He himself had thought this negative spirit of the past few years a philosophy, but apparently, it was nothing of the sort. Or where was it now? For he was suddenly all nervously alive, a man of vigor and pride, a man of urgent emotional need....

"I will try," he said.

She clung to his hand. "I have your promise?"

He bowed. "I must think. I should not like to fail. There will be time. He will"—it was hard to phrase this—"he will wait, surely, until he is at home. But you must not stay longer here. And we must not meet again like this. I will try my best to help you."

It seemed a pitifully inadequate speech. But the wild impulse was upon him to clasp her lovely person in his arms—claim her, fight for her, live again a man's life through and for her. It was, he deliberately thought, almost insane in him. A man with nothing to offer, not even the great hope of youth, struggling against an emotion, a hunger, that it was grotesque to indulge. He compressed his lips tightly.

She seemed breathless. For a moment she pressed her hands to her cheeks and eyes; then waved to him and went lightly down the ladder.

CHAPTER V
RESURGENCE

THE upper-deck passengers awoke in the morning to find the engines still at rest, and the now familiar View of Kiu Kiang still to be seen from port-side windows; the *Yen Hsin* had merely been moved a hundred yards or so below the landing hulk and anchored. There was grumbling about the breakfast table. The captain did not appear. The huge mate was preoccupied; explaining with grave courtesy that he had no further news. He assumed that orders to proceed to Hankow would be forthcoming during the day. It was understood now that the republican troops were everywhere protecting white folk, and, in any event, the foreign concessions up the river were well guarded by the war-ships.

The outstanding fact was that they were to spend at least another night on the river. The sensible thing to do, or so decided the younger men, was to have a dance. Accordingly, before tiffin, committees were hard at work planning decorations for the social hall. Miss Means proved a fertile source of entertaining ideas. And it was agreed, during the day, that Miss Andrews had a pretty taste at hanging flags.

The Chinese day begins with the light. And little Mr. Kato, sitting smilingly through breakfast, had already passed hours among his below-decks acquaintance. After breakfast he sat outside with the Kanes, senior and junior, talking rapidly. There Miss Carmichael observed them; later, when Rocky stood by the rail throwing brass cash down into the crowding, nosing sampans of the water beggars, she strolled his way—looking incredibly young—carrying a book from the boat's library, a thin finger between the pages as a mark. She smiled at the quarreling beggars below. But he, at sight of her, grew sulky.

"You didn't come last night," he said, very low, his voice thick with suddenly rising feeling.

"No, I couldn't. You can't always plan things."

"Well, you said—"

"Rocky, please! You mustn't talk like that. We can be seen."

"Well—" he closed his lips. It was the first time she had called him by his name. That seemed something. And she was right; they must keep up appearances. He felt that she was extremely clever; living her own life as a business woman, away out here, doing as she chose, like a man, never losing her head for a moment. Well, he would show her that he could be a sport.

"Kato picked up some queer news this morning, prowling around. There's a mutiny brewing below decks. He hasn't got all the facts, yet. He's down there now. It's the viceroy's soldiers. First thing we know they'll be blowing up the boat." He was gloomy about it; boyishly turning his heavy burden of self-pity and reproach into the new channel.

"Well," said she, "we'll all have to take our chances, I suppose," and moved away a step, pausing and balancing gracefully on the balls of her feet and smiling at him.

"Wait," he muttered—"don't go!"

"It's better. No good in our being seen too much together—"

"Too much?"

"I'll save you some dances to-night."

"A lot! All of them!"

She smiled again at this outburst; said, "We can visit afterward, anyhow," and moved away.

On the other side of the deck she found the Manila Kid leaning in a doorway, moodily chewing a match. His listless eyes at once sought her wrist.

"You're not wearing it," he muttered.

"You know why, Jim."

"Sure! Young Kane."

"Oh, Jim, where are your brains? Don't try to tell me that Tex hasn't seen that watch.... Well, do you want him to know there's something between us—just now—"

"I don't know's I—"

Her pale cool eyes swept the deck. Then she leaned beside him; opened her book, then looked out over it at the shipping and the dimpling river beyond; smiled in her easy way. "Jim, why didn't you tell me that Tex has started this thing without me?"

"I've been watching for a chance to."

She considered this. He went on:

"Look here, Dixie, this is big stuff!"

"Of course."

"I've been trying to figure out how we stand. I didn't quite get you last night. Tex and his boy Tom have got a bunch of the soldiers now. But they're moving careful because there's another show been started. One of the regular revolutionary crowd is below there stirring 'em up. Some of 'em are full of this republic idea, want to die for it and all that stuff, and Tex has to move cautious to buy 'em off. Say, what does he want so many for?"

"The more the better."

"But how're you going to pay 'em?"

"Let them loot."

"But Tex—and Tom—are promising them part of the real stuff, jewels."

"Oh, you'd probably have to promise. But when they get into it, with plenty of loot and liquor and women, it'll be easy enough to get away from them."

"But how're you going to keep 'em in hand before that? Do you know what some of 'em are whispering around now? They want to carve up the boat. Come right up here and go through the viceroy's outfit."

"But he hasn't much stuff here, Jim. We've got bigger game than that."

"I know—and anyway it'd bring a gunboat down on us. That's what Tex is trying to make Tom see. Tom's in Tex's room now. But my God, Dixie, when I think of what you've started in that offhand way o' yours...."

"Tex'll hold them down, Jim. That's one good thing about him, he's not weak. You're nervous. Better go in and help the teachers hang flags. That'll soothe you. You and I mustn't talk any more either. If there's any news for me, better send me a chit by a boy."

The Kid looked mournfully at her. He was a grotesque, this Jim Watson, tall, angular, thin bony face under the tipped-back cap, bald salients running up into his hair on either side the plastered-down front locks. And as he gazed on this wisp of a girl who had slipped mysteriously in among the adroit swindlers and adventuresses of the coast but a few brief years back and had from the very beginning cleverly made her way, his disorganized spirit yearned toward her. She had brains, and used them. She knew how to be nice to a fellow, and the Kid hungered for sympathy. And she was piquantly desirable: in part because men sought her without success. Except perhaps that young naval officer at Hong Kong, the name of no man had been seriously linked with hers; and the fact that he was an eldest son of one of the richest and greatest families in England in a measure removed the incident beyond the confines of normal human experience. No, the Kid could hardly feel that he ought to resent that. He knew, as he so moodily surveyed her, that her sympathy—the word was his own—could be bought only at a high price. The price, indeed, frightened him. He couldn't think along with Dixie and Tex. Nor could he easily conceive of opposing Tex, for the man was strong and merciless. Still....

"See here, Dixie, if I wasn't so fool crazy over you, do you think for a minute I'd let you drag me into this kind of a mix-up? Why, my God!—when I got to thinking about it last night—the risks you're running—"

"It's big stakes, Jim. You can't expect a million to fall into your lap. Got to play for it. Tell me—does this Tom Sung understand English?"

"Of course! He was a farm laborer in California, and a cook in the United States Navy. Why?"

"I may have to talk to him myself before we get through with it."

"Of course you know Tex means to rob you?"

"Of course," said she, smiling a little for the benefit of a customs man who appeared up forward. "You run along now, Jim. This is no game for weak nerves. Remember, I need you."

"Well—just this—"

"Careful!"

"—You listen, now! You won't find me getting cold feet—"

"I'm sure of that."

"And I ain't afraid o' Tex Connor, either! If you mean that I've got to go up against him—Well, say, look here! If I go through—if I do everything you say—how're we going to stand, you and me?"

"I let you give me the watch, didn't I?"

"Well—that's all right—but I asked you once to go to the Islands with me, and you wouldn't."

"Not over there. I know too many people."

"Well, somewhere else, then! Tell me straight, now! If we pull this off—shake down a real pile—will you go with me?"

She looked thoughtfully at him for a brief moment; then turned again to the river. "You know I'm fond of you, Jim."

"It's a trade, Dixie? If I stick to you, you'll stick to me?"

She considered this; finally, very quietly, barely parting her lips, replied, simply: "Yes."

He drew in his breath with a whistling sound.

She added, then: "Careful, Jim! I know how you feel, but don't let yourself talk."

"I know, Dix, but my God! When I think of how you've kept me dancing this year—and now—"

"I'll say this, Jim. Just this. If you knew everything about Tex Connor—"

"You mean, he's tried to—"

"I mean certain things he's said to me. If you're as fond of me as that you'd understand why I've felt, once or twice, like killing him. That man is a devil, Jim."

Then she slipped away.

Miss Carmichael sat deliberately through tiffin; discreetly quiet, as always; apparently without nerves. The Kid ate rapidly, speaking not a word, seldom looking up from his plate. Tex Connor was calmly wooden, as always, though at intervals Miss Carmichael felt his eye on her as she daintily nibbled her curry.

After tiffin she was stretched comfortably in her deck chair, reading, or seeming to, when Connor appeared, strolling along the deck, hands deep in pockets, chewing the inevitable Manila cigar. He wore a neat cap, and his large person was clothed in an outing suit of gray flannel. On his feet were shoes of whitened leather with rubber soles. To any but a shrewd student of physiognomy he might have passed for a prosperous American business man or politician, of the bluff western sort.

He paused at her careless nod; bent his face around and stared coldly at her. Nothing of the real man showed; even his rough vulgarity was concealed behind the mask and the manner. He ought to have a woman to tell him, she thought, that he was altogether too stout to wear a Norfolk jacket.

"Sit down?" she asked.

He dropped into the chair beside her.

"Looks as if we'd be hung up here till night anyhow," he said gruffly. "All foolishness, too. It's safe enough between here and Hankow. The Jardine boat came down this morning. And we land at the concessions— don't have to go clear up to the city." He drummed on the chair; shifted his cigar. "I can't hang around here. Got to get up to Peking before they close off the railroad."

She listened quietly to this little tirade; then remarked: "Thought over my proposition, Tex?"

"What proposition?.... Oh, that scheme? Sure, I've thought it over. Nothing in it, Dix."

"Why not?"

"Too complicated. Did you ever see a lot of soldiers on the loose—their killing blood up? You could never handle 'em in the world."

"Oh, of course," said she, "if you tried any coarse work. But I wouldn't pin that on you, Tex."

"It's easy to talk." Connor's voice rose slightly; he noted the fact himself; paused and spoke with greater deliberation. "But I wouldn't tackle a gamelike that. It ain't practical. Anyhow, Dix, I wouldn't go it blind. I'd have to know where I was going every minute. If you wanted to talk real business, it might be different. I might see a way to start something. But even at that"—he got heavily to his feet...."No, thing for me's to stick to my own line."

He was moving slowly away when her slow light voice brought him up short. "Tex," she said, "I see you're just a cheap liar, after all."

Then she watched the color sweep over his face. It was something to stir that wooden countenance with genuine emotion. She even found a perverse thrill in the experience.

He stood motionless for a long moment. Finally he said, none too steadily: "You know what would happen to a man that said that to me."

"What would you do? Shoot?.... Where would that get you? No, Tex, listen! Sit down here."

But he stood over her.

"I know everything you're doing."

"Oh—you do?"

"You're crossing me. But you can't get away with it. You know where you are—in China! And you're tampering with the troops of the viceroy of Nanking. My God, Tex, haven't you *any* brains? Did you really think I'd show my hand?"

He chewed the cigar in silence, staring down.

"I'll give you your choice," she went on. "You can work with me. fifty-fifty, or I'll have Tom Sung beheaded. And then you'll be out a meal ticket. And all your expenses with Tom up to now. And the three thousand you lost to the Kanes."

"You don't know what you're talking about! I haven't even seen Tom Sung in twenty-four hours."

"That's another lie. He was in your room this morning."

"How do you know that? Say, if Jim Watson's been talking...."

"He hasn't, Tex. I've got my information—and there's a lot of if—from Kato the Japanese. Go and talk to him, if you like. Or to your friends the Kanes."

Connor, the color gone from his face now, looked steadily down at her. Slowly he drew from an inner pocket a gold-mounted case of alligator skin and selected a fresh cigar, lighting it on the stump of the old one. Finally he said:

"Dix, I'm taking some rough talk from you. But never mind—now. You say you know where the stuff is, but you won't tell me."

"Not now. I'll keep that information to trade with, Tex."

"Well and good. I'll tell you that you can't get it without a little help from me. And you're not going to get it. Tell me where it is, and I'll put it through and split with you. It'll have to be pretty quick, too. If you won't, you don't get your loot. And you give up my boy Tom—"

"What'll you do, Tex?" She was faintly smiling.

"Oh, I won't shoot you. I'll protect myself better'n that. But I'll run you off the coast. You'll have turned your last card out here."

To this she said simply nothing. For a moment her two eyes met his one full. Then he strolled away. And the day passed.

Doane stood by the rail in the dusk of early evening looking in through the open doorway. The social hall was gay with flags, the dragon of China hung flat over the talking machine with the American and British colors draped on either hand. The little teachers had on their brightest and best. Miss Andrews in particular, wore a pink party gown that might have been made by a village dressmaker—or, more likely, by herself—and flushed prettily as she chatted with young Braker. The men were all in their dinner coats.

Dixie Carmichael, in the inevitable blue middy blouse, sat quietly reading in a corner. A strange creature, always imperturbably girlish.

Duane had observed her casually on the boat and about the Astor House at Shanghai, and despite the curious tales that drifted along the coast—already the girl had acquired an almost legendary fame—he had never seen her other than discreetly quiet. Men who had observed her on the steamer from Hong Kong after the outraged British wives as good as drummed her out of town asserted that she exhibited not so much as a ruffle of the nerves. A girl without emotion, apparently; certainly without a moral sense.

She had for a time managed a gambling house on Bubbling Well Road, Shanghai, but this year seemed to be more active up Peking way. At least she had made several trips to the north. There were moments when her thin, nearly expressionless face bore a look of infinite age; yet she was young. It would be interesting, he reflected, to know of her home and her youth, of the remarkable deficiency (or the equally remarkable gift) that had sent her out alone, with her hair down her back, to pit her uncanny quickness of thought and her sordid purpose against the desperately clever rascals of the coast.

When again he passed the doorway they were dancing—a waltz. Dixie and young Kane were together. Miss Means, primmer than ever, moved about with a tall Australian. Braker was with little Miss Andrews. The others of the younger men danced humorously with one another. The Manila Kid stood lankily, gloomily, by the talking machine, sorting records.

There was a bustling outside the farther door; musical voices; the shimmering of satin in the light; and the viceroy came in, escorting his daughter and attended by all his suite. At the sight of Miss Hui Fei as she appeared in the doorway and stepped lightly over the sill Doane caught his breath. She wore an American costume, a gown of soft material in rose color trimmed with silver, the stockings and little slippers in silver as well. A girl at any college or suburban dance back home might have dressed like that. Her richly black hair was parted on the side; masses of it waved carelessly down over her temples and part of the broad forehead. Her color was high, her eyes were bright. The eagerly Western quality he had sensed in her was dominant now, triumphant as youth can be triumphant.

Doane, for a moment, pressed a hand to his eyes. He could not relate this radiantly Western girl with the quaintly Oriental figure he had last seen by moonlight on the boat deck. It was difficult, too, to understand her bright happiness. Had her insistently modern spirit prevailed over her father's resolve to die? Or was she, after all, carried away by girlishly high spirits at the thought of a party? On the latter possibility Doane set his teeth; it raided thoughts of Oriental fatalism and surface adaptability that he could not face.

Surely the girl who had talked so earnestly, who had so clearly exhibited a Western view of her father's predicament, was more than Oriental at heart.

The most deeply sobering thought, of course, was that he should so poignantly care. The mere sight of her thrilled him, shook him. All night and during this day he had been fighting the new shining sense of her in his heart; it was clear now that the battle was a losing one. It was true, then; the last broken shards of his elaborately built up, wholly mental philosophy of life had crashed hopelessly about his ears.

The pity of it seemed to him, even then, to be that he was possessed of such abounding vitality of body and mind. He felt a young man. He was never ill, never even tired. Only accident, he felt, could shorten his life. Certainly he wouldn't take it himself; he had gone all through that. He would have to go dully on and on; he was like an engine that is using but a fraction of its proper power. He had not known that his need was a woman until he met this woman. To no other, he felt, could he give the rich upwellings of emotion in his heart; and vital emotion, he had tragically learned three years earlier, can not be repressed indefinitely. There was a breaking point... He was, even now, bringing up favorable arguments. This young woman, as she had admitted, like himself, stood between the worlds. She could never be happy in China; hardly out of it. If.... If.... Thoughts came, bitter thoughts, of his years, of his poverty. The thing had the grip of a demoniac possession. He had seen other men mad over the one woman, and had pitied them; but now he.... He called himself savagely, in his heart, a fool. Yet the wild hopes mounted.

The waltz was over. The Kid changed the records and ground the machine. An interpreter left the group of mandarins and spoke with one of the Australians; led the man back to his excellency. A moment later the music sounded again, and the Australian danced lightly away with Miss Hui Fei in what Doane had no means of knowing was the very new one-step. He had never danced; plainly she loved it. She moved like a fairy— light, utterly graceful, her oval face, when she turned, flushed a little and soberly radiant.

Hating the man who held her so close, he turned away. He did not know that his excellency, glimpsing him outside there in the shadows, leaned forward and bowed; he did not observe (or care) that Dixie Carmichael was dancing with the German customs man, while Rocky Kane, suddenly white, lighting one cigarette on another, stood in a corner devouring with his eyes Miss Hui Fei. A little later, when the young man spoke, there at his side, he started; for he had heard no one approach. Rocky was hatless; hair rumpled as if he had been running nervous fingers through it, cheeks deeply flushed, eyes staring rather wildly. He threw his cigarette overboard and squarely faced the huge man in blue.

"I don't know what you'll think of me—" he began, in a breathless, unsteady voice; then his eyes wavered.

Doane turned with him, Dixie Carmichael stood in the doorway, watching them. Rocky, with a nervous gesture, as if he would brush her away, looked up again into the stern older face. He was plainly lost in himself, burning with the confused fires of youth.

"I don't know what you'll think of me—" he came again to a stop. Apparently the words, "Mr. Doane," would have completed the sentence, but failed for some reason to find voice. Perhaps it was the habit of his wealthy environment that restrained him even now from speaking with more than casual respect to a uniformed employee of a river line; yet, contradictorily, here he was, all boyish humility!.... "I'm a damn fool, of course, I know that. But—you've seen her."

Doane glanced again toward the door. Dixie Carmichael had disappeared.

"No—not that one!" cried the boy hotly; then dropped his voice. "The girl in there! The—princess, isn't she?"

Doane inclined his head.

"Then she'd be the one I—well, you remember."

"She's the same. The Princess Hui Fei—"

"Hughie Fay? Like that?"

"Yes."

"What a lovely name!.... You—I know you won't understand! It's so hard to—I *am* young, of course. I''ve been sort of in wrong. I guess you think I''m a pretty wild lot. I seem to have been trying about everything. But until to-night—oh, there's no use pretending I'm not hit all of a heap. I am. I never saw anything like her—never in my life. I don't know what the pater would say—me falling for a Manchu girl—you think I'm crazy, don't you?"

"No."

"Perhaps I am. My head's racing. Just watching her in there makes my pulse jump. I get bewildered. Tell me—she was all Chinese the—the other time—all painted up. Big head-dress with flowers on it. Why did she do that?"

"Out of respect to her father. The rouge and the head-dress were according to Oriental custom." He looked directly down at the boy, and added, deliberately, "Veneration of parents is the finest thing in Chinese life. I sometimes think we have nothing so fine in America."

The boy's eyes fell. He mumbled. "Ouch! You landed there, I guess." Then he raised his eyes. "I can't help myself—whatever I am—but I can start fresh, can't I? That's what I'm going to do, anyhow—start fresh." He squared himself. His lip quivered.

"Will you take me in there to the viceroy, and translate my apology?"

Doane stood a moment in silence. Then he replied, quietly, "Yes." And led the way into the social hall. He found himself watching, like a spectator, the little scene.... the viceroy rising, with a quiet smile, a gentle old man, awaiting with perfect courtesy of bearing whatever might be forthcoming; Rocky Kane, seeming younger than before, with, in fact, the appearance of an excited boy, the wild look still in his eyes but the face set with supreme determination. Doane observed now that he had a good forehead, wide and not too high. The nose was slightly aquiline, like his father's. The eyes, so dark now, were normally blue; the mouth sensitive; the skin fine in texture.

"Tell him"—thus the boy—"tell him I acted like a dirty cad, that I know better, and—and ask his pardon."

Doane translated discreetly. A dance was just ending, and curious eyes were bent on the group. The mandarins stood behind the viceroy, all gracefully at ease in their rich rubes.

His excellency, without relaxing that smile, replied in musical intonation.

"What is it?" asked Rocky Kane, under his breath, all quivering excitement; "what does he say?"

"That he accepts your apology, with appreciation of your manliness."

Young Kane's nervous frown relaxed at this. He was pleased.

"Will you," he was saying now, "will you ask if I may dance with the princess?"

Doane complied. He felt now a strain of fineness in this ungoverned boy that was oddly moving to his own emotion-clouded brain.... Hoi Fei was approaching, the Australian at her side.

"He suggests"—Doane found himself translating—"that you ask her. He does not know what engagements she may have made."

The boy bit his lip. And then the princess was greeting the mate. "It's nice to see you, Mr. Doane," she was saying. "I wondered if you weren't coming to the party."

It seemed to Doane that he could feel young Kane's devouring eyes fastened on her. The moment had come in which he must act. The Australian, sensing a situation, thanked the princess and slipped away. Quietly, Doane said: "Miss Hui Fei, this is Mr. Kane, who has asked permission to meet you."

She drew back a very little; Doane caught that; yet the courtesy of her race did not fail her. She inclined her pretty head; even smiled.

"Should I speak English?" asked the boy, out of sheer confusion; then: "Miss Hui Fei" —he was white; the words came slowly, almost coldly, between set teeth — "I am sorry for my rotten behavior the other night."

That was all. He waited. Miss Hui's smile faded.

No Oriental could have come out so bluntly with it. She seemed to be considering him. Gradually the smile returned, and with it an air of courteous dismissal.

"I have forgotten it."

Kane gathered his courage.

"May I have a dance with you?"

For a moment the silence was marked. Perhaps Miss Hui was gathering herself as well. But it was only a moment; she spoke, smiling as if she were happy, her manner gracious, even kind: "I am sorry. I have promise' every dance. The ladies are so few to-nigh'."

That was all. The boy seemed somewhat slow in comprehending it. He stood motionless; then the color returned slowly to his face, flooding it. He bowed to her stiffly, then to her father, and rushed out on deck.

Miss Hui smiled up at the mate. "I have save' the dance you ask'," she said pleasantly. "It is this nex' one, if you don' mind."

The Manila Kid adjusted the needle and released the catch.

"I'm sorry," said Doane, as they moved away, "I don't dance."

The commonplace remark fell strangely on his own ears. It could hardly be himself speaking. He was all glowingly warm with impulse, his logic gone.

"We'll sit it out," said Miss Hui pleasantly.

And during the brief walk across the room, beside this buoyantly graceful girl, even while aware of the eyes upon him, he felt the magic wine of youth thrilling through his arteries. What a fairy she was! Snatches of poetry came; one—=

"Were it ever so airy a tread...."=

—and lingered fragrantly after they were seated and he found himself looking down at her, listening with something of the gravity and kindliness of long habit when she so quickly spoke.

CHAPTER VI
CONFLAGRATION

A BEWILDERED, crushed Rocky Kane stood tightly holding the rail; staring down at the softly black water that ran so smoothly along the hull beneath; muttering in whispers that at intervals broke out into heated speech. This strange princess had humiliated him perfectly, completely; there had been nothing he could say, nothing to do but go; and she had let him go without a look or a further thought. He told himself it was unfair. He had swallowed his pride and apologized. Could a man do more?

But pressing upward through this chaotic mental surface of hurt pride and insistent self-justification came an equally insistent memory of his outrageous conduct toward her. As the moments passed, the memory intensified into a painfully vivid picture. His native intelligence, together with the undeveloped decency that was somewhere within him, kept at him with dart-like, stinging thoughts. He had insulted not only herself but her race as well, in assuming a ruthless right to make free with her.

Then self-justification again; how could he know that she spoke English and dressed like the girls back home? Was it fair of her to masquerade like that?

He was miserably wrong, of course. And his nerves were terribly upset. That was at least part of the trouble, his nerves; he lighted a cigarette to steady them. The match shook in his hand. This nervous trembling had been increasing lately; he found it an alarming symptom. Perhaps the trouble was inherent weakness. Ability like his father's often skipped a generation; and character. Yes, he was weak, he had failed at everything. His college career was a wreck; a monstrous wreck, he believed, echoes from which would follow him through life. To his incoherent mind it seemed that he had about all the vices—drinking, gambling, pursuing helpless girls, even smoking opium. His one faith had been money; but now he suddenly, wretchedly, knew that even the money might fail him. It was as easy to toss away a million as a hundred on the red or the black. And then young men who wasted themselves acquired diseases from the terrors of which no fortune could promise release; a thought that had long dwelt uncomfortably in a sensitive, deep-shadowed corner of his brain.... a brain that was racing now, beyond control.

Her unfairness lay in so publicly snubbing him. Her father knew the facts, as did Miss Carmichael, and the big mate, that old preacher with a mysterious past. Who was he, anyhow—setting up to regulate other people's lives?

Then rose among these turbulent thoughts a picture of the princess as she was now, there in the social hall. Tears welled into his eyes; he brushed them away, lighted a fresh cigarette and deeply inhaled the smoke. He had rushed out; suddenly, wildly, he desired to rush back. She was beautiful. She had quaintly moving charm. A rare little lady! It seemed almost that he might compel her to listen while he explained. But what was it that he was to explain? That he was some other than the dirty sort they all knew him to be, that he had proved himself to be?

The wild thoughts were like a beating in his brain. It was his father's fault, this crazy nervousness, and his mother's.... He hated that big mate. Self-pity rose like a tidal wave, and engulfed him. He stared and stared at the softly dark water. Beginning with about his sixteenth year he had wrestled often with the thought of suicide, as so many sensitive young men do. Now the water fascinated him; it was so still, it moved so resistlessly on to the sea. "A pretty easy way to slip out. Just a little splash—-I could climb down. Nobody'd know. Nobody'd care much of a damn. Oh, the old man would think he cared, but he wouldn't. He'll never make a bank president out of me. And that's all he wants."

A voice, guardedly friendly, said, "Better not let yourself talk that way."

He turned with a start. Miss Carmichael was standing there by the rail. So he had talked aloud—another unpleasant symptom.

"You—you saw what—"

She inclined her head. "What's the good of letting it upset you? Lie down for a while. A pipe or two wouldn't hurt you. You're nervous as a witch. It would soothe you." He stared at her.

"Better lie down anyway," she said, taking his arm and moving him toward his cabin. "You don't want them to see you like this."

He yielded. His will was powerless. He dropped on the seat, while she lingered, almost sympathetically, in the doorway, an unbelievably girlish figure in the half light. Something of the influence she had been exerting on him—which had seemed to die when Miss Hui Fei entered the social hall— fluttered to life now. He found relief, abruptly, in recklessness.

"Come on in," he said huskily. "Have a pipe with me!"

Quietly, wholly matter-of-fact, she closed and locked the door. "We'll shut the window, too, this time," she said.

"You needn't turn on the light." He was reaching for his trunk. "Excuse me—a minute! I can see all right. I know just where everything is."

"Leave the trunk out," said she. "And lay your suit-case on it. Then we can put the lamp on that."

Miss Hui Fei led Doane to a seat under the curving front windows.

"We mus' talk as if ever'thing were ver' pleasan'." The question rose again, but without bitterness now, how she could smile so brightly. "I have learn' some more. It is ver' difficul' to tell you, but—it is difficul' to think, even.... so strange that at firs' I laugh'.".... Yes, there were tears in her eyes. But how bravely she fought them back and smiled again. He felt his own eyes filling, and turned quickly to the window; but not so quickly that she failed to see. She was sensitively observant, despite her own trouble. For a moment, then, they were silent, lost in a deep common sympathy that was bread to his starving heart.

It was in that moment that their little conspiracy nearly broke down. Had any of the others in the big room looked just then, gossip would have spread swiftly; certainly sharp-eyed mandarins would have found matter for consideration; for Hui Fei impulsively found his hand as it rested between them on the seat, and was met with a quick warm pressure.

And then, in another moment, she was speaking, quite herself. "My maid has foun' out tha' they are sending the head eunuch from the Forbidden C'ty to our home. An' that is agains' the law."

"Of course," said he. "Even the Old Buddha never tried but once to send out a eunuch on government business. That was the notorious An Te-hai. And he never returned; he was caught in Shantung—in a barge of state on the Grand Canal—and beheaded. Even the Old Buddha couldn't do that. This woman is amazing. But of course there is really no government at Peking now—only this strange anachronism."

"He has orders to seize all father's beautifu' things the paintings an' stones an' carvings."

"The rebels may catch him. They'd make short work of him."

"I ask about that. The rebels have cross the river from Wu Chang to Han Yang, but they have not yet reach the railway. That comes into Hankow from this side."

"Even so," he mused, "the train service from Peking must have broken down. Though they're running troop trains south, of course."

"I haven't tol' you all of it." Her voice was low and unsteady. "This eunuch, Chang Yuan-fu, is ordered, by the empress, to take me to Peking too. They are all whispering about it. The empress is angry at my foreign ways, and will marry me to a Manchu duke. She di'n' like it when my father tol' her I mus' marry no man I di'n' choose myself.... I think you ough' to smile."

Mechanically he obeyed.

"It seems almos' funny." murmured Miss Hui. "Sometimes I can no' believe tha' such a thing could happen. When I think of America an' England and all the worl' we know to-day, I can no' believe that such wicked things can happen."

It was anything but unreal to Doane. He knew too well that America and England, even all the white peoples, make up but a fraction of the inhabitants of this strange earth. His eyes filled again as he considered the possible—yes, the probable fate of the lovely girl at his side. In such a time of disorganization the reckless Manchu woman at Peking could do much. Chang might lose his head at the sound of gunfire in Han Yang and fly back to the capital, or he might not. A capable and corrupt eunuch would run heavy risks to gain such a prize. For a huge prize the viceroy's collection would indeed be; many of the priceless stones and paintings would never reach the throne.

The thought came of trying to persuade her to save herself; a thought that was as promptly discarded. She would not leave her father while he lived. He, of course, would not take his own life elsewhere than in his ancestral home. And to that home, with his inevitable escort of underlings and soldiers, was hurrying—if not already there—this Chang Yuan-fu, one of those powerfully venomous creatures that have figured darkly at intervals in the history of China.

Doane spoke low and quickly: "Can you find out when Chang's train left Peking, Miss Ilui?"

"No, I have try ver' har' to learn. I think they don' know that. It is so importan' to know that, too, because my father"—Her voice faltered. Doane once again, with a swift glance to left and right, took her hand and, for a brief moment, gripped it firmly. "You haven' yet spoken to my father?"

"Not yet, dear Miss Hui.... you must smile!.... I have found it very difficult to think out a way of approaching him. Your father is a great viceroy. He might take it ill that I should venture to interfere in what he would feel to be the supreme sacred act of his life. He might"—Doane hesitated—"even for you he might feel that he couldn't turn back."

"I know," she said, very low. "I have thought of tha', too. But they shall never take me to Peking."

He understood. The suicide of girls as a protest against unwelcome marriage was a commonplace in China. It was, indeed, for thousands the only way out. She knew that, of course. And she spoke there out of her blood.

"I will speak to-morrow," he murmured. "Before we reach Huang Chau. We have nothing to lose. He can only rebuff me."

He felt now that in this tragic drama was bound up all that might be left to him of happiness. The guiding motive of his life was—there was a divine recklessness in the thought—to save Hui Fei, to make her smile again, with a happy heart. She whispered now:

"Thank you."

He asked her, abruptly changing his manner, almost distantly courteous, about her life in an American college. Little by little, as she made the effort to follow him into this impersonal atmosphere, her brightness returned.

The record was scraping its last. Applause came from the dancers, in which she joined. The Manila Kid wound the machine again, and the dancers swung again into motion.

"I am asking too much of you," she murmured. "But I have been frighten'. I coul'n' think wha' to do."

He had to set his teeth on the burning phrases that rushed from his long unpractised heart, eager for utterance. "I will take you back to your father," he said.

In his mind it was settled. Whatever strange events might lie before them, they should not take her to Peking. His own life, as well as hers, stood in the way. It had come to that with him.

It was near to midnight when the *Yen Hsin*, on advices from Hankow, headed again upstream. At the first throb of the engine the white passengers stopped dancing and came out on deck. There was gaiety, even a little cheering.

It was perhaps two hours later when Doane, asleep in his cabin, heard the shots, confused with the incidents of a dream. But at the first screams of the women below decks he sprang from his berth. Some one was banging on his door; he opened; the second engineer stood there, coatless and hatless, a revolver in his hand, and a little blood on his cheek.

"All hell's broken loose below," said the young Scotchman. "Chief's down there. I tried to get to him, but—God, they're all over the place—fighting one another."

"Who are, MacKail?" Doane hurriedly drew on trousers and coat, and thrust his feet into his slippers.

"The viceroy's soldiers. Revolutionary stuff."

Doane got his automatic pistol from a drawer in the desk; quickly filled an extra clip with cartridges; went forward. The Scotchman had already gone aft.

The engine was still running, the steamer moving steadily up the moonlit river. The uproar below decks sounded muffled, far-away. It might have been nothing more than a little night excitement in a village along the shore. The shooting continued. Men were shouting. There were more shrill screams; and then splashes overside. As he hurried forward, staring over the rail, Doane caught a passing glimpse of a face down there in the foam and a white arm. The white men were stumbling drowsily out of their cabins; he saw one of the customs men, in pajamas, and Tex Connor. They hurled questions at him but he brushed them aside.

Captain Benjamin stood over the cringing pilot with a revolver.

"Engine room don't answer!" he shouted coolly enough. "And we can't get to it. Take MacKail and try to get through. I'll make this rat keep her in the channel."

Doane ran back. More of the men were out, talking excitedly together. He paused to say: "Get any weapons you have, every man of you, and see that none but women get up to this deck! Keep the men down!"

MacKail stood at the head of the port after stairway, outside the rear cabins, a big Australian beside him.

"They're just naturally carving one another up," observed the Australian.

"Come," said Doane, and went down the steps.

The noise and confusion were great down here. Women were crowding out of the lower cabins, sobbing hysterically, tearing their hair and beating their breasts, crowding forward and aft along the deckway or climbing awkwardly over the rail and slipping off into the river.

Doane shouted a reassuring word in their own tongue; pointed to the steps; finally drew one girl forcibly back from the rail and started her up. Others followed, screaming all the way. Still others clung to the white men.

Doane broke away and plunged into the dim interior of the boat. Most of the lights were out. Dark figures were wrestling. There were grunts, groans, savage cries of rage and triumph. A huge pole-knife caught the light as it swung. Doane was aware of men breathing hard as they struggled.

He stumbled over an inert body; would have fallen had not the Australian caught him. A tall soldier who lunged toward them with a dripping bayonet was shot by MacKail.... There were no means here of distinguishing the parties to this savage struggle, but in the inner corridor it was lighter. Near at hand two of the republicans—queues cut off, dressed in an indistinguishable but odd-appearing uniform of some light gray stuff with a white cloth tied about the left arm, had heaped bodies across the corridor and were shooting over them at a darker mass just forward of the engine room.

Doane shouted at the republicans, ordering them to withdraw. They shook their heads angrily. One, even as he tried to reply, sank into a limp heap with a dark stream trickling from a hole in his forehead. His comrade bent low to reload his rifle. With the shouting of many hoarse voices the dark mass up forward came charging down the corridor. Doane was firing into them when MacKail and the Australian caught his arm and drew him back through the doorway. From that position, however, all three could shoot the blue-clad attackers as they plunged by the opening. Then, however, they had to defend themselves. The soldiers came on by dozens. Doane had his second clip of cartridges in his pistol.

"Get back!" he shouted to the others. "Guard the steps—they'll be coming up for loot!"

They retreated. Two bodies lay huddled on the steps they had left but a few moments earlier. A few dead women were on the deck and one or two men.

Even as they stepped over the bodies and mounted to the deck above, all three men, their faculties sharpened to a supernatural degree by the ugly thrill of combat, took in the details of what was evidently accepted among these republican rebels as their uniform—a suit of unmistakably American woolen underwear, the drawers supported by bright-colored American suspenders; socks worn outside (like the suspenders) with garters that bore the trademark name of an American city, and finally, American shoes. So the enthusiasm of these young revolutionists for the greatest of republics found expression! And across the breast of each, lettered on a strip of white cloth, was the inscription that Sun Shi-pi had so glibly translated as "Dare to Die." Sun must have brought along these supposedly Western uniforms in his pedler's trunks.

It was never to be known what surprising incidents had preceded this sudden slaughter. The chief engineer might have told, but his mutilated body Doane found, on his second attempt to get through, lying just across the sill of the engine room, as if he had been stepping out to reason with them.

The entire battle lasted barely half an hour. It was, for the white folk, a period of confusion and terror. Toward the end, the blue men, utter outlaws now, made rush after rush up the various stairways and ladders, only to be fought back at every point by the white men and the few surviving officers of his excellency's force. They were like the most primitive savages, knowing neither fear nor reason. The blood-lust that at times captures the spirit of this normally phlegmatic and reasonable people drove them for the time to the point of madness.

At last, however, they drew off below. Two of the boats were within their reach. These they lowered, and despite the speed of steamer and current, though not without evident loss of life, they got them over, tumbled into them, and fell away into the night astern. Then for the first and last time this night Doane saw the redoubtable Tom Sung. He stood in the nearer boat, brandishing a rifle and screeching wild phrases in Chinese.

MacKail took the engine room. Captain Benjamin, still, grimly, pistol in hand, held the pilot to his task. There was no crew to clean the shambles below decks, yet with the few loyal soldiers who had managed to hide away now at the furnaces, the steamer wound her way steadily up-stream.

Doane found what had once been the earnest Sun Shi-pi in the starboard corridor, below. On his body were the uniform, white brassard and motto of the "Dare to Dies." They had beheaded him.

The passengers, clad and half clad, nervous, talkative, hung about the decks. The two teachers, curiously self-possessed, sat side by side at the dining table. From the quarters of his excellency, aft, came the continuous sound of women moaning and wailing.... It was, to the eye, but a river steamer plowing up-stream in the moonlight. But to the senses of those aboard the situation was a nightmare, already an incredible memory while sleep-drugged eyes were slowly opening.... To the mighty river it was but one more incident in the vivid, often bloody drama of a long-suffering, endlessly struggling people....

In his spacious cabin, his eyes shaded from the electric light by a screen of jade set in tulip wood, dressed in his robes of ceremony, wearing the ruby-crowned hat of state with the down-slanting peacock feather, his excellency sat quietly reading the precepts of Chuang Tzü.

"Hui Tzü asked," (he read) 'Are there, then, men who have no passions? If he be a man, how can he be without passions?'

"'By a man without passions,' replied Chuang Tzü, I mean one who permits neither evil nor good to disturb his inner life, but accepts whatever comes.... The pure men of old neither loved life nor hated death. Cheerfully they played their parts, patiently awaited the end. This is what is called not to lead the heart away from Tao.... The true page ignores God; he ignores man; he ignores a beginning; he ignores matter; he accepts life as it may be and is not overwhelmed. If he fail, what matters it? If he succeed, is it not that he was provided through no effort of his own with the energy necessary to success.... The life of man passes like a galloping horse, changing at every turn. What should he do; what should he not do? It passes as a sunbeam passes a small opening in a wall—here for a moment, then gone.... let knowledge stop at the unknowable. That is perfection.'"

It is to be doubted if even Doane gave regard at the moment to the possible origin of the fire. It had spread through two or three of the upper cabins by way of the ventilating grills and was roaring out through a doorway by the time he heard the new outcry and ran to the spot. The white men were rushing about. Rocky Kane, collarless, disheveled, was fumbling ineffectually at the emergency fire hose; him Doane pushed aside. But the flames spread amazingly; worked through the grill-work from cabin to cabin; soon were licking at the walls and furniture of the social hall.

Doane left Dawley Kane and Tex Conner—an oddly matched couple— manning the hose, others at work with the chemical extinguishers, while he went forward through the thickening smoke to the bridge.

Captain Benjamin said, huskily, almost apologetically—his eyes red and staring, his face haggard: "I'm beaching her."

And in another moment she struck, where the channel ran close under an island.

Lowering the boats without a crew proved difficult. Already the fire had reached those forward. Doane, the other mate and MacKail did what they could. The Chinese women crowded hither and thither, screaming, rendering order impossible. In the confusion one boat drifted off with only Connor, the Manila Kid, and Miss Carmichael.

Captain Benjamin was cut off by the quick progress of the flames. The whole forward end of the cabin structure was now a roaring furnace, fortunately working forward on the down-stream breeze rather than aft. The flames blazed from moment to moment higher; sparks danced higher yet; the heat was intense. Doane sent the viceroy and his suite below, aft, where the deck was still strewn with bodies and slippery with blood. With three available boats, fighting back the crowding women and the more excitable among his excellency's secretaries, he sent ashore, first the women, then his excellency and the men. Hui Fei—she had slipped hastily into the little Chinese costume she wore at their midnight talk, and had thrown about it an opera cloak from New York—went in one of the first boats; Doane himself handed her in. The two teachers, pale, very composed, followed. At the oars were two of the customs men, faces streaked with grime and sweat.

To his excellency, as the last boats got away, Doane said: "I will follow you soon. I must look once more for the captain."

"I will send back a boat," said the viceroy.

Doane ran up to the upper and promenade decks. There was no sound save the roaring and crackling of the fire. There seemed no chance of getting forward. In the large after cabin stood the six-fold Ming screen. Quickly he folded it; there seemed a chance of getting it ashore. He thought, with a passing regret, of the *pi* of jade; but there was no reaching his own cabin now. He stepped out on deck. There, clear aft, leaning against the cabin wall, stood Rocky Kane, like a man half asleep, rubbing his eyes; and crouching against his knee, clinging to his hand, was the little princess in her gay golden yellow vest over the flowered skirt and her quaint hood of fox skin.

Doane caught the young man's shoulder; swung him about; looked closely into the dull eyes with the tiny pupils.

"So!" he cried, "that again, eh!"

"I can't understand"—thus Rocky—"I don't see how it could have happened. It couldn't have been my fault."

Doane saw now that his head had been burned above one ear; and the hand that pressed his face was blistered white.

"It *wasn't* my fault! I found myself out on deck. I tried to get the hose."

"Yes, I saw you. Quick—get below."

Doane tenderly lifted the little princess.

Rocky was still incoherently talking; promising reform; blaming himself in the next breath after hotly defending himself. His voice was somewhat thick. He was drowsy—swayed and stumbled as he moved toward the stairs.

Doane, speaking gently in Chinese to the child, stood a moment considering. The heat was becoming intolerable. It wouldn't do to keep the little one here. He carried her down the stairs.

Below, the boy faced him. "I'm no good," he whimpered. "I can't wake up. Hit me—do something—I won't be like this."

Doane considered him during a brief instant. They were standing under a light, their feet slipping on the deck, bodies lying about. With the flat of his hand, then, Duane struck the side of the boy's head that was not burned; struck harder than he meant, for the boy went down, and then, after sprawling about, got muttering to his feet.

"It's all right!" he cried unsteadily. "I asked you to do it. I'm going to get hold of myself. I've been no good—rotten. I've touched bottom. But I'm going to fight it out—get somewhere." His egotism, even now amazingly held him. Even as he spoke he was dramatizing himself. But his pupils were widening a little; he was in earnest, crying bitterly out of a drugged mind and conscience. And Doane, looking down at him, felt stirring in his heart, though curiously mixed with a twinge of jealousy for his youth and the hopes before him, something of the sympathy his long deep experience had instilled there toward blindly struggling young folk. Boys, after all, were normally egotists. And Heaven knew this boy had so far been given no sort of chance!

Doane led the way clear aft. The heat was terrific. From a row of fire buckets he sprinkled the little princess; bathed her temples. The water was warm, but it helped.

Young Kane, with a nervous movement, suddenly picked up one, then another, of the buckets and dashed them over himself. Distinctly he was coming to life. "We may never come out of this, Mr. Doane," he said. "It's a terrible fix." More and more, as he came slowly awake, he was dramatizing the situation and himself. "But I want to say this. I've never known a man like you. You're fine—you're big—you've helped me as no one else has. I'll never be like you—it isn't in me. I've already gone as close to hell as a man can go and perhaps still save himself—"

"Can you swim?" asked Doane shortly.

"I—why, yes, a little. I'm not what you'd call a strong swimmer."

Doane was wetting the princess's face and his own. There would be little time left. There was smoke now. He found a slight difficulty in breathing; evidently the fire had eaten through, forward, to the lower decks.

"They won't be able to get a boat back here," he said, and quietly pointed out the still blazing pieces of board that, after whirling into the air, were drifting by. A terrific blast of heat swept about them, indicating a change of wind.

"Wait here a moment for me," he added. "I must make one more effort to find Captain Benjamin. If that fails, we can swim ashore."

He tried working his way forward when the heat proved too great in the corridor, climbing out on the windward side of the hull. But the flames were eating steadily aft; he could not get far. Beaten back, he returned to the stem to discover that the child and Rocky Kane were gone. After a moment he saw them in the water, a few rods away, first a gleam of yellow that would be the jacket of the little princess, then their two heads close together.

He lowered himself down a boat-line and swam after them. In the water this giant was as easily at home as in any form of exercise on land. Within the year he had swum at night, alone, for the sheer vital pleasure the use of his strength brought him, the nine miles from Wusung to Shanghai—slipping between junks and steamers, past the anchored war-ships and a great P. & O. liner from Bombay. The water was cool, refreshing. He stretched his full length in it, rolling his face under as one arm and then the other reached out in slow powerful strokes.

Young Kane was having no easy time of it. He was clearly out of wind. And the child whimpered as she clung tightly about his neck.

"I gave you up," he sputtered weakly. Then added, with an evidence of spirit that Doane found not displeasing: "No, don't take her, please! Just steady me a little." He was struggling in short strokes, splashing a good deal. "We ought to touch bottom now pretty quick."

Sampans and the boats of the cormorant fishers were edging into the wide circle of light about the steamer. Along the shore of the island clustered the groups of mandarins, their silk and satin robes forming a bright spot in the vivid picture.

Doane found the sand then; walked a little way and helped the nearly exhausted boy to his feet.

"They're coming down the shore," said Rocky, trying, without great success, to speak casually.

Doane looked up and saw them running—white men, Chinese servants, mandarins holding up their robes, women, and last, walking rapidly, his excellency.

It was Hui Fei, throwing off her cloak and running lightly ahead, who took the frightened child from young Kane's arms and carried her tenderly up the bank. There as the attendants gathered anxiously about them, she tossed the child high, petted her, kissed her, until the tears gave place to laughter. The tall eunuch wrapped the little princess then in his own coat; and Hui Fei accepted the opera cloak that transformed her again in an instant from a slimly quaint Manchu girl to a young woman of New York.

Doane stood by. Toward him she did not look. But to Rocky Kane, who lay on the bank, she turned with bright eagerness. He got, not without effort, to his feet.

Smiling—happily, it seemed to the bewildered, brooding Doane—she gave him her hand; led him to meet her father.

"You have met Mr. Kane," she said. "It was he who save' little sister. He risk' his life to bring her here, father."

Rocky, throwing back his hair and brushing the water from his eyes, stood, his sensitive face working nervously, very straight, very respectful, and took the hand of the viceroy.

There was, then, manhood in him. The viceroy recognized the fact in his friendly smile. Hui Fei plainly recognized it as she walked, chatting brightly, at his side, while he bent on her a gaze of boyish adoration.

As for Doane, he moved away unobserved; dropped at length on a knoll, rested his great head on his hands, and gazed out at the blazing steamer. She would soon be quite gone. Poor Benjamin was gone already; a strange little man, one of the many that drift through life without a sense of direction, always bewildered about it, always hoping vaguely for some better lot. It had been a tragic night; and yet all this horror would soon seem but an incident in the spreading revolution. It had always been so in China. In each rebellion, as in the mighty conquests of the Mongols and the Manchus, death had stalked everywhere with a casual terribleness. Life meant, at best, so little. Genghis Khan's men had boasted of slaying twenty millions in the northwestern provinces alone within the span of a single decade. The new trouble must inevitably run its course; and what a course it might prove to be! From the mere effort to face this immediate future Doane found his mind recoiling; much as strong minds were to recoil, only three years later, when the German army should march through Belgium.

He gave up that problem, came down to the particular thought of this swiftly growing new love that had stolen into his heart. The hope of personal happiness had passed now. Self seemed, like the life to which it so eagerly clung, not to matter. Instead that hope was growing into a profound tenderness toward the girl. She was, after all—the thought came startlingly—about the age of his own daughter, Betty, whom he had not seen during these three strange years. Betty and her journalist husband would be somewhere in Turkestan now; he was studying central Asia for a book, she sketching the native types. For a long time no letter had come.... It was a fine experience, this unbidden stir of the emotions, this thrill. There was mystery in it, and wonder. Merely to have that almost youthful responsiveness still at call within his breast was an indication that life might yet hold, even for him, the derelict, rich promise. And it was a reminder, now, to his clearing brain that his life must be service. He must find terms on which to offer himself, his gifts. His spirit had been molded, after all, to no lesser end.

The viceroy drew away then from the group about the child; came deliberately along the bank. The increasing tenderness Duane felt toward Hui Fei reached also to her father, who was facing with such fine dignity the grim ending of a richly useful life. Now, perhaps, he could plead with him for the daughter's sake. Somehow, certainly, happiness must be found for her. In pleading he would be serving her.

His brain was swinging into something near balance; it was, after all, a good brain, trained to function clearly, mellowed through patient years of unhappiness. It would help him now to fight for the girl, to save her, if he might, from the dark ways of the Forbidden City. She called herself so naively an "American." The West had thrilled her. She must not be given over to the eunuch, Chang.

So, even as he contrived a sort of self-control, even as he determined to forget his own little moment of romantic hopefulness, the lover within him stood triumphant over all his other selves.

CHAPTER VII
THE INSCRUTABLE WEST

DOANE knew nothing of the dignified figure he presented as he took the viceroy's hand, a profoundly sobered giant, his huge frame outlined beneath his wet garments like a Greek statue of an athlete.

"You have helped to save the life of my child, Griggsby Doane"—thus his excellency, in what proved to be a little set speech—"and with all my heart I thank you. I am old. Little time is left to me. But life follows upon death. Death is the beginning of life. It has been said by Chuang Tzü that the personal existence of man results from convergence of the vital fluid, and with its dispersion comes what we term death. Therefore all things are one. All vitality exists in continuing life. And I, when what I have thought of as my self arrives at dispersion, shall live on in my children. My words are inadequate. My debt to you is beyond my power to repay. Command me. I am your servant."

Doane bowed, hearing the words, catching something of the warm gratitude in the heart of the old man, yet at the same moment flogged on to action by the sense of passing time and present opportunity. It was no simple matter, it seemed, to approach this seasoned, calmly determined mind regarding the final personal matter of life and death. But he plunged at it; stating simply that he had heard the gossip of the impending tragedy, and that in conversing with the lovely Hui Fei, who was in obvious difficulty in existing between the two greatest civilizations without a solid footing in either, he could not bear to think of her possible fate.

Rang Yu listened attentively.

"Your Excellency," Doane pressed on, "it is not right that you should listen to the command of a decadent throne. Forgive my frankness, my presumption, but I must say this! True, you are a Manchu. While this revolution continues it will be difficult for you. But before another year shall have gone by there will be a new China. The bitter animosities of to-day will pass. Though a Manchu, your wise counsel will be needed. Your knowledge of the Western World will temper the over-emphatic policies of the young hot-heads from the universities of Japan."

The viceroy considered this appeal during a long moment; then, soberly, he looked up into the massive, strongly lined face of the white man and asked, simply: "But what would you have me do, Griggsby Doane?"

"Your Excellency knows of the plan to seize your property?"

Kang inclined his head.

"If you go on to your home, it may be that everything will be taken, even the money on your person."

Kang bowed again.

"Then, Your Excellency, why not now—while you yet have the means to do so—escape down the river with your daughter and myself? Can you not trust yourself and her in my hands? I will find means to convey you safely to Shanghai—perhaps to Japan or Hong Kong—where you will be secure until further plans may be laid."

"Griggsby Doane," replied the viceroy with simple candor, "you speak indeed as a friend. And I would be false to the blood that flows in my veins did I not prize the friendship of man for man, second only to the love of a son for a parent, above every other quality in life. Friendship is most properly the theme of many of the noblest poems in our language. It is to us more than your people, who place so strong an emphasis on love between the sexes, can perhaps bring themselves to understand. And therefore, Griggsby Doane, your feeling toward myself and my daughter moves my heart more deeply than I can express to you.

"It is not surprising that news of my sorrow—of this sad ending that is set upon my long life—should have reached you. But since you know so much, I will tell you, as friend to friend, more. Do you know why this sentence has been passed upon me? It is because I could not bring myself to obey the order of the throne that the republican agitator, Sun Shi-pi who had sought sanctuary at my yamen in Nanking should be at once beheaded. Instead I sent for Sun Shi-pi to counsel him. I permitted him to go to Japan on condition that he engage in no conspiracies and that he remain away. Instead of complying with my condition he hastened to organize revolutionary propaganda. He returned to China, appeared in disguise on the steamer that is burning out yonder, and is now dead, there, in his republican uniform."

So his information was complete! A picture rose in Doane's mind of the headless trunk of Sun Shi-pi amid the horrors of the lower deck.

His excellency continued: "I was denounced at the Forbidden City as a traitor. The sentence of death followed, in the form of an edict from the empress dowager in the name of the young emperor. Were I now to follow Sun Shi-pi into exile in a foreign land I would mark myself for all time as a traitor indeed; as one who, while sharing as an honored viceroy the prosperity and dignity of the reigning dynasty, conspired toward its downfall."

"But, Your Excellency, the empress dowager and the young emperor no longer speak with the voice of the Chinese people."

"That could make no difference, Griggsby Doane. By edict of the Yellow Dragon Throne of Imperial China I have been instructed to go to my ancestors. My allegiance is only to that throne. I will obey.... Already, Griggsby Doane, you have done for me more than one can ever demand of a friend. And yet one more demand I must make upon you. There is no other to whom I can turn. I have no other friend to-night. Within a short time my secretaries will secure a launch or a junk to convey us to my home near Huang Chau. Will you come with us there?"

Doane, surprised, bowed in assent.

"Thank you. The gratitude of myself and all my family and friends will remain with you. You are a princely man.... Until later, then, good night, Griggsby Doane."

He was gone.

Doane walked farther along the bank; stood for a time absorbed in thought that led, at length, to what seemed a new ray of light in the darkness that was his mind. And he strode back, hunting in this group and that for Dawley Kane. That man had offered help. Now he could give it.

Dawley Kane, fully dressed, unruffled, quietly smoking a cigar and looking through a pocket notebook by the light from the river, seemed a note of sanity in an unbelievably confused world. To him, apparently, the nightmare of fighting and slaughter on the steamer, like the fire, were but incidents. The only evidence the man gave out of quickened nerves was that he talked a little more freely than usual. To Doane he presented a surface as clear and hard as polished crystal, impenetrable, in a sense repelling, yet, as we say, a gentleman.

They even chatted casually, as men will, standing there looking out at the fire (which now had reached the stem and eaten down to the lower decks, incinerating alike the bodies of men who had died for faith and for lust) and at the wide circle of light on the rim of which floated the vulture-the boats of the rivermen. Doane forced himself into the vein of the man's interest; riding roughshod over a desperate sense of unreality. For he knew that the great masters of capital were often proud and even finicky men who must be approached with skill. They were kings; must be dealt with as kings.

Kane was interested to learn what relation the fight below decks might have to the rebellion up the river. That, clearly, was characteristic of the man—the impersonal gathering in and relating of observable data. His interest was deeper in the agriculture and commerce of the immense Yangtze basin, to which subject he easily passed. His questions came out of a present fund of knowledge—questions as to the speed, cargo-capacity and operation-cost of the large junks that plied the river by thousands, as to the cost of employing Chinese labor and the average capacity of the coolie. He knew all about the slowly developing railroads of North and Central China; commented in passing on the surprising profits of the young Hankow-Peking line.... He seemed to Doane to have in his mind a map or diagram of a huge, profitmaking industrial world, to which he added such bits of line or color as occurred in the answers to his questions. But he gave out no conclusions, only questions. Famines, other wide-spread suffering so tragically common in the Orient, interested him only as an impairment of trade and industrial man power. The opium habit he viewed as an economic problem.

Doane, settling doggedly to his purpose, found himself analyzing the power of this quiet man. It lay of course, in the control of money. And money would be only a token of human energy. The religion of his own ardent years had taken no account of earthly energy or its tokens; it had directed the eyes of the bewildered seeker toward a mystical other world. Yet human life, in the terms of this earth, must go on. To this point he always came around, of late years, in his thinking, just as the church had always come around to it. Money was vital. The church was endlessly begging for it; in no other way could it survive to continue turning away the puzzled eyes of the seekers.

And the immense energy created in the human struggle to live and prosper must continually be gathering up, here and there, into visible power that shrewd human hands would surely seize. He felt this now as a law. Religion had not left him. He felt more strongly than ever before that this miraculously continuing energy implied a sublime orderly force that transcended the outermost bounds of human intelligence. Religion was surely there: it only wanted discovering. It had, as surely, to do with primitive energy, with the heat of the sun and the disciplined rush of the planets, with the tragic struggle of human business, with work and war and sex and money.... And then he indulged in a half-smile. For this primitive undying energy could be no other than the Tao of Lao-tzu and Chuang Tzü.

And so, after all these groping years of his errant faith, he had fetched up, simply in Taoism.

But that law seemed to stand. The human struggle created power that tended to gather at convenient centers. And here beside him, smoking a cigar, stood a man whose uncommon genius fitted him to seize that power as it gathered and administer it; a man to whom money came—the very winds of chance heaped it about him. And to Doane, just now, money—even in quantity that would be to Kane hardly the income of a day or so—meant so much that the grotesque want of it (the word "grotesque" came) stopped his brain.

For it was coming clear to him how completely the throne could at will, obliterate the worldly establishment of Kang Yu. That throne, however politically weak, yet held the savage instruments of despotic power. Kang's sad end would come within the twenty-four hours, perhaps; certainly he would wait only to prepare himself and to write his final papers. The eunuch's men would be everywhere about the household; nothing could be hidden from them, or from the spies among the servants.... With money—a little money—Hui Fei might be saved from an end as tragic as her father's.... The thing, surely, could be managed. For the moment it seemed almost simple. She could be spirted away. There might he missionaries to escort her down the river on one of the steamers.

It was then, while Doane's thoughts still raced hither and thither, that Kane himself broached the vital topic.

"This viceroy"—thus Kane—"seems to be quite a personage. He's been a diplomat, I believe. And Kato tells me has an excellent collection of paintings."

Doane felt himself turning into a trader. "You are interested in Chinese paintings, are you not, Mr. Kane?" he asked guardedly.

"Oh, yes. I have something of a collection. And now and then Kato picks up something for me."

"I don't know, of course, how far you would care to go with it Mr. Kane"—Doane was measuring every word as it passed his lips—"but there is a possibility that a bargain could be struck with his excellency at this time."

"Indeed?"

"It would be advisable to act pretty quickly, I should say."

"Well! This is interesting. You are informed about his collection?"

"In a general way. It is very well known out here. His collection of landscapes of the Tang and Sung periods is supposed to be the most complete in existence, with fine works of Ching Hao, Kuan Tung, Tung Yuan and Chu-jan. The best known paintings of Li Chang are his. He has several by Kao Ke-ming, and, I know, an original sixfold landscape screen by Kuo Hsi. Then there are works of the four masters of southern Sung—Li Tang, Lui Sungnian, Ma Yuen and Hsia Kuai. You would find nearly all the great men of the Academy represented."

Doane stopped; waited to see if this list of names impressed the great American. If he knew, in his own person, anything whatever about Chinese painting he must exhibit at least a little feeling. But Dawley Kane said nothing; merely lighted, with provoking deliberation, a fresh cigar.

"It is commonly understood, too"—Doane could not resist pressing him a little further—"that he has authentic paintings by Wu Tao-tzu, and Li Lung-mien." Surely these two names would stir this man who seemed at moments no more than a calculating machine with manners. But Kane smoked on.... "And I understand that he has a fairly complete collection of portraits by the men of the Brush-strokes-reducing Method."

He finished rather lamely; fell silent, and looked out over the still brilliantly lighted river; the river of a hundred thousand dramatic scenes— battles and romances and struggles for trade—the great river with its endless memories of gold and bloodshed—the river that for a brief day was running red again. The fire out there, though red flame and rolling smoke and whirling sparks still roared upward, was consuming now the lower deck and the hull. Within the hour the *Yen Hsin* would be no more than a curving double row of charred ribs; one more casual memory of the river.

Still Dawley Kane smoked on. He clearly knew no enthusiasm. He was an analyst, an appraiser, a trader to the core. He felt no discomfort, even in friendly talk, in letting the other man wait. But Doane would say no more. And finally, knocking the ash off his cigar with a reflective finger, Kane remarked; "You really think that this collection would be a good buy?"

"Unquestionably."

"Have you any idea what he would ask?"

"I don't even know that he would consider selling it."

"But if he were properly approached.... there are reasons____"

"You know of his predicament?"

"I gather that there is a predicament."

"Oh.... well, yes, there is. But I don't know how even to guess at the value. Many of the paintings are priceless. In New York, at collector's prices, and without hurrying the sale...."

"A hundred thousand dollars?"

"Many times more."

"But if he is anxious to sell—must sell"

"There is that, of course."

"A hundred thousand is a good deal of money. If I were to place that sum to his credit to-morrow, for instance, by wire, at a Shanghai bank, don't you suppose it would tempt him?"

"It might. Though Kang knows the value of every piece." Doane was finding difficulty in keeping pace with the situation. Kane would shave every penny, as a matter of principle. That, of course, explained him; was the secret of his wealth and power. Paintings, after all, mattered to him only in a remote sense; you could always buy them if you chose, if people would, as apparently they did, think better of you for buying them. It came down to the desirability of building up and solidifying one's name, of what Doane had heard spoken of everywhere in America during his last visit as "publicity." The word irritated him. It suggested that other word, also heard everywhere in America, "salesmanship." These words, to the sensitively observant Doane, had connoted an unpleasant blend of aggressive enterprise with an equally aggressive plausibility.

But his wits were sharpening fast. If this man was a buyer, he would be a seller.

"His excellency has another collection that might or might not interest you—the value of it would be only slightly artistic—his precious stones." Doane threw this cut carelessly. "There is no estimating the value of those. It might run into the millions...." He saw Kane's eyes come to a sudden hard focus behind the veil of smoke. He was really interested at last. And Doane, with mounting pulse, quietly added, "He has historical jewels from many parts of Asia—head ornaments, bracelets, ropes of matched pearls from Ceylon, old careen jade from Khotan, quantities of the jewelry taken from Khorassan and Persia by Genghis Khan and his sons, including a number of famous royal pieces, and some of the jeweled ornaments brought from the temples of India by Kublai Khan."

This, Doane knew, was enough. He waited, now, himself. Waited and waited.

"Mr. Doane"—Kane, at last, was speaking—"I would be glad to have you approach the viceroy for me. To-night, if you think best. I will be glad, of course, to pay you a commission."

"Shall I make a definite offer—for the paintings and the jewels?"

"No." Kane considered. "Let him set a price. Then we will make our offer."

"It is safe to say, Mr. Kane"—Doane was remembering experiences of men in church and educational work who had had to approach the great capitalists for gifts of money—"that you could sell half the paintings for what you might pay for the two collections at this time. That would enable you to give the other half, as a collection bearing your own name, to one of the art museums at home, at no cost to yourself."

Kane smoked thoughtfully. "I presume, Mr. Doane," he said, "that the predicament you spoke of can not interfere in any way with the safe delivery of the collections."

Doane considered. How much did this man know? That Japanese, behind his mask of a smile, would be deep, of course. With a sudden sinking of the heart, Doane perceived that Kane might easily know the whole story. But even if he did he would admit nothing. He trusted no one; that was his calm cynical strength. He would trade to the last.... Another swift, if random, perception of this tense moment was that much of the common talk regarding the "inscrutable" East was utter nonsense. Read in the light of history and habit the Oriental mind was anything but deeply mysterious; it was, indeed, very nearly an open book. Whereas the Western mind, with its miraculous religion, its sentimentality and materialism and (at the same time) its cynically unscrupulous financial power, could be baffling indeed.

Desperate now, seeing no other way through, Doane spoke out from his tortured heart. "Mr. Kane, the simple fact is that his excellency has been condemned to death, and his daughter to a fate that will almost certainly end in death for her as well. They are seizing his property...."

"Who are they?"

"The Imperial Government—the empress dowager and her crew. They are sending the chief eunuch, Chang Yuan-fu, to take his paintings and jewels, and his daughter, to Peking. Frankly, it may be necessary to hurry matters—smuggle the things out. But the fan paintings can be packed in parcels, the scrolls rolled small on their ivory sticks, the jewels gathered in a few boxes. Once in white hands they would be safe. I think. I believe I can arrange it. The porcelains and carvings you would probably have to leave behind."

His voice died out. Dawley Kane was coolly appraising him. Their minds were not meeting.

"As you are stating it now, it is a different situation altogether," said Kane, the ring of tempered metal in his voice. "Obviously the man to deal with is the eunuch, What's-his-name."

"But—really—"

"He would have the collections complete including the porcelains and the carvings. I should want them all. He would be ignorant and corrupt, of course; we could buy him for a song. And there would be no risk. Yes, let him get possession. Then if you would like to approach him for me I will be glad to see that you make something for yourself."

Doane drew in his breath. Slowly he said: "But that, Mr. Kane, seems a good deal like taking a profit out of the viceroy's misfortune."

But he caught himself. To Kane, who had made enormous profits out of wrecked railways, who had cornered stocks and produce and mercilessly squeezed the short sellers, this would be sentimentality.

Doane heard himself saying: "I'm sorry. I could hardly undertake it, Mr. Kane." And walked away. His failure was complete. Worse, if there had been any gaps in the information supplied by the ubiquitous little Kato, they were filled now. The finely balanced machine that served so smoothly as a brain in the head of the great American, would be working on and on. Through the Japanese he could easily enough reach Chang Yuan-fu from Hankow after the tragedy that now hovered so close over the old viceroy and all that was his. He could make what he and his suave kind would doubtless regard—the slang word came grimly—as a killing.

The white men had made a small fire of dry rushes and thwarts from the boats. There sat Hui Fei, the sleeping little princess in her arms; and, beside her, Rocky Kane. Near by, where the men had spread coats on the ground, Miss Means and Miss Andrews slept side by side.

Doane walking toward the group—stopping, moving away only to turn irresolutely back—saw young Kane reach over and take the child into his own arms, and saw Hui Fei smile at him. He strode away then, struggling to believe that she could do that. But she had.... After all, she knew only that he had acted outrageously toward her, had then apologized publicly, boyishly, and now had brought her little sister ashore, himself falling exhausted on the bank. With those few facts, out of her impulsively young judgment she could strike a balance in his favor. Even at his worst he had bluntly admired her; for that she might, in the end, forgive him. And his youth would call to her.

Deane, indeed, forced himself to consider the boy dispassionately. The wild oats of any spoiled youth with too much money at his disposal, if brought together, and closely scrutinized, would make an appalling showing. Wild young men did, of course, recover. There was in this boy a note of intensity—passionate, eager—that was by no means all egotism. And there was in the father a hard sort of character that had proved itself indomitable, and that must be taken into account. Yes, it was a simple fact, that many a young fellow had gone farther wrong than had Rocky Kane without wrecking his adult life. You couldn't tell. And there they were, the eager moody boy and the lovely girl, who was oddly, quaintly conspicuous in her opera wrap, sitting very close, talking in low tones while he walked alone. It was torture.... yet it wras an awakening. He told himself that it was better so... Pacing back and forth, dwelling on the quick changeableness of youth, its ardor and sensitive hopefulness, he thought—reaching out for fellowship as will always the hurt soul—of other lonely lives, of Abelard and Jean Valjean, of St. Francis, even of Christ. It was odd—from his present philosophical position of something near Taoism he felt the legendary Christ as a profoundly human and friendly spirit, immeasurably more tender, finer, gentler than the theological structure of thought and conduct that had been erected in His name. He had thought himself very nearly around the circle, back to essential good.... This process could bring only humility. Life began to matter less. Love was a tormenting problem of self; the mature soul must in some measure attain selflessness if it were not to go down in the trampled dust of life. Worldly success was an accident. It was hardly desirable; hardly mattered. That he had within the hour pinned his hope to money, fairly fought for it, began to seem incredible.

The viceroy found him standing quietly by the river, turning from the slowly dying fire out there to the slowly spreading glow in the eastern sky.

"I like to think," remarked his excellency, smiling in friendly fashion, "that when the first Buddhist patriarch, Bodhidharma, miraculously crossed the river on a reed plucked from the southern bank, it was not far from here, near my home."

"Was not your city of Huang Chau the home of Li To?" asked Doane.

"Indeed, yes!" cried his excellency. "In some of his excursions on the river he undoubtedly passed the site of my home."

Doane quoted from that most famous of rhapsodists in musical Chinese: "'One who has hearkened to the waters roaring down from the heights of Lung, and faint voices from the land of Ch'in; one who has listened to the cries of monkeys on the shores of the Yangtze Kiang and the songs of the land of Pa'.... That"—he was musing aloud, reflectively as the Chinese do—

"was written three full centuries before William of Normandy first set foot on British soil.... Li Po so described himself."

They talked on, of life and philosophy, in, language interwoven with classical allusions. Friendship, the finest relationship in Chinese civilization, as it stood, had come to them.... It brought a kind of peace. Doane failed to recognize this sensation as in some degree but a phase of his painful exaltation. It seemed to him then that his struggle, no matter what atonement might lie before, was over. He forgot again the Western vigor that was, and to the last would be, driving his spirit.

Meanwhile the swiftly growing acquaintanceship of Huj Fei and Rocky Kane was weaving its bright-tinted weft in and out through the dark warp of Rocky's ill-spent youth. His eyes followed the slightest movement of her slim hands and rested dog-like on her finely modeled head about which the shining wet black hair lay close. To his quick youth she was an exquisite fairy. He felt her as perfume in the air he breathed. Her voice, when she drowsily, prettily spoke, fell on his ear like music in an enchanted land. He could say little; he had never before so lost himself.

She tried daintily to conceal a yawn. And he, clasping the child in both arms, turned away to hide its brother. Then, very softly, she laughed and he laughed.

"You must try to sleep," he said gently.

"I can no' let you keep my sister. You, too, are ver' tire'."

"It's nothing. I love to hold her. Really! You see, my life hasn't been this way. Maybe, if I'd had a sister..." He stopped; suddenly, vividly sensing what he had been; a hot flush flooded his sensitive face. He could only add then: "I want you to sleep. It may be hours before the boat comes for you. It's been such a horrible night—such a nightmare...."

"But you mus' res', too. One of the servan's will take my sister."

"No!" he cried, low, fiercely, "I won't let any one else have her!" Sensing crudely that the child was a chord between them, he tightened his hold. The little head rolled back on his arm; he bent over, tenderly kissed the soft cheek, then looked over it at Hui Fei, staring. During one brief moment their eyes met full in the flickering yellow light.

She turned away; in lieu of speech looked about for a spot to lay her head.

"Here!" He laid the child on the ground; and, surprised to find himself collarless and coatless, took off his waistcoat, rolled it up and placed it for a pillow. "It's really pretty well dried out," he added, with an embarrassed little laugh.... Then, as she still said nothing, went on, "Do just lie down there. I'll keep awake. We can't count on the servants; they're all scared to death."

Still she hesitated. "I'm afraid I am ver' tire'," she finally remarked unsteadily. "I can't think ver' clearly."

"Listen!" said he, hardly hearing. "I've got to tell you something. I'm not good enough so much as to speak to you."

"Please!" she murmured. "I don' wan' you to talk abou' —"

"I don't mean that. It's other things too." His voice broke, but after a moment he pressed on, a determined look on his curiously youthful face. "I've done every rotten thing I could think of. I'm—well, I guess I'm just a criminal. No, listen—please! It's true. I'm to blame for this awful fire— smoking opium in my cabin. It was my lamp—it must have been. I fell asleep. But I knew better, of course.... Oh, God, it's terrible! All those lives, all this suffering! And you—I've nearly killed you—when it was you...." Here, creditably, he caught himself. "Don't think I'm talking wildly. I'm getting at something. Seeing you, meeting you—and now, this—well, I've never seen anybody like you. It's bowled me off my feet. I know what love is, now—Oh, please! I've got to get this out. I love you. I'm crazy about you. I can say that because pretty soon that boat'll come and you'll go and I'll never see you again. It's right, too! I've got to start again—alone and prove that there's good stuff in me somewhere..."

"I'm ver' tire'," she murmured wistfully; and resting her head on the rolled-up waistcoat she lay still.

If she had only let him finish! There had been something—some point— he was getting at. He hadn't meant to tire her or hurt her.... When the tall eunuch came for the little princess he angrily drove the fellow away. For Hui Fei was sleeping now, peacefully, like the warm little child in his arms.

An English gunboat was the first relief craft to arrive; in the cool dawn; a tiny craft, built for the river, with a white freeboard low as a monitor's and bridge structure forward of the thin high funnel. The small boat that came ashore made a number of trips, taking off the passengers and the surviving white officers of the *Yen Hsin*.

His excellency refused, with calm courtesy, to set foot on the English gunboat that was built for the river; he would wait for the junk that had been sent for.

Dawley Kane found his son, nodding, with the picturesquely-clad child in his arms. The boy, glancing at the sleeping Hui Fei whose head rested comfortably on the rolled-up waistcoat, gave the child now to the patiently waiting eunuch, then fairly dragged his father to the boat. With the Japanese, Kato, and oddly distant to the big mate and the suddenly exotic-appearing viceroy in his richly embroidered satins who had been after all only casually, for a few days, in their lives, they embarked.

They had nearly reached the gunboat when those on the bank heard young Kane's voice raised in hot protest. There was a moment of argument; then a splash. The boy could be seen then swimming back to shore. And Dawley Kane, turning his back, went on to the gunboat, stepped aboard, and disappeared. Rocky clambered, dripping, up the bank; came straight to Duane, a staring, exhausted youth, very white.

"I can't do it." he panted. "They've just told me—Kato and the pater—about this terrible trouble of the viceroy's and—and Miss Hui Fei's.... The pater said it was time I—got clear of any new entanglement. I quit him. Oh, I suppose you'll think me a—damn fool, but"—at this point he nearly broke into tears—"but I love that girl, Mr. Doane! If I can't be of some use to her—now, in this awful trouble—I don't want to live. Will you—help me? And let me help?".... And, all blind confidence, he offered his hand to the big mate; who took it.

The gunboat hoisted anchor and swung about, heading down-stream. Passing her, upward bound, came a large junk, with the rig of a trader from Szechuen, her single huge rectangular sail, brown-umber 'n tint and closely ribbed with battens of bamboo, flat against the one mast that towered clumsily amidships. The eight long sweeps, in the low waist and forward, moved rhythmically in time with the syncopated, wailing chant of nearly a hundred oarsmen. The *tai-kung* crouched, bamboo pole in hand, just within the prow.

The hull was of cypress, stained from stem to stern with yellow orpiment and rubbed to a polish with oil. The high after-deck structure, all of fifty feet in length, terminating in a projecting gallery-twenty feet or higher above the water, was carved everywhere in intricately decorative designs; as were, also, the roof over the tillerman's stand on the deck house and the gallery railing (just within which stood a row of flowering plants in yellow and green pots). The many small windows along the sides were glazed with opalescent squares of ground oyster shells and glue; those across the stern (under the gallery) with stained glass.

To no one aboard the gunboat or among the still waiting groups on the bank did the thought occur that this craft might be engaged in other than peaceable business. Her like were not an uncommon sight along the always crowded river. The passing attention she drew was merely that aroused by a richly decorative object moving beautifully (with a remarkably detailed reflection) through the flat water, that itself glowed under the red and gold of the early morning sky like a great sheet of burnished old copper. It was not observed that three white faces peered warily out of the shadow, behind as many opened windows; nor could it easily be seen that the figure in blue, sitting, knees drawn up, on the deck house just behind the *laopan* who mercilessly urged on the sweat-shining oarsmen, was none other than the redoubtable Tom Sung.

CHAPTER VIII
ABOARD THE YELLOW JUNK

IN making their escape from the steamer, Tex Connor and the Manila Kid seized one of the small boats, manning, one at either end, the tackle-falls. Connor was quick, rough, profane. The Kid, breathless with excitement, hesitant, glancing back over the rail for a thinly girlish face that did not, then, appear, worked with ten thumbs at the ropes. Connor's end, the boat, fell first, a short way, nearly pitching him out. He cursed this futile man, his jackal, roundly; then clung to the tackle as the stern fell.... The Kid moaned with pain as the slipping hemp burned the skin off his fingers, but held it just short of disaster.

Hot red flames licked out overhead as the boat jerkily dropped. The women were screaming up there. A white man, the second mate, leaned over, swearing vigorously at them. They passed an open freight gangway, where bodies lay.

"Ready, now!" cried Connor. "Let go with me!"

"Wait a minute, can't you?" whined the Kid. He was peering into the dark interior of the steamer; grasping a moment more; wrapping a handkerchief about his left hand. "My God! Can't a fellow tie up his hand."

A thin blue figure appeared, stepped lightly over into the boat and dropped on a middle thwart.

"Dixie!" cried the Kid in falsetto.

She wore a cap, and carried an oddly lady-like shopping bag.

"Where'd you come from?" growled Connor.

"I saw you start," said the girl casually. "Come on—let's get away."

Connor stared at her; then turned back to his work. The boat struck the water and drifted rapidly away down-stream. Connor, roaring angrily at the Kid, got out an oar.

"What are you doing?" asked Miss Carmichael very quietly.

"Going ashore?" said Connor.

"Oh, come, Tex!" said she. "Use your head."

He looked sharply, inquiringly, doubtingly at her.

"You two better row straight down-stream as hard as you can," she added. "You can bet Tom Sung and that gang aren't going to show themselves at Kiu Kiang. They've stopped somewhere below here."

The Kid, who was nursing his hand, looked up; wrinkled his low forehead that was hatless, and then softly whistled. Connor made no remark, but continued studying the girl with his one eye. Finally, with an effort at reasserting his authority, he growled:

"Take an oar, Jim!"

"But my hands! My God, that rope took all the—"

"Do you expect me to do the rowing, Jim?" said Miss Carmichael.

The Kid yielded then. The girl settled herself comfortably in the stern, looking back at the fire. Soon they were out of the circle of light.

Suddenly Connor drew in his oar; stowed it away.

"Dixie," he remarked. "You've made up your mind to go through with this business, eh?"

"Certainly," she replied.

"You'll have to come across if you want my help. I won't go it blind."

Miss Carmichael glanced back at the red glow in the sky, then out toward the slightly paling East.

"I'll tell you by sunrise," she said. "The thing won't keep much longer than that, anyhow. It'll have to be fairly quick work."

"All right," said Connor. "That's an agreement. Now I'm going to take a nap. This current's taking us down fast enough. When you sight Tom's outfit, wake me up." With which he curled up in the bow, and soon was snoring.

The Kid stowed his own oar, and crept to the girl's side.

"Careful!" she whispered. "If he should wake up...." She extricated herself from an encircling arm. "Jim—sit still now!—It's time you and I had an understanding. I need you, and I'm going to use you. I don't propose to have you all steamed up, either. You'll need all the nerve you've got. Perhaps more. I'm not at all sure that you're big enough for what you've got to do. That's the difficulty."

"You promised, Dixie." He was still absurdly breathless. "You said it was a trade—if I'd stick to you, you'd stick to me!"

"Certainly. But it's during the next eight or ten hours that you're going to find out what sticking to me, means. You can have me, all right, Jim, but you've got to earn me."

"I guess I'll earn you, all right."

"I wonder if you have the courage."

"By God, for you, Dixie—"

Her hand fell lightly on his; and her voice, very small and calm, broke in with: "Supposing I told you to kill a man. Would you do it?"

She heard, felt, his breath stop. Then he whispered, with one swift glance at the sleeping Connor: "If I say yes, Dixie, will you kiss me? Right now!"

She pressed her lips slightly; then replied: "No. Not yet. And you needn't kill anybody until I tell you to."

"Is it—is it"—his whisper was huskier—"is it—him, Dixie?" He was staring with less certainty now, at Connor.

"No"—said she slowly—"nobody in particular. But anything may happen to-night, Jim. And we can't falter. Not now."

She let him press her hand during a brief moment; then made him resume his seat. And from behind lowered lids she watched him.

Once he came back, to ask hoarsely: "You said he was rough with you, Dix. Did he—did you and he—my God, if I thought that Tex had—"

She caught his shoulder and placed a hand over his mouth: held him thus while she said: "If he catches you back here, Jim, he'll kill you. No fear! Now you go back there and show me that you can play cards. You're sitting in the biggest game of your life. Jim Watson."

He crept back; puzzled, something hurt. There was a sting in her voice. Could it be that the girlish Dixie was as cold-blooded as that? Treating him like a child! Hadn't she any feelings? The question came around and around in his muddy brain, confused with frantic uprushes of jealousy against the big man who slept and snored in the bow.... hadn't she any feelings?.... She was excitingly desirable.

Just as a conquest, now; something to brag about.

It was Dixie who sighted the soldiers, sitting in heated argument on the bank not a hundred yards below a big junk that lay moored to stakes in an eddy. She called sharply to Connor; they pulled straight in beside the other two boats.

Tom Sung came to the water's edge, a rifle (with set bayonet) in his hand. Connor stepped out, holding the boat. The Kid, with a furtive, glance at the big yellow fighter, and the abruptly silent shadowy group on the bank, cautiously got out an automatic pistol and held it beside him on the thwart.

Dixie said sharply, for Connor's ears: "Put up that gun, Jim!"

The Kid obeyed.

She spoke then to Connor direct.

"Tell your man we want that junk," she said. "Get out these other boats and take it, quick. Then we'll start back up stream."

For a moment Connor was nonplussed. The girl's assumption of authority was complete. Even the slow-thinking Tom Sung felt her presence and turned abruptly from himself toward her.

But, though angered, Connor controlled himself. She meant, after all, business. Dixit wasn't a girl to make careless mistakes. She knew, none better, what any success, little or big, might be worth in risks run. So, speaking sharply, he gave his orders to Tom.

Quietly the twenty or more outlaw soldiers came down to the boats and pushed off. Rowing and paddling they crept up on the junk. A drowsy watchman peeped over at the rail, forward.

Then they were alongside. Catching at the mooring poles, the soldiers stepped out on the wide sponson that curved down, amidships, nearly to the water-line. Quickly, rifles slung on backs but revolvers at their girdles and knives in their teeth, they went up the ropes hand over hand, their bare feet dinging monkeylike to the smooth side.

There were cries aboard now, and a confusion of running feet. The first soldier to get a leg over the rail came tumbling back with a split skull, bounding off the sponson into the water and sinking as he drifted away.

Connor and the Kid caught together at the sponson. Connor stepped out; and calling on a belated soldier to give him a back, climbed laboriously, puffing but determined, up over the rail, pausing at the top only to call back for the Kid to follow.

But that worthy hesitated, crouching, clutching at the boat painter. "I've got to hold the boat here!" he shouted back; but Connor had disappeared.

There was much noise up there now—shouts, groans, appalling screeches, shots, and that insistent pattering of feet.

Dixie, watching critically the crouching figure on the sponson—for the Kid was shivering and making little sounds, obviously caught in the acute physical distress into which extreme sudden fear will at times plunge a man—called abruptly: "Jim—look up!"

A nearly naked Chinese was lowering himself in a deliberate gingerly manner down a moving rope nearly overhead.

"Kill him, Jim!" Dixie added.

Singling out her clear voice from the tumult, the yellow man looked fearfully down.

The Kid, at the same moment, looked up; then, fumbling in a curiously absent way for his pistol, glanced back at Dixie.

"I'll hold the boat," said she. "Go on—kill him!" She sat quietly, one thin arm reached out to the nearest mooring pole, looking steadily up.

The Kid, nerving himself, suddenly burst into a storm of wild oaths and shot three times into the body above him. At the first shot the man slipped down a little way.

"Push him away!" Dixie cried sharply. "I don't want him falling into the boat!"

He was shooting again; and then with an effort diverted the falling body.

Dixie got up, and stood steadying herself in the gently rocking boat; and the Kid—quit; out of breath now, and muttering, as he fondled the hot pistol, "Well, I did it, didn't I? I did what you said!"—found in her eyes, shining through the dusk of early dawn, a bright white light that was, to him, disconcerting and yet profoundly thrilling. He shivered again as he felt the spell of her strange genius. What a woman, he was thinking again, but wildly, madly, now, to conquer.

And she was saying, "I guess your nerve's all right."

Other shining yellow bodies were tumbling over the side and floating away.

"Help me up there, Jim!" she commanded. "Never mind tying the boat—let it go! It's only a giveaway. Quick—give me a hand!"

She was beside him on the sponson. He clasped her in his arms; but before he could kiss her she slapped him sharply. "Keep your head!" she commanded. "Put me up there!"

He lifted her high; until she could kneel, then stand, on his shoulder. She went over the rail as lightly as a boy. She found the soldiers in small groups cornering one or another of the crew, torturing and hacking at them with bayonets and knives, and during a brief moment looked on with a curious keen interest. The master, or *laopan*, crouched, whimpering, on the poop.... She saw Connor standing by the mast, just above the well, amidships and forward, where were huddled the survivors among the crew (their number surprisingly large); Connor was panting, revolver in hand, and scowling about him.

Dixie stepped to his side.

"You've got to save enough of this crew to work the boat up the river, Tex," she remarked.

"I'm saving enough of 'em," he replied gruffly. "We've only killed a dozen or so. There was more'n a hundred."

The heavily evil-looking Tom Sung reluctantly detached himself from one of the groups and came over, wiping his bayonet casually on his sleeve. Mr. Connor roughly ordered to gather his men together and make ready to get under way. To the Kid, who came awkwardly over the rail just then, Connor gave merely a glance. Then to Dixie, he said:

"Come up here!"

He led the way up the steps with the carven hand rail to the poop; gave the *laopan* a careless kick; stepped around the steersman''s covered pit and out astern on the high projecting gallery.

"Now," he said, fixing his one eye on Her, "where's this place?"

She turned away to the pots of flowers that stood closely spaced just within the elaborate woodwork of the railing. There were chrysanthemums, white, yellow and deep Indian red; highly cultivated double dahlias; red lotus blossoms; and tuberoses that filled the fresh morning air with their heavy perfume. "Well?" Connor added explosively.

"I said I'd tell you by sunrise, Tex," she said, coolly pleasant; and hummed, very softly, a music-hall tune, bending over a spreading lotus blossom with every appearance of ingenuous girlish interest. After a moment, she went on, "The thing now is to get this junk up the river as fast as it will go."

"Where to?" He was controlling his voice, but his face, usually expressionless, was brutally clouded...."Push me just a little farther, Dix, and you'll go overboard. And there won't be any flowers at the funeral. By God, I'm not sure I wouldn't enjoy it. You got me into this business! Now if you—"

"Better control yourself, Tex," said she; straightening up before him. "I may have got you in, but it's a real job now. You've got to go through. And you're going to need me. The place is a few miles this side of a town called Huang Chau, on the north hank."

"Beyond Hankow?"

"No, below. It's only a matter of hours getting up there, if you'll just get this junk started."

"How'll we know it when we get there?"

"All we've got to do is ask a native, anywhere along the bank, where Kang Yu lives—his old home."

"Who's he?"

"The viceroy of Nanking. Why don't you use that eye of yours once in a while, Tex—look around you a little?"

Slowly his mind, so quick at the vicious games of his own race, picked up and related the facts. His face relaxed, as he thought, into the familiar wooden expression.

"You're sure the stones are there?" he asked, quietly now.

She nodded; hummed again; caressed the flowers.

"All right, Dix," he said then, as he turned to go forward, "that sounds square enough. I guess I can handle it all right. And I'll see that you get your share all hunky dory."

"What are you figuring my share to be?" she asked, glancing casually up from a lotus blossom.

"Oh," he cried without hesitation, almost playfully, "you and I aren't going to have any trouble about that."

He went then; and she lingered among the flowers.

From beyond the long deck house came shouts and wailing. The great sweeps were got overside. The mooring poles were hoisted out and lashed along the sponsons. The clumsy craft swung out into the river and moved slowly forward.

At the sound of a hasty light step Dixie looked up into the haggard gray face of the Kid.

"What was it?" he whispered, glancing fearfully behind him. "Wha'd he say to you?"

She dropped her eyes; turned away.

"Quick! Tell me, or by God, I'll—"

She threw up a frail white hand.

"Not now, Jim!"

"When?"

"He'll have to sleep. There's work ahead."

"If you think *I* can sleep—"

"I can't either, Jim. It's dreadful. But I'm going to tell you everything. You have a right to know. Wait till we're past the steamer. We'd better get below now anyhow. We mustn't be seen. If we aren't, they'll never suspect this junk. Then make sure he's asleep and come up here. I'll be waiting."

The Kid brought Dixie's breakfast of rice and eggs and tea to the gallery.

"The cook was only wounded a little," he explained. "Tom's got him working now."

Dixie was reclining on a Canton chair of green rushes over a bamboo frame, her head resting languidly near the tuberoses. Now and again she drew in deeply the rich odor. And beyond the fringe of flowers and the carven railing she could see the river. Junks moved slowly by, sliding down with the current—somber seagoing craft out of Tientsin and Cheefoo and Swatow and even Canton. By a village were clustered open sampans, and slipper-boats with their coverings of arched matting. The small craft of the fishermen with suspended nets or with roosting, crowding cormorants clustered here and there along the channel-way. Everywhere farmers and their coolies were at work in the fields. A family—father, mother, boys and girls—worked tirelessly with their feet a large irrigating wheel at the water's edge.

The Kid seated himself on the deck and mournfully looked on while she ate. Perversely she delayed her narrative, playing with time and life. In her oblique way she was happy, exercising her gift for gambling on a scale new in her experience. Indeed, for the thrill she now experienced, Dixie Carmichael would have paid almost any price. Life itself—the mere existing—-she held almost as cheaply as the Chinese. Deliberately, with nerves steady as steel instruments, she finished her simple breakfast and then put the bowls aside on the deck.

Lying back, averting her face, gazing off down the river, she began the narrative that she had framed within the hour. Her manner, calm at first, soon offered evidences of deeply suppressed emotion. Her voice exhibited the first unsteadiness the Kid had ever heard in it. She drew out an embroidered handkerchief from the pocket of her blouse and pressed it once or twice to her eyes, as, with an air of dogged determination, she talked on.

The narrative itself dealt with her girlhood near San Francisco, her chance meeting with Tex Connor, then a well-known character on the western coast of America, her girlish infatuation with him, and an elopement that she had supposed would end in marriage. Instead she found her life ruined. Connor had beaten her, degraded her, driven her into vice. She ran away from him; reached the China Coast; settled down with every intent to become what she termed, in his and her language, a square gambler.

"When I took up with you a little last year, Jim, it seemed to me that at last I'd found a man I could tie to. You never knew my real feelings. I'm not the kind that tells much or shows much. I guess perhaps my life's been too hard. But—oh, Jim!—well, you're, seeing the real girl now. I'm pretty well beaten down, Jim.... You're getting the truth from me at last. I've got to tell it—all of it—for your own sake. You're in worse trouble than you know, right now. The cards are stacked against you, Jim. Your life even"—her voice broke; but she got it under control—"I'm going to save you if I can."

Moodily he watched her.

"If it was anybody but Tex! He's merciless. He's strong. He never forgets.... Listen, Jim! Tex came clear from London to find me. And he found out about—us—you and me. That I was growing fond of you. He never forgets and he never forgives. Oh. Jim, can't you see it! Can't you see that that's why he took you on—so he could watch you, keep you away from me? Can't you see what a game I've had to play? God, if you'd heard what he said to me back here this very morning—Oh, it's too awful! I can't tell you! He's so determined! He gets his way, Jim—Tex gets his way!.... Oh, what can I do!"

"No, wait—I've got to tell you the whole thing. You said he was planning to cross me. He'll do that, of course. I don't think I care much about that. But you, Jim—oh, you poor innocent boy! If you could only see! You'll never get your hands on one of the viceroy's jewels."

She turned her face toward him. Her eyes now were swollen and wet with tears.

Jim, gray of face, held in his two hands a Chinese knife, balancing it. There were stains on the blade. He must have picked it up, she reflected, here on the junk. For it wouldn't be like him to carry such a weapon. It seemed to her then that he was holding his breath. She saw him moisten his blue lips with the tip of an ashen tongue. He was trying to speak. At least his lips parted again. She waited. When the voice did finally come, it was so hoarse that he had evident difficulty in making it intelligible.

"Tex may be strong—but if you think I'm afraid—"

"Oh, Jim.... no, I don't mean that! Not that! Oh, I don't know what I'm saying-! It's only when I think how happy you and I might be—think of it! really rich! able to go and live decently somewhere, like regular folks!"

Silently, with surprising stealthy swiftness, he got to his feet. His right hand, with the knife, busied itself in a side pocket of his coat.

"Say the word, Dixie"—his face was contorted with the muscular effort necessary to produce this small sound—"say the word, and I'll kill him."

"Oh, no, Jim!" she covered her face with her thin hands, and sobbed, very low. "Oh God, what can we do? Isn't there some other way?"

"Say the word," he whispered.

"Would it be"—she broke down again—"would it be—where a man's a devil, where he's threatened—wouldn't it be like defending ourselves?"

"Say the word!"

"Oh, Jim—-God forgive me!.... Yes!"

Her lips barely framed the word. But he read it. She watched him as he stepped around the huge coils of tracking rope on the roof of the steersman's pit; watched until he dropped softly down and disappeared.

Then, lying back, very still, she listened. But the oarsmen were chanting up forward, the *laopan* shouting; nearer, the steersman was singing an apparently endless falsetto narrative (as if there had never been bloodshed). The minutes slowly passed. She drew in the sweet exhalation of the tuberoses.... still no unusual sound. She herself exhibited no sign of excitement beyond the hint of a cryptic smile and the white light in her eyes.... Her shopping bag lay on her lap. Opening it, she looked at the bracelet watch, that nestled close to a small triangular bottle of green corrosive sublimate tablets.... The gentle wash of the current against the hull gave out a soothing sound. The slowly rising sun beat warmly down, and the polished deck radiated the heat. A sensation of drowsiness was stealing over her. For a short while she fought it off; but then, deciding that no anxiety on her part could be of value, she yielded, closed the bag on her lap, and drifted into slumber.

It was pleasantly warmer still. She felt her eyes about to open—slowly—on a presence. This languor was delicious. As an almost ascetic epicure in sensations she rested a moment longer in it, thinking dreamily of priceless gems heaped in her hollowed hands; of luxurious idleness in some exotic port—Singapore, or Penang (she had loved the tropical splendor of Penang), or in Burmah or India—Rangoon say, or even Lucknow, Lahore and Simla. They would know less about her there. And with the means to operate on a larger scale she should be able to add enormously to her wealth. She decided to dress and act differently; make a radical change in her methods.

Her lips parted. The presence before her—coatless, little cap pushed back off the low forehead—was Connor. He had pushed aside a flower pot to make a seat on the rail.

She closed her eyes again. He still wore the gray flannels and the white shoes with the rubber soles-It would be the shoes that had enabled him to approach without awakening her. He was smoking a cigar And the face was wooden again—save for his eye—He at stared oddly at her. And she thought his breathing somewhat short, just at first.

She opened her eyes again.

"I've had a good nap," she said.

He smoked, and stared.

"Where's Jim?" she asked then; quite casually: raising herself on an elbow.

He made no reply; smoked on, still a thought breathless, fixing her with his eyes.

"He brought me some breakfast, just before I fell asleep.... What time is it?"

For what seemed a long space he did not even answer this; merely smoked and stared. She had never, sensitively keen as were her perceptions, felt so curious a hostility in Connor. She had hitherto supposed that she understood him, short as had been their actual acquaintance—-her narrative of a past with him in America, as related to Jim, was false—but the man before her now, sitting all but motionless on the railing, smoking with an odd rapid intensity, holding that cold eye on her, was wholly alien.

Finally he replied: "It's afternoon."

"No!" She sat up. "Have we been going right along?"

"Right along."

She stood erect; covered a yawn; then with her thin hands smoothed down the wrinkled blue skirt about her hips.

"I look like the devil," she remarked. The thin hands went to her hair. "You haven't noticed any sort of a mirror in the cabin, have you, Tex?"

He did not reply.

Faintly through the still air came a faint sound—a boom—boom-bom.

"What's that?" she asked sharply.

"Fighting around Hankow."

"We're not way up there?" She stepped to the side and looked out ahead. "There's a city!"

"Tom says it's Huang Chau."

"Hello! We're there!"

He inclined his head.

"What are you going to do?"

"Tie up here."

She heard now other and more confused sounds. The junk was slowing down; working in toward the yellow shallows.

"Now listen!" said he. She glanced at him, then away, apparently considering the quiet landscape; alien he was indeed, and hostile, his manner that of an inarticulate man struggling with a set speech.... "Listen! You're smart enough. But I want you to understand I don't trust you."

"Don't you, Tex?"

"When I go ashore, you're to stay here—right here on this deck—where you are now."

"What's the big idea, Tex?"

"There'll be men to see that you do stay here. I want you to get this straight."

"Of course," said she musingly, "you won't be able to rob me outright. You'll have to give me enough of a share to keep me quiet afterward."

He said nothing.

"But what's to prevent the crew from getting away with the junk. I'm not very keen about being carried off that way."

"You needn't worry. I'm taking the master along with me."

He stood then; looked meaningly at her; then went forward. She noted that his two hip pockets bulged.

Slowly the long narrow craft was worked in toward the land. Trackers sculled ashore in sampans and made the great hawsers fast to stakes. Then the crew, with a deal of shouting and many casual blows, were assembled in the long well forward of the mast, where they huddled abjectly.

Keeping around the steersman's house, Dixie contrived to take in much of the scene. There was quarreling among the soldiers. Tom Sung towered over them, shouting rough orders. The two men that were told off (she judged to guard her and the junk) appeared to be objecting to their part in the affair. Obviously there would be small loot here.

Connor came back over the deck house; stood angrily over her. She sensed the mounting brutality in him. For that matter, his sort and their ways with women were familiar enough to her. She had learned to take brutal men for granted. But it had not occurred to her that Connor would strike her. However, he did. Knocked her to her knees; then to her face; even kicked her as she lay on the deck. He was suddenly loud, wild.

"None o' this peeking around!" he cried. "Keep your eyes where they belong!" And left her there.

After a little she was able to creep to the rail and peer out through the flowers. Frightened members of the crew were sculling the sampans back and forth, until at length the whole party, every man except the *laopan* armed, fully assembled, set off inland.

Beyond an unpleasant headache she felt no injury. She sat for a little while; then again looked forward. The two guards were on the deck house, talking excitedly together. While she watched they climbed down, shouted at the huddled crew, fired a careless shot or two into the mass of them that brought down at least one. At length two of the crew went over the side, followed by the soldiers. A moment later the sampan appeared moving toward the shore, the two soldiers loudly urging on the oarsmen.

Dixie, swiftly then, rearranging her disordered hair as she walked, went down into the cabin.

A corridor extended along one side from the *laopans* quarters under the steersman''s house—sounds of stifled weeping came from there, apparently a woman or a girl—forward to the open space amidships. The rooms all gave on this corridor, the doorways hung with curtains of blue cotton cloth. Into one and another of these rooms she looked. There was bentwood furniture and bedding in each——the latter tossed about. On the walls hung neat ideographic mottoes. The grillwork about the windows and over the doors was of a uniform and quaint design.

Connor had taken for himself the rear room. There she found, beneath the window a heap of matting and bedding. Thoughtfully, deliberately, she lifted it off, piece by piece, exposing first a foot and leg, then a bony hand, finally the entire figure of what had been Jim Watson, known, of recent years, along Soochow Road and Bubbling Well Road as the Manila Kid. His clothing was slashed and torn in many places. About his middle, and about his head, were wide pools of blood that during a number of hours, evidently, had been drying into the boards of the deck. The neck, she observed, on closer examination, had been cut through nearly to the vertebrae.

During a swift moment she considered the grew-some problem; then carefully replaced the matting and bedding.

She went forward then to the end of the corridor; paused to look in her shopping bag, open the triangular bottle and drop a few of the green pills into the pocket of her middy blouse, under her handkerchief; closed the bag and stepped out on the low midships deck.

The sampan had just returned to the junk. The two soldiers were walking; rapidly inland after Connor's party. She let herself quickly over the side; stepped into the sampan; waved toward the shore. Meekly the cowed oarsmen obeyed the pantomime order.

She stepped out on the bank, very slim, almost pretty; tossed a Chinese Mexican dollar into the boat, watched, with a faint, reflective smile, the two primitive creatures as they fought over it; then walked briskly, not without a trace of native elegance in her carriage, after the soldiers, lightly swinging her shopping bag.

CHAPTER IX
IN A GARDEN

THE road—narrow, worn to a deep-rutted little canyon—circled a brown hill, rose into a mud-gray village, where a few listless children played among the dogs, and a few apathetic beggars, and vendors of cakes, and wrinkled old women stared at the thin white girl who walked rapidly and alone; wound on below the surface of the cultivated fields; came, at length, to a wall of gray-brick crowned with tiles of bright yellow glaze and a ridge-piece of green, and at last to a gate house with a heavily ornamented roof of timbers and tiles. Other roofs appeared just beyond, and interlacing foliage that was tinged, here and there, with the red and yellow and bronze of autumn.

The great gates, of heavy plank studded with iron spikes, stood open, apparently unattended. Dixie Carmichael paused; pursed her lips. Her coolly searching eyes noted an incandescent light bulb set in the massive lintel. This, perhaps, would be the place. Almost absently, peering through into tiled courtyards, she took two of the green tablets from her pocket; then, holding them in her hand, stepped within, and stood listening. The rustling of the leaves, she heard, as they swayed in a pleasant breeze, and a softly musical tinkling sound; then a murmur that might be voices at a distance and in some confusion; and then, sharply, with an unearthly thrill, the silver scream of a girl.... Yes, this would be the place.

The buildings on either hand were silent. Doors stood open. Paper windows were torn here and there, and the woodwork broken in. But the flowers and the dwarf trees from Japan that stood in jars of Ming pottery were undisturbed.

She passed through an inner gate and around a screen of brick and found herself in a park. There was a waterfall in a rockery, and a stream, and a tiny lake. A path led over a series of little arching bridges of marble into the grove beyond; and through the trees there she caught glimpses of elaborate yellow roofs. On either hand stood *pai-lows*—decorative arches in the pretentious Chinese manner—and beyond each a roofed pavilion built over a bridge.... She considered these; after a moment sauntered under the *pai-low* at her right, mounted the steps and dropped on the ornamented seat behind a leafy vine. Here she was sheltered from view, yet her eyes commanded both the main gate and the way over the marble bridges to the buildings in the grove.

She looked about with a sense of quiet pleasure at the gilded fretwork beneath the curving eaves of the pavilion, the painted scrolls above them, and the smooth found columns of aged nanmu wood that was in color like dead oak leaves and that still exhaled a vague perfume. The tinkling sound set up again as another breeze wandered by; and looking up she saw four small bells of bronze suspended from the eaves.... She sat very still, listening, looking, thinking, drawing in with a deep inhalation the exquisite fragrance of the nanmu wood. It might be pleasant, one day, to lease or even buy a home like this. So ran her alert thoughts.

The murmuring from the buildings in the grove continued, now swelling a little, now subsiding. It was not, of itself, an alarming sound, except for an occasional muffled shot. Her quick imagination, however, pictured the scene—they would be running about, calling to one another, beating in doors, rummaging everywhere. The drunkenness would doubtless be already under way. There would be much casual but ingenious cruelty, an orgiastic indulgence in every uttermost thrill of sense. It would be interesting to see; she even considered, her nerves tightening slightly at the thought, strolling back there over the bridges; but held finally to her first impulse and continued waiting here.

A considerable time passed; half an hour or more. Then she glimpsed figures approaching slowly through the grove. They emerged on the farthest of the little marble bridges. One was Tex Connor; the second perhaps— certainly—Tom Sung. They carried armfuls of small boxes, at the sight of which Dixie's pulse again quickened slightly; for these would be the jewels. Tom appeared to be talking freely; as they crossed the middle bridge he broke into song; and he reeled jovially.... Connor walked firmly on ahead.

They stopped by the gate screen. Connor glanced cautiously about; then moved aside into a tiled area that was hidden from the gate and the path by quince bushes. He called to Tom who followed.

Miss Carmichael could look almost directly down at them through the leaves. She watched closely as they hurriedly opened the boxes and filled their pockets with the gems. Tom used a stone to break the golden settings of the larger diamonds, pearls and rubies.

A low-voiced argument followed. She heard Tom say, "I come back, all light. But I got have a girl!" And he lurched away.

Connor, looking angrily after him, reached back to his hip pocket; but reconsidered. He needed Tom, if only as interpreter; and Tom, singing unmusically as he reeled away over the marble bridges, knew it.

Connor waited, standing irresolute, listening, turning his eye toward the gate, then toward the trees behind him. The girl in the pavilion considered him. She had not before observed evidence of fear in the man. But then she had never before seen him in a situation that tested his brain and nerve as well as his animal courage. He was at heart a bully, of course: and she knew that bullies were cowards.... What small respect she had at moments felt for Tex left her now. She came down to despising him, as she despised nearly all other men of her acquaintance. Still peering through the leaves, she saw him move a little way toward the gate, then glance, with a start, toward the marble bridges, finally turning back to the remaining boxes.

He opened one of these—it was of yellow lacquer richly ornamented— and drew out what appeared to be a tangle of strings of pearls. He turned it over in his hands; spread it out; felt his pockets; finally unbuttoned his shirt and thrust it in there.

It was at this point that Dixie arose, replaced the green tablets in her pocket, smoothed her skirt, and went lightly down the steps. He did not hear her until she spoke.

"Do you think Tom'll come back, Tex?"

He whirled so clumsily that he nearly fell among the boxes and the broken and trampled bits of gold and silver; fixed his good eye on her, while the other, of glass, gazed vacantly over her shoulder.

She coolly studied him—the flushed face, bulging pockets, protruding shirt where he had stuffed in those astonishing ropes of pearls.

He said then, vaguely: "What are you doing here?"

"Thought I'd come along. Suppose he stays back there—drinks some more. You'd be sort of up against it, wouldn't you?"

"I'd be no worse off than you." He was evasive, and more than a little sullen. She saw that he was foolishly trying to keep his broad person between her and the boxes.

"You couldn't handle the junk without Tom. Not very well.... Look here, Tex, it can't be very far to the concessions at Hankow. We could pick up a cart, or even walk it."

"What good would that do?"

"There'll be steamers down to Shanghai."

"And there'll be police to drag us off."

"How can they? What can they pin on you?" Connor's eye wavered back toward the grove and the buildings. He was again breathing hard. "After all this.." he muttered. "That old viceroy'll be up here, you know. With his mob, too. And there's plenty of people here to tell...." He was trying now to hold an arm across his middle in a position that would conceal the treasure there.

Her glance followed the motion, and for a moment a faintly mocking smile hovered about her thin mouth. She said: "Saving those pearls for me, Tex?"

He stared at her, fixed her with that one small eye, but offered not a word. A moment later, however, nervously signaling her to be still he brushed by and peeped out around the quinces.

"What is it?" she asked quickly; then moved to his side.

Immediately beyond the farthest of the marble bridges stood a group of ten or twelve soldiers in drunkenly earnest argument. Above them towered the powerful shoulders and small round head of Tom Sung. In the one quick glance she caught an impression of rifles slung across sturdy backs, of bayonets that seemed, at that distance, oddly dark in color; an impression, too, of confused minds and a growing primitive instinct for violence. Tom and another swayed toward the bridge; others drew them back and pointed toward the buildings they had left. The argument waxed. Voices were shrilly emphatic.

"Looks bad," said the girl at Connor's shoulder. "You've let 'em get out of hand, Tex." Then, as she saw him nervously measuring with his eye the width of the open space between the quinces and the gate screen, she added, "Thinking of making a run for it, Tex?"

He slowly swung that eye on her now; and for no reason pushed her roughly away. "It's none of your business what I'm going to do," he replied roughly.

But the voice was husky, and curiously light in quality. And the eye wavered away from her intent look. This creature fell far short of the Tex Connor of old. She spoke sharply.

"Come up into this summer-house, Tex!" she indicated it with an upward jerk of her head. "They won't see us there, at first. You didn't see me. You've got your pistols. You can give me one. We ought to be able to stand off a few Chinese drunks."

She could see that he was fumbling about for courage, for a plan, in a mind that had broken down utterly. His growl of—"I'm not giving you any pistol!"—was the flimsiest of cover. And so she left him, choosing a moment when that loud argument beyond the bridges was at its height to run lightly up the steps and into the pavilion.

From this point she looked down on the thick-minded Connor as he struggled between cupidity, fear and the bluffing pride that was so deep a strain in the man. The one certain fact was that he couldn't purposelessly wait there, with Tom Sung leading these outlawed soldiers to a deed he feared to undertake alone.... They were coming over the bridges now, Tom in the lead, lurching along and brandishing his revolver, the others unslinging their rifles. The argument had ceased; they were ominously quiet.

Dixie got her tablets out again; then sat waiting, that faint mocking smile again touching the corners of her mouth. But the smile now meant an excitement bordering on the thrill she had lately envied the savage folk in the grove. Such a thrill had moved those coldeyed women who sat above the combat of gladiators in the Colosseum and with thumbs down awaited the death agony of a fallen warrior. It had been respectable then; now it was the perverse pleasure of a solitary social outcast. But to this girl who could be moved by no simple pleasure it came as a gratifying substitute for happiness. Her own danger but added a sharp edge to the exquisite sensation. It was the ultimate gamble, in a life in which only gambling mattered.

Connor was fumbling first at a hip pocket where a pistol bulged, then at a side pocket that bulged with precious stones. His eye darted this way and that his cheeks had changed in color to a pasty gray. The girl thought for a moment that he had actually gone out of his head.

His action, when it finally came, was grotesquely romantic. She thought, in a flash, of the adventure novels she had so often seen him reading. It was to her absurd; even madly comic. For with those bulging pockets and that gray face, a criminal run to earth by his cruder confederates, he fell back on dignity. He strode directly out into the path, with a sort of mock firmness, and, like a policeman on a busy corner, raised his hand.

Even at that he might have impressed the soldiers; for he was white, and had been their vital and vigorous leader, and they were yellow and low-bred and drunk. As it was, they actually stopped, just over the nearest bridge; gave the odd appearance of huddling uncertainly there. But Connor could not hold the pose. He broke; looked wildly about; started, puffing like a spent runner, up the steps of the pavilion where the girl, leaning slightly forward, drawing in her breath sharply through parted lips, looked through the leaves.

Several of the rifles cracked then; she heard bullets sing by. And Connor fell forward on the steps, clawed at them for a moment, and lay still in a slowly widening pool of thick blood. He had not so much as drawn a weapon. Tex Connor was gone.

They came on, laughing, with a good deal of rough banter, and gathered up the jewels. Tom and another mounted the steps to the body and went through the pockets of his trousers for the jewels that were there and the pistols. As there was no coat they did not look further. And then, merrily, they went back over the marble bridges to the buildings in the grove where were still, perhaps, liquor and women.

When the last of their shouts had died out, when laying her head against the fragrant wood she could hear again the musical tinkling of the bronze bells and the pleasant murmuring of the tiny waterfall and the sighing of the leaves, Dixie slipped down to the body, fastidiously avoiding the blood. It was heavy; she exerted all her wiry strength in rolling it partly over. Then, drawing out the curious net of pearls she let the body roll back.

Returning to her sheltered seat she spread on her lap the amazing garment; for a garment of some sort it appeared to be. There was even a row of golden clasps set with very large diamonds. At a rough estimate she decided that there were all of three thousand to four thousand perfect pearls in the numerous strings. Turning and twisting it about, she hit on the notion of drawing it about her shoulders and found that it settled there like a cape. It was, indeed, just that—a cape of pearls. She did not know that it was the only garment of its precise sort in the world, that it had passed from one royal person to another until, after the death of the Old Buddha in 1908 it fell into the hands of his excellency, Kang Yu.

She took it off; stood erect; pulled out her loosely hanging middy blouse; and twisting the strings into a rope fastened it about her waist, rearranging the blouse over it. The concealment was perfect.

She sat again, then, to think out the next step. Returning to the junk was out of the question. It would be better to get somehow up to the concessions and trust to her wits to explain her presence there. For Tex had been shrewd enough about that. The concessions were a small bit of earth with but one or two possible hotels, full of white folk and fuller of gossip. She had had her little difficulties with the consuls as with the rough-riding American judge who took his itinerant court from port to port announcing firmly that he purposed ridding the East of such "American girls" as she. Dawley Kane would surely be there, and other survivors of the fire.... It all meant picking up a passage down the river at the earliest possible moment; and running grave chances at that. But her great strength lay in her impregnable self-confidence. She feared herself least of all.

Another problem was the getting to the concessions. It was not the best of times for a girl to walk the highway alone. To be sure, she had come safely through from the junk; but it had not been far, and she hadn't had to approach a native army. She decided to wait an hour or so, until the plunderers there in the grove should be fully drunk; then, if at the moment it seemed the thing, to slip out and make a try for it.

And then, a little later, evidently from the road outside the wall, came a new sort of confused sounds; music, of flageolets and strings, and falsetto voices, and with it a low-pitched babel of many tongues. Whoever these new folk might be, they appeared to be turning in at the open gate. The music stopped abruptly, in a low whine of discord, and the talk rose in pitch. Over the brick screen appeared banners moving jerkily about, dipping and rising, as if in the hands of agitated persons below; a black banner, bearing in its center the triple imperial emblems of the Sun, the other two yellow, one blazoning the familiar dragon, the other a phoenix.

A few banner men appeared peeping cautiously about the screen; Manchu soldiers of the old effete army, bearing short rifles. They came on, cautiously into the park, joined in a moment by others. An officer with a queue and an old-fashioned sword and a military cap in place of a turban followed and, forming them into a ragged column of fours, marched them over the marble bridges and into the grove, where they disappeared from view.

Then a gorgeously colored sedan chair came swaying in, carried by many bearers walking under stout bamboo cross-poles. Others, in the more elaborate dress of officials, walked beside and behind it. Then came more soldiers, who straggled informally about, some even dropping on the gravel to rest their evidently weary bodies.

The chair was opened in front and a tall fat man stepped rather pompously out, wearing a robe of rose and blue and the brightly embroidered insignia and button of a mandarin of the fourth rank. At once a servant stepped forward with a huge umbrella which he opened and held over the fat man. And then they waited, all of them, standing or lying about and talking in excited groups. Several of the officials hurried back around the screen as if to examine the deserted apartments just within the gate, and shortly returned with much to say in their musical singsong.... An officer espied the body of Connor lying on the steps of the pavilion, and came with others, excitedly, to the foot of the steps. The key of the confused talk rose at once. There was an excited conference of many ranks about the tall fat man under the umbrella.

Then came, from the grove, that same sound of muffled shots, followed by a breathless pause. More shots then, and increasing excitement here by the screen. A number of the soldiers who had crossed the bridges appeared, running. The man in the lead had lost turban and rifle; as he drew near blood could be seen on his face. And now, abruptly, the officials and the ragtag and bobtail by the screen—pole-bearers, lictors, runners, soldiers—lost their heads. Some ran this way and that, even into the bushes, only to reappear and follow their clearer-headed brethren out to the gate. The umbrella-bearer dropped his burden and vanished. The fugitives from the grove were among the panic-stricken group now, racing with them for the gate and the highway without; scurrying around the end of the screen like frightened rabbits; and in pursuit, cheering and yelling, came many of the soldiers from the junk.

They caught the tall fat mandarin, as he was waddling around the screen, wounded by a chance shot; leaped upon him, bringing him down screaming with fear; beat and kicked him; with their knives and bayonets performing subtle acts of torture which gave them evident pleasure and of which the coldly observant Dixie Carmichael lost no detail. When the fat body lay inert, not before, they took the sword of a fallen officer and cut off the head, hacking clumsily. The head they placed on a pole, marching noisily about with it; finally setting the pole upright beside the first of the little marble bridges. Then, at last, they wandered back into the grove and left the grisly object on the pole to dominate obscenely the garden they had profaned.

Dixie leaned against the smooth sweet surface of the nanmu wood and listened, again, to the pleasantly soft sounds of waterfall and moving leaves and little bronze bells. Her face was chalk white; her thin hands lay limp in her lap; she knew, with an abrupt sensation of sinking, that she was profoundly tired. But in her brain burned still a cold white flame of excitement. Life, her instinct as the veriest child had informed her, was anything, everything, but the simple copybook pattern expounded by the naive folk of America and England. Life, as she critically saw it, was a complex of primitive impulses tempered by greeds, dreams and amazing subtleties. It was blindly possessive, carelessly repellent, creative and destructive in a breath, at once warm and cold, kindly and savage, impersonally heedless of the helpless human creatures that drifted hither and yon before the winds of chance. Cunning, in the world she saw about her, won always further than virtue, and often further than force.

She could not take her eyes, during a long period, from the hideous object on the pole. Her over-stimulated thoughts were reaching quickly, sharply, far in every direction. The feeling came, grew into belief, that she was, mysteriously, out of her danger. She felt the ropes of pearls under her blouse with an ecstatic little catch of the breath; and (finally) letting her eyes drop to that other ugly object on the steps beneath her, slowly opened her bag, drew out the bracelet watch (that the Manila Kid had given her out of an absurd hope) and fastened it about her wrist. And her eyes were bright with triumph.

CHAPTER X
YOUTH

THERE came for his excellency, as the sun mounted the sky, a large junk of his own river fleet—great brown sails flapping against the five masts of all heights that pointed up at crazily various angles, pennons flying at each masthead, hull weathered darkly, mats and fenders of woven hemp hung over the poop-rail, and a swarming pigtailed crew at the sweeps and overside on the spunson and hard at the tracking ropes as the *tai-kung* screamed from the bow and the *laopan* shouted from the poop.

They were ferried aboard in the small boat, Kang with his daughters and his suite and servants, a handful of pitifully wailing women, young Kane and Griggsby Doane. Then the trackers cast off from the shore and the mooring poles, the sweeps moved, and with the *lao pan* musically calling the stroke the junk moved laboriously up-stream toward the home of his excellency's ancestors.

Crowded into the uninviting cabins the weary travelers sought a few hours of rest. Even the servants and the mourning women, under the mattings forward, fell swiftly asleep. Only Rocky Kane, his eyes staring widely out of a sensitively white face, walked the deck; until the thought—a new sort of thought in the life of this headstrong youth—that he would be disturbing those below drove him aft, out beyond the steersman to the over-hanging gallery. Here he sat on the bamboo rail and gazed moodily down at the tireless, mighty river flowing off astern.

The good in the boy—made up of the intelligence, the deep-smoldering conscience, the fineness that were woven out of his confused heritage into his fiber—was rising now like a tide in his spirit; and the experience was intensely painful. It seemed to his undisciplined mind that he was, in certain of his aspects, an incredible monster. There had been wild acts back home, a crazy instinct for excess that now took on distinctness of outline; moments of careless evil in Japan and Shanghai; the continuous subtle conflict with his father in which any evasion had seemed fair; but above all these vivid memory-scenes that raced like an uncontrollably swift panorama through his over-alert brain stood out his vicious conduct on the ship. It was impossible at this moment to realize mentally that the Princess Hui Fei was now his friend; he could see her only in the bright Manchu costume as she had appeared when he first so uncouthly spoke to her. And there were, too, the ugly moments with the strange girl known as Dixie Carmichael. That part of it was only a nightmare now.... The racing in his brain frightened him. He stared at the dimpling yellow river, at a fishing boat, and finally lifted his hurt eyes to the bright sky.... He had been going straight to hell, he told himself, mumbling the words softly aloud. And then this lovely girl had brought him into confusion and humility. Suddenly he had broken with his father; that, in itself, seemed curiously unaccountable, yet there the fact stood.... Life—eager, crowding had rushed him off his feet. He felt wildly adrift, carried on currents that he could not stem.... He was, indeed, passing through one of life's deepest experiences, one known to the somewhat unimaginative and intolerant people whose blood ran in his veins as conviction of sin. His own careless life had overtaken and confronted him. It had to be a bitter moment. There was terror in it. And there was no escaping; it had to be lived through.

A merry voice called; there was the patter of soft-clad feet, and in a moment the little princess in her yellow hood with the fox head on the crown was climbing into his lap. Eagerly, tenderly, he lifted her; cuddled her close and kissed her soft cheek. Tears were frankly in his eyes now.

He laughed with her, nervously at first, then, in the quick responsiveness of youth, with good humor. She came to him as health. Together they watched the diving cormorants and the wading buffalo. Then he hunted about until he found a bit of board and a ball of twine; whittled the board into a flat boat, stuck a little mast in it with a white sail made from a letter from his pocket, and towed it astern. Together they hung on the rail, watching the craft as it bobbed over the little waves and laughing when it capsized and lost its sail.

She climbed into his lap again after that, and scolded him for making the unintelligible English sounds, and made signs for him to smoke; and he showed her his water-soaked cigarettes.

At a low-pitched exclamation he turned with a nervous start. The tall eunuch stood on the cabin roof; came quickly forward for the child. And beside him was Miss Hu Fei, still of course wearing the Chinese coat and trousers in which she had escaped from the steamer. She had, under the warm sun, thrown aside the curiously modern opera wrap. She was slim, young, delicately feminine. The boy gazed at her reverently. She seemed to him a fairy, an unearthly creature, worlds beyond his reach. In his excitement, but a few hours back—in what he had supposed to be their last moment together, in what, indeed, had seemed the end of the world—he had declared his love for her. That had been an uprush of pure emotion.... He recalled it now, yet found it difficult to accept as an occurrence. The actual world had turned unreal to him, as it does to the sensitively young that suffer poignantly.

To this grave young woman, oddly his shipmate, he could hardly, he felt now, have spoken a personal word. Their acquaintance had begun at a high emotional pitch; now it must begin again, normally. So it seemed to him.

"We were looking for my li'l sister," she explained, and half turned. The eunuch had already disappeared with the child.

"Won't you sit out here—with me?" He spoke hesitantly. "That is, unless you are too tired to visit."

"I coul'n' sleep," said she.

Slowly she came out on the gallery.

"There aren't any chairs," said he. "Perhaps I could find—"

"I don' mind." She sank to the floor; leaned wearily against the rail. He settled himself in a corner.

"I couldn't sleep either. You see—Miss Hui—Miss Fei"—he broke into a chuckle of embarrassment—"honest I don't know what to call you."

The unexpected touch of boyish good humor moved her nearly to a smile. Boyish he was, sitting with his feet curled up, stabbing at the deck with his jackknife, coatless, collarless, his thick hair tousled, blushing pleasantly.

"My frien's call me Hui," she replied simply.

"Oh—really! May I—If you would—of course I know that—but my friends call me Rocky. The whole thing is Rockingham Bruce Kane. But...."

"I'll call you Misser Kane," said she.

His face fell a very little; but quickly he recovered himself.

"You must have wondered—I suppose it seems as if I've done a rather crazy thing—it *must* seem so..." She murmured, "Oh, no!"

"Attaching myself to your party this way—-at such a difficult time. I know it was a pretty impulsive thing to do, but...."

His voice trailed into silence. For a brief moment this wild act seemed, however different in its significance to himself, of a piece with his other wild acts. It was, perhaps, like all those, merely ungoverned egotism. Her voice broke sweetly in on this moment of gloomy reverie.

"We know tha' you woul' help us if you coul'. An' you were so won'erful."

"If I only could help! You see when I spoke that way to you—I mean telling you I loved you—"

"Please! We won' talk abou' tha'."

"No. We won't. Except just this. I was beside myself. But even then, or pretty soon afterward, I knew it was just plain selfishness."

"You mus'n' say that, either. Please!"

"No—just this! Of course you don't know me. What you do know is all against me—"

"I have forgotten—"

"You will never forget. But even if you were some day to like me more than you could now, I know it would take a long time. I've got to earn the right to be really your friend first. I'm going to try to do that. I've started all over—to-day—-my life, I mean. I'm just simply beginning again. There's a good long scrap ahead of me. That's all about that! But please believe that I've got a little sanity in me."

"Oh, I'm sure—"

"I have. Jumping overboard like that, and swimming back to you—it wasn't just crazy impulse, like so many of the things I've done. You see, my father knows you and your father—yes, I mean the terrible trouble you're in. Oh, everything comes to him, sooner or later. All the facts. You have to figure on that, with the pater. He—well, he wanted me to stop thinking about you. He was afraid I'd be writing to you, or something. You see, he'd watched us talking there by the fire. And he told me about this—this dreadful thing. And then I had to come back. Don't you see? I couldn't go on, leaving you like this. Of course, it's likely enough I'm just in the way here—" She was smiling wearily, pathetically, now.

"Oh, no—" she began.

"It's this way," he swept impetuously on. "Maybe I *can* help. Anyway, I''ve got to try. If your father—really—" He saw the slight shudder that passed through her slender body, and abruptly checked the rapid flow of words. "We've got to take care of you," he said, with surprising gravity and kindness. "You'll have to get back with the white people. You mustn't be left with the yellow."

"I know," said she, the strength nearly gone from her voice. "It always seems to me that I'm an American. Though sometimes I ge' confuse'. It isn' easy to think."

"I'm simply wearing you out. I mustn't. But just this—remember that I know all about it. I've broken with my father, for the present, and I'm happy about that. I have got some money of my own—quite a little. I've even got a wet letter of credit in my pocket. I had just sense enough last night to get it out of my coat. It's no good, of course, outside of the treaty ports, but it's there. I'm here to help. And I do want to feel that you'll call on me—for anything—and as for the rest of it—"

He had thought himself unusually clear and cool, but at this point his voice clouded and broke. He glanced timidly at her, and saw that her eyes were full of tears. He had to look away then. And during a long few moments they sat without a word.

Then the thought came, "I'm here to help!" It was a stirring thought. He had never helped, never in his life that he could remember. And yet the Kanes did things; they were strong men.

He was moodily skipping his knife over his hand, trying to catch the point in the soft wood. Abruptly, with a surprising smile, he looked up and asked: "Ever play mumbletepeg?"

Her troubled eyes for an instant met his. He chuckled again in that boyish way. And she, nervously, chuckled too. That seemed good.

"It's sort of hard to make the blade stick in this wood," he said eagerly. "But we can do some of the things."

Griggsbv Doane, too, was far from sleep. For that matter, he was of the strong mature sort that needs little, that can work long hours and endure severe strain without weakening. Moving aft over the poop he saw them, playing like two children, and stepped quietly behind the slanting short mast that overhung the steersman.

They made a charming picture, laughing softly as they tossed the knife. It hadn't before occurred to him that young Kane had charm. Plainly, now, he had. And it was good for Hui Fei, in this hour of tragic suspense. Youth, of course, would call unto youth. That was the natural thing. He tried to force himself to see it in that light but he moved forward with a heavy heart.

The junk plowed deliberately against the current. The monotonous voice of the chanting *lao pan*, the rhythmical splash and creak of the sweeps, the syncopated continuous song of the crowded oarsman, an occasional warning cry from the tai-kung—these were the only sounds. Elsewhere, lying in groups about the deck, the castaways slumbered.

But Doane knew that his excellency was awake, shut away in the *laopan's* cabin, for repeatedly he had heard him moving about. Once, through a thin partition, had come the sound of a chair scraping. It would mean that Kang was preparing his final papers. These would be painstakingly done. There would be memorials to the throne and to his children and friends, couched in the language of a master of the classics, rich in the literary allusions dear to the heart of the scholar, Manchu and Chinese alike.

Doane found a seat on a coil of the heavy tracking rope. His own part in the drama through which they were all so strangely living could be only passive. He would serve as he might. His little dream of personal happiness, with a woman to love and new strong work to be somehow begun, was wholly gone.

Slowly, foot by foot, the clumsy craft crept up the river. And strangely the scene held its peaceful, intensely busy character. Everywhere, as if there were no revolution, as if the old river had never known wreckage and bloodshed, the country folk toiled in the fields. Junks passed. Irrigating wheels turned endlessly. Fishermen sat patiently watching their cormorants or lowering and lifting their nets. A big English steamer came booming down, with white passengers out of bloody Hankow (the looting and burning of the native city must have been going on just then, before the reinforced imperial troops drove the republicans back across the river). They layabout in deck chairs, these white passengers; or, doubtless, played bridge in the smoking-room. And Doane, as so often during his long life, felt his thoughts turning from these idle, self-important whites, back to the oldest of living peoples; and he dwelt on their incalculable energy, their incredible numbers, their ceaseless individual struggle with the land and water that kept them, at best, barely above the line of mere sustenance.

It was difficult, pondering all this, to believe that any revolution could deeply stir this vast preoccupied people, submerged as they appeared to be in ancient habit. The revolution could succeed only if the Manchu government was ready to fall apart from the weakness of sheer decadence. It was nothing, this revolution, but the desperate work of agitators who had glimpsed the wealth and the individualistic tendencies of the West. And the hot-blooded Cantonese, of course. Most of the Chinese in America were Cantonese. The revolution was, then, a Southern matter; it was these tropical men that had come to know America. That was about its only strength. The great mass of yellow folk here in the Yangtze Valley, and through the coast provinces, and all over the great central plain and the North and Northwest were peaceable at heart; only those Southerners were truculent, they and the scattered handfuls of students.

And yet, China, in the hopeful hearts of those who knew and loved the old traditions, must somehow be modernized. Sooner or later the Manchus would fall. The vast patient multitude must then either learn to think for themselves in terms of modern, large-scale organization or fall into deeper degradation. The European trading nations would strike deep and hard in a sordid struggle for the remaining native wealth. The Japanese, with iron policy and intriguing hand would destroy their institutions and bring them into a pitiful slavery, economic and military.

His own life, Doane reflected, must be spent in some way to help this great people. The individual, confronted by so vast a problem, seemed nothing. But the effort had to be made. Since he was not a trader, since he could not hope now to find himself in step with the white generation that had passed him by, all that was left was to pitch in out here. The call of the martyred Sun Shi-pi pointed a way.

The personal difficulty only remained. The man who loses step with his own people and his own time must submit to being rolled under and trampled on. There is no other form of loneliness so deep or so bitter. And seeing nothing above and about him but the hard under side of this hard white civilization, the unfortunate one can not hope to retain in full vigor the incentive to effort that is the magic of the creative white race. Every circumstance now seemed combined to hold him down and under. The philosophy of the East with which his spirit was saturated argued for contemplation, submission, negation (as did, for that matter, the gospel of that Jesus to whose life the peoples that called themselves Christian, in their every activity, every day, gave the lie). His only driving power, then, must come out of the white spark that was, after all, in his blood. It was only as a discordantly active white that he could help the yellow men he loved.... And the one great incentive love, companionship, for which his strong heart hungered—had flickered before him only to die out. He must somehow, at that, prove worthy. It was to be just one more great effort in a life of prodigiously wasted effort.... He thought, as he had thought before, in bitter hours, of Gethsemane. But he knew, now, that he purposed going on. Once again he was to dedicate his vigor to a cause; but this time without the hope of youth and without love walking at his side.

And then, quaintly, alluringly, the picture of Hui Fei took form before his mind's eye, as if to mock his laborious philosophy, charm it away. Like that of a boy his quick imagination wove about her bright youth, her piquant new-old worldliness, shining veils of illusion. It was, then, to be so. He was to live on, sadly, with a dream that would not die.... He bowed his head.

Their play brought relief to the overwrought nerves of the two young people. After a time they settled comfortably against the rail.

"You lost all your things on the steamer?" said he. "Ever'thing."

"So did I." He smiled ruefully. "Even part of my clothes. But it doesn't matter."

"I di'n' like to lose all my pretty things." said she. "But they're gone now. All excep' my opera cloak. An' I'm jus' a Manchu girl again. It's so strange—only yes'erday it seem' to me I was a real American. I los' my books, too—all my books."

He glanced up quickly. "You're fond of reading?"

"Oh, yes. Aren' you?"

"Why—no, I haven't been. The fellows and girls I've known didn't read much."

"Tha' seems funny. When you have so much. And it's so easy to read English. Chinese is ver' hard."

"What books have you read mostly?"

She smiled. "Oh, I coul'n' say. So many! I've read the classics, of course—Shakespeare an' Milton and Chaucer. Chaucer is so modern—don' you think? I mean the way he makes pictures with words."

"What would you think," said he, "if I confessed that I cut all those old fellows at school and college?"

"I've thought often," said she gravely, "tha' you Americans are spoil' because you have so much. So much of everything."

"Perhaps. I don't know. The fellows feel that those things don't help much in later life."

"Oh, bu' they *do!* You mus'' have a knowledge of literature an'' philosophy. Wha'' do they go to college for?"

"Well—" Inwardly, he winced. He felt himself, without resentment, without the faintest desire to defend the life he had known, at a disadvantage. "To tell the truth, I suppose we go partly for a good time. It puts off going into business four years, you know, and once you start in business you've got to get down to it. Then there's all the athletics, and the friends you make. Of course, most of the fellows realize that if they make the right kind of friendships it'll help, later, in the big game."

"You mean with the sons of other rich men?" she asked.

"Why, no, not—yes, come to think of it, I suppose that's just what I do mean. Do you know here with you, it doesn't look like much of a picture—does it?" Thoughtfully she moved her head in the negative. "I know a goo' deal about it," said she. "I've watch' the college men in America. Some of them, I think, are pretty foolish."

"I suppose we are," said he glumly. "But would you have a fellow just go in for digging?"

She inclined her head. "I woul'. It is a grea' privilege to have years for study."

He was flushing. "But you're not a dig! You—you dance, you know about things, you can wear clothes...."

"I don' think study is like work to me. I love it. An' I love people—every kin', scholars, working people—you know, every kin'."

His moody eyes took in her eagerly mobile face; then dropped, and he stabbed his knife at the deck.

"Of course, we know that all is no' right 'n America. The men of money have too much power. The govemmen' is confuse', sometimes very weak and foolish. The newspapers don' tell all the things they shoul'. But it is so healthy, jus' the same! There is so much chance for ever' kin' of idea to be hear'! An' so many won'erful books! Often I think you real Americans don' know how' won'erful it is. You get excite' abou' little things. I love America. The women are free there. There is more hope there than anywhere else in the worl'. An' I wish China coul' be like that."

"I quit college," said he. "You see, I've never looked at things as you do."

"Bu' you have such a won'erful chance!"

"I know, And I've wasted it. But I'm changing. I—it wouldn't be fair of course to talk about—about what I was talking about—not now—but I am seeing things—everything—through new eyes. They're your eyes. I'm going at the thing differently. You see, the Kanes, when you get right down to it, don't think about anything but money."

"I like to think about beauty," said she.

"I wonder if I could do that."

"Why no'?"

"Well—it's kind of a new idea."

"Listen!" she reached out, plainly without a personal thought, and took his hand. "I'm going to reci' some poetry that I love."

Thrilled by the clasp of her hand, his mind eager wax to the impress of her stronger mind, his gaze clinging to her pretty mouth, he listened while she repeated the little poem of W. B. Yeats beginning:=

"All the words that I utter,

And all the words that I write..."=

At first he stirred restlessly; then watching, doglike, fell to listening. The disconcerting thing was that it could mean so much to her. For it did—her dark eyes were bright, and her chin was uplifted. Her quaint accent and her soft, sweet voice touched his spirit with an exquisite vague pain.

"It is music," said she.

"I don't see how you remember it all," said he listlessly.

"Jus' the soun's. Oh, it woul' be won'erful to make words do that. So often I wish I ha' been born American, so it woul' be my language too."

She went on, breathlessly, with Yeats's—=

"When you are old and gray and full of sleep..."=

And then, still in pensive vein, she took up Kipling's *L'Envoi*—the one beginning—"There's a whisper down the field." Clearly she felt the sea, too; and the yearning of those wandering souls to whom life is a wistful adventure, and the world an inviting labyrinth of beautiful hours. She seemed to know the *Child's Garden of Verses* from cover to cover, and other verse of Stevenson's. It was all strange to him, except "In winter I get up at night." He knew that as a song.

And so it came about that on a dingy Yangtze junk, at the feet of a Manchu girl from America, Rocky Kane felt for the first time the glow and thrill of finely rhythmical English.

She went on, almost as if she had forgotten him. William Watson's *April, April* she loved, she said, and read it with a quick feeling for the capricious blend of smiles and tears. It dawned on him that she was a born actress. He did not know, of course, that the theatrical tradition lies deeper in Manchu and Chinese culture than in that of any Western people.

She recited the beautiful *Song* of Richard Le Galliene, beginning:=

"She''s somewhere in the sunlight strong...."=

And followed this with bits from Bliss Carman, and other bits from Henley's *London Nocturnes*, and from Wilfred Blunt and Swinburne and

Mrs. Browning. She had a curiously strong feeling for the color of Medieval Italy. She spoke reverently of Dante. Villon she knew, too, and Racine and the French classicists. She even murmured tenderly de Musset's *J'ai dis à mon coeur*, in French of which he caught not a word and was ashamed. For he had cut French, too.

And then, as the sun mounted higher and the gentle rush of the river along the hull and the continuous chantey of the oarsmen floated, more and more soothingly to their ears, they fell quiet, her hand still pleasantly in his. Together they hummed certain of the current popular songs, he thinking them good, she smiling not unhappily as her voice blended prettily with his. And Griggsby Doane heard them.

At last she murmured: "I think I coul' rest now."

"I'm glad," said he, and drew down a coil of rope for a pillow, and left her sleeping there.

Doane heard his step, but for a moment could not lift his head. Finally the boy, standing respectfully, spoke his name: "Mr. Doane!"

"Yes."

"May I sit here with you?"

"Of course. Do."

"I've got to talk to somebody. It's so strange. You see, she and I—Miss Hui Fei—it's all been such a whirl I couldn't think, but...."

That sentence never got finished. The boy dropped down on the deck and clasped his knees. Doane, very gravely, considered him. He was young, fresh, slim. He had changed, definitely; a degree of quiet had come to him. And there could be no mistaking the unearthly light in his eyes. The love that is color and sunshine and exquisite song had touched and transformed him.

Doane could not speak. He waited. Young Kane finally brought himself with obvious, earnest effort in a sense to earth. But his voice was unsteady in a boyish way.

"Mr. Doane," he asked, "do you believe in miracles?"

Thoughtfully, deliberately, Doane bowed his great head. "I am forced to," he replied.

"You've seen men change—from dirty, selfish brutes, I mean, to something decent, worth while?"

"Many times."

"Really?.... But does it have to be religion?"

"I don't knew."

"Can it be love? The influence of a woman, I mean—a girl?"

"Might that not be more or less the same thing?"

"Do you really think that?"

Again the great head bowed. And there was a long silence. Rocky broke it

"I wish you would tell me exactly how you feel about marriage between the races."

"Why really "

"You must have observed a lot, all these years out here. And the pater tells me that you're an able man, except that you've sort of lost your perspective. He did tell me that he'd like to have you with him, if you could only bring yourself around to our ways." Rocky, even now, could see this only as a profound compliment. He rushed on: "Oh, don't misunderstand me! She doesn't love me yet. How could she? I've got to earn the right even to speak of it again. But if I should earn the right—in time—tell me, could an American make her happy?"

"I'm afraid I can't answer that general question." But Rocky felt that he was kind. "The pater says I'd be wrecking my life. He says she'd always be pulled two ways—you know! God! He seemed to think I had only to ask her, and she'd come. He doesn't understand."

"No," said Doane—"I'm afraid he couldn't understand."

"You feel that too? It's very perplexing. I know I've spoken carelessly about the Chinese and Manchus. I looked down on them. I did! But oh, if I could only make it clear to you how I feel now! If I could only express it! We've been talking a long time, she and I. I don't mind telling you I'm taking a pretty bitter lesson, right now. She knows so much. She has such fine—well, ideals—"

"Certainly."

"Oh, you've noticed that!.... Well, I feel crude beside her. Of course, I am."

"Yes—you are. Even more so than you can hope to perceive now."

The youth winced; but took it. "Well, suppose—just suppose that I might, one of these days, prove that I'm decent enough to ask her to be my wife.... Oh, don't think for a minute that I don't understand all it means. I do. I tell you I'm starting again. I'm going to fight it out."

"That is fine," said Griggsby Doane, and looked squarely, gravely, at the very young face. It was a white face, but good in outline; the forehead, particularly, was good. And the blue eyes now met his. "I believe you will fight it out. And I believe you have it in you to win."

"I'm going to try, Mr. Doane. But just suppose I do win. And suppose I win her. It's when I think of that, that I.... I'll put it this way—to my friends, to everybody in New York, she'd be an oddity. A novelty, not much more. You know what most of them would think, in their hearts. Either they'd make an exception in her case—partly on my account, at that—or else they'd look down on her. You know how they are about people that aren't—well, the same color that we are. Probably I couldn't live out here. The business is mainly in New York, of course. And she's such an enthusiastic American herself—she'd want to be there. Some, anyway. And she's got to be happy. She's like a flower to me, now; like an orchid. Oh, a thousand times more, but.... What could I do? How could I plan? Oh, I'd fight for her quick enough. But you know our cold rich Americans. They wouldn't let me fight. They'd just...."

"My boy," said Doane. quietly but with an authority that Rocky felt, "you can't plan that. You can do only one thing."

"What thing?"

"Stay here in China a year before you offer yourself to that lovely girl. Study the Chinese—their language, their philosophy, their art. A year will not advance you far, but it should be enough to show you where you yourself stand."

"A year....!"

"Listen to what I am going to try to tell you. Listen as thoughtfully as you can. First I must tell you this—the Chinese civilization has been—in certain aspects still remains—the finest the world has known. With one exception, doubtless."

"What exception?"

"The Grecian. You see, I have startled you."

"Well, I'm still sort of bewildered."

"Naturally. But try to think with me. The Chinese worked out their social philosophy long ago. They have lived through a great deal that we have only begun, from tribal struggles through conquest and imperialism and civil war to a sort of republicanism and a fine feeling for peace and justice. And then, when they had given up primitive desire for fighting they were conquered by more primitive Northern tribes—first the Mongols, and later the Manchus. The Manchus have been absorbed, have become more or less Chinese.

"And now a few more blunt facts that will further startle you. The Chinese are the most democratic people in the world. No ruler can long resist the quiet force of the scores of thousands of villages and neighborhoods of the empire.

"They are the most reasonable people in the world. You can no more judge them from the so-called Tongs in New York and San Francisco, made up of a few Cantonese expatriates, than you can judge the culture of England by the beachcombers of the South Seas.

"They developed, centuries before Europe, one of the finest schools of painting the world has so far known. There is no school of reflective, philosophical poetry so ripe and so fine as the Chinese. They have had fifty Wordsworths, if no Shakespeare.

"You will find Americans confusing them with the Japanese, whom they resemble only remotely. All that is finest in Japan—in art and literature—came originally from China."

"You take my breath away," said Rocky slowly. But he was humble about it; and that was good.

"But listen, please. What I am trying to make clear to you is that in old Central China—in Hang Chow, and along this fertile Yangtze Valley, and northwest through the Great Plain to Kai Feng-fu and Sian-fu in Shensi—where the older people flourished—germinated the thought and the art, the humanity and the faith, that have been a source of culture to half the world during thousands of years.

"But you can not hope to understand this culture through Western eyes. For you will be looking out of a Western background. You must actually surrender your background. It is no good looking at a Chinese landscape or a portrait with eyes that have known only European painting. Can you see why? Because all through European painting runs the idea of copying nature—somehow, however subtly, however influenced by the nuances of color and light, copying. But the Chinese master never copied a landscape He studied it, felt it, surrendered his soul to it, and then painted the fine emotion that resulted. And, remember this, he painted with a conscious technical skill as fine as that of Velasquez or Whistler or Monet."

The youth whistled softly. "Wait, Mr. Doane, please.... the fact is, you're clean over my head. I—I don't know a thing about our painting, let alone theirs. You see I haven't put in much time at—" He stopped. His smooth young brows were knit in the effort to think along new, puzzling channels. "But she would understand," he added, honestly, softly.

"Exactly! She would understand. That is what I am trying to make clear to you."

"But you're sort of—well, overwhelming me."

"My boy." said Doane very kindly, "you could go back home, enter business, marry some attractive girl of your own blood who thinks no more deeply than yourself, whose culture is as thinly veneered as your own— forgive me. I am speaking blunt facts."

"Go on. I'm trying to understand."

"—And find happiness, in the sense that we so carelessly use the word. But here you are, in China, proposing to offer your life to a Manchu princess. You do seem to see clearly that there would be difficulties. It is true that our people crudely feel themselves superior to this fine old race. As a matter of fact, one of the worthiest tasks left in the world is to explain East to West—draw some part of this rich old culture in with our own more limited background. But as it stands now, the current will be against you. So I say this—study China. Open your mind and heart to the beauty that is here for the taking. Try to look through the decadent surface of this tired old race and see the genius that still slumbers within. If, then, you find yourself in the new belief that their culture is in certain respects finer than ours—as I myself have been forced to believe—if you can go to Hui Fei humbly—then ask her to be your wife. For then there will be a chance that you can make her happy. Not otherwise."

Doane stopped abruptly. His deep voice was rich with emotion. The boy was stirred; and a moment later, when he felt a huge hand on his shoulder he found it necessary to fight back the tears. The man seemed like a father; the sort of father he had never known.

"Don't ask her so long as a question remains in your mind. Defiance won't do—it must be faith, and knowledge. I can't let you take the life of that girl into your keeping on any other terms."

The odd emphasis of this speech passed quite by the deeply preoccupied young mind.

"You're right," he replied brokenly. "I've got to wait. Everything that you say is true—I really haven't a thing in the world to offer. I'm an ignorant barbarian beside her."

"You have the great gift of youth," said Doane gently.

But a moment later Rocky broke out with: "But, Mr. Doane—how can I wait? She—after her father—they're going to take her away—make her marry somebody at Peking—somebody she doesn't even know—"

"I don't think they will succeed in that plan," said Doane very soberly.

"But why not? What can she do? A girl—alone—"

"There are tens of thousands of girls in China that have solved that problem."

"But I don't see—"

"You must still try to keep your mind open. You are treading on ground unknown to our race." A breathless quality crept into Doane's voice; his eyes were fixed on the distant river bank. "I wonder if I can help you to understand. Death—the thought of death—is to them a very different thing—"

"Oh!" It was more a sharp indrawing of breath than an exclamation. "You don't mean that she would do that?"

Doane bowed his head.

"But she couldn't do a cowardly thing."

Doane brought himself, with difficulty, to utter the blunt word. "Suicide, in China, is not always cowardice. Often it is the finest heroism—the holding to a fine standard."

"Oh, no! It wouldn't ever—"

"Please! You are a Westerner. Your feelings are those of the younger—yes, the cruder half of the world. I must still ask you to try to believe that there can be other sorts of feelings." Again the great hand rested solidly on the young shoulder; and now, at last, the boy became slightly aware of the suffering in the heart of this older man. Though even now he could not grasp every implication. That human love might be a cause he did not perceive. But he sensed, warmly, the ripe experience and the compassionate spirit of the man.

"You have stepped impulsively into an Old-World drama," Doane went quietly on—"into a tragedy, indeed. No one can say what the next developments will be. You can win, if at all, only by becoming yourself, a fatalist; You must move with events. Certainly you can not force them."

"But I can take her away," cried the boy hotly; finishing, lamely, with "somehow."

"Against her will?"

"Well—surely—"

"She will not leave her father."

"But—oh, Mr. Doane...."

He fell silent. For a long time they sat without a word, side by side. Here and there about the junk sleepers awoke and moved about. A few of the women, forward, set up their wailing but more quietly now. The craft headed in gradually toward the right bank, passing a yellow junk that was moored inshore and moving on some distance up-stream. At a short distance inland a brown-gray village nestled under a hillside.

"That junk passed us before we left the island," Rocky observed, gloomily making talk.

Doane's gaze followed his down-stream; then at a sound like distant thunder, he turned and listened. "What's that?" asked the boy.

Doane looked up into the cloudless, blazing sky. "That would be the guns at Hankow," he replied.

The lictors were landed first to seek carts in the village. Then all were taken ashore in the small boat. His excellency smilingly, with unfailing poise, talked with Doane of the beauties of the river; even quoted his favorite Li Po, as his quiet eyes surveyed the hills that bordered the broad river:=

"'The birds have all flown to their trees,

The last, last lovely cloud has drifted off,

But we never tire in our companionship—

The mountains and I,'"=

The line of unpainted, springless carts, roofed with arched matting, yellow with the fine dust of the highway, moved, squeaking, off among the hills. Following close went the women and the servants. The junk swung deliberately out and off down the river.

Doane, declining a cart, walked beside that of his excellency; Rocky Kane, deadly pale, his mouth set firmly, beside Miss Hui Fei. And so, through the peaceful country-side they came to the long brick wall and the heavily timbered gate house by the road, and, pausing there, heard very faintly the soft tinkling of the little bronze bells within. It was late afternoon. The shadows were long; and the evening birds were twittering among the leafy branches just within the wall.

CHAPTER XI
THE LANDSCAPE SCROLL OF CHAO MENG-FU

ROCKY KANE, the few hours that followed were to exist in memory as a confused sequence of swift-pressing scenes, all highly colored, vivid; certain of them touched with horror, others passing in a flash of exotic beauty; while the fire of hot, unreasoning young love burned all but unbearably within his breast.

He would remember the crowded line of carts in the sunken narrow road, the unruly mules that plunged and entangled their harness; the huddled women; the yellow dust that clung thickly to the bright silks of the mandarins; the confusion about the gate, and the handful of soldiers that came hurrying forward to help in a strange business up there; the trains of other carts that struggled to pass in the narrow way, while tattered muleteers shouted a babel of invective.

He would remember the sad face of Miss Hui Fei-drawn back within the shadow of the cart and the faint smiles that came and so quickly went; and the efforts he made, at first, to cheer her with boyishly bright talk of this and that.

He would remember how he made his way forward through the press, without recalling what had just been said, or what, precisely, could have been the impulse driving him on; past his excellency—sitting yet in his cart, calmly waiting, while the drabbled mandarins stood respectfully by; and how he found the soldiers carrying oddly limp Bodies into one of the gate houses, hiding them there.

He would remember the picture on which he stumbled as he rounded the inner screen of brick; Mr. Doane and an officer and two or three soldiers standing thoughtfully about a fat body in spattered silks that was hideously without a head; standing there in the half dusk—for the shadows were lengthening softly into evening here under the trees—Mr. Doane then bending over, the officer kneeling, to examine the embroidery on the breast; and then two soldiers bringing up a pole on the end of which grinned the missing head; and then the sound of his own voice—curiously breathless and without body, asking, "What is it, Mr. Doane? What terrible thing has happened?" And then, even while he was speaking, four soldiers carrying another body by, this of a stout man in shirt and flannel trousers, that he felt he had seen somewhere before.

He would remember—when they had carried out the last awful reminder of the bloodshed that had been, and while Mr. Doane pressed a hand to his eyes as if in prayer—how he stood silent there on the gravel area, looking up into the trees and about at the dim quaint *pai-lows* on either hand and at the pavilions behind them, each on its arch of stone over placid dark water; and how the lightly moving air of evening whispered through the trees, stirring, with the foliage, faintly musical little bells; and how, into this moment of calm, appeared, light of step, swinging her shopping bag as she descended the marble steps of the pavilion at the right and came forward under the *pai-lows*, the pale girl, Dixie Carmichael, who glanced respectfully toward Mr. Doane, and at Rocky himself raised her black eyebrows while her thin lips softly framed the one word, "You?" And then, after a few words—the girl said that Tex Connor and the Manila Kid made her come; it had been a terrible business; she thought both must have been, killed; she had contrived to hide—how Mr. Doane asked him to take her back to the women; and how they went, he and she, his heart beating hotly, out through the darkening gate where paper lanterns now moved about. He felt that for the first sharp blow at his new life. There would be other blows; doubtless through this girl; for the old life would not give him up without a fight.

He was to forget what they said, he and this unaccountable, cool girl, as he left her out there and hurried back; but would remember the picture he found on his return—Mr. Doane striding off deliberately into the darkness beyond the little white bridges, while the officer followed with a lantern, and the few soldiers, also with lanterns, straggled after. He would remember crowding himself past all of them, snatching one of the lanterns as he ran, and falling into step at the side of the huge determined man.

There were broad courtyards, then, and buildings with heavily curving roofs and columns richly colored and carved, with dim lights behind windows of paper squares. There were drunken soldiers, who ran away, and screaming women, and other women who would never scream or smile again. There was litter and splintered furniture and a broken-in door here and there. There was a familiar big soldier who plunged at Mr. Doane with a glinting blade in his hand; and then a sharp struggle that was to last, in retrospect, but an instant of time, for the clearer memory was of himself binding with his handkerchief a small cut in Mr. Doane's forearm while the soldiers carried out a wounded struggling giant, and then shouts and shots from the courtyard when the giant escaped. And he would remember picking up an unset ruby from the tiling and handing it to Mr. Doane. There was the picture, then, of a melancholy procession winding slowly through the grove with bobbing gay lanterns.

And finally, to the boy incredibly, the place came into a degree of order and calm. Women and men disappeared into this building and that. Rocky sat alone on the steps of a structure that might have been a temple, hands supporting his throbbing head. The moonlight streamed down into the courtyard; he could see the grotesque ornaments on the eaves of the buildings, and the large blue-and-white bowls and vases in which grew flowering plants and dwarfed trees from Japan, and, in the farther gate, a sentry lounging. Now and again faint sounds came from within the largest of the buildings, voices and footsteps; and he could see lights again dimly through the paper. He wondered what they might be doing.... His thoughts were a fever. The spirit of Hui Fei hovered like an exquisite dream there, but crowding in with malignant persistence came, kept coming, pictures of Dixie Carmichael. He wondered where they had put her. Perhaps she was already asleep. It would be like her to sleep. She was so cold, so oddly unhealthy. Doubtless, surely, he would have to speak with her.

He must have dozed. Soldiers were dragging themselves sleepily about the courtyard, rifles in hand. Two officers and a mandarin in a gown were examining a paper by the light of a lantern. Then Mr. Doane came out and read the paper. They talked in Chinese, Mr. Deane's as fluent as theirs. Rocky thought drowsily about this; considered vaguely the years of study and experience that must lie back of that fluency.

Mr. Doane, indeed, seemed to be assuming a sort of command. With great courtesy, but with impressive finality, he appeared to be outlining a course to which the mandarin assented. The officers bowed and went out through the gate. And when the mandarin and Doane then turned and entered the largest building it was the white man who held the paper in his hand.

Rocky fell again into a doze; slept until he found Mr. Doane shaking him.

"Come with me now. You can help." Thus the huge grave man with the deep shadows in his face.

And Rocky went with him, guided by a servant with a lantern, through corridors and courtyards, glimpsing dimly massive pillars and panels in black wood and softly red silk and railings of marble carved into exquisite tracery.

With the paper that the boy had drowsily observed Doane sought his excellency. Dominated by the white man the attendant mandarin tapped at an inner door, then hesitatingly opened; and Doane alone stepped within.

The room was long, plain, obscurely seen by the light of a single incandescent lamp over the formal *kang* or platform across the farther end. Doane had not thought of electric light in here and found it momentarily surprising. The walls were paneled in silk; the ceiling was heavy with beams. Against either side wall, mathematically at the center, stood a square small table and a square stool, heavily carved. Seated on the *kang*, with papers spread about and brushes and ink pot directly under the light, in short quilted coat and simple black cap, was Kang; a serenely patient figure, quietly working. He had merely looked up; a frail old man, quite beyond the reach of annoyance, whose eyes gazed unafraid over the rim of mere personal life into the eternal, tireless energy that would so soon absorb all that was himself. Then, recognizing the stalwart figure that moved forward into the light, he rose and clasped his hands and smiled.

"Only an unexpected crisis would lead me to intrude thus," began Doane in Chinese, bowing in courtly fashion and clasping his own hands before his breast.

"No visit from Griggsby Doane could be regarded as an intrusion in my home," replied his excellency.

"I will speak quickly, in the Western fashion," Doane went on. "His Excellency, the General Duke Ma Ch'un, commanding before Hankow, writes that he regrets deeply the violent death of the eunuch, Chang Yuan-fu on your excellency's premises while dutifully engaged on the business of her imperial majesty, and cordially requests that your excellency come at once to headquarters as his personal guest to assist him in making an inquiry into the tragedy. He supplements this invitation with a copy of a telegram from His Excellency, Yuan Shih-k'ai, commanding him to guard at once your person and property."

The simple elderly man, who had been a minister, a grand councilor and a viceroy, seemed to recoil slightly as his eyes drooped to the papers about him; then he reached, with a withered hand that trembled, for this new paper and very slowly read it through.

"His Excellency, Duke Ma Ch'un." Doane added gently, "has sent a company of soldiers to escort you fittingly to his headquarters. They are waiting now at the outermost gate. I took it upon myself in this hour of sorrow and confusion to advise them, through the mouths of your loyal officers, that your excellency is not to be disturbed before dawn."

Slowly, with an expressionless face, the viceroy folded the paper and laid it on the *kang*. He sank, then, beside it; with visible effort indicating that his visitor sit as well. But Doane remained standing—enormously tall, broad, strong; a man to command without question of rank or authority; a man, it appeared, hardly conscious of the calm power of personality that was so plainly his.

"Your Excellency is aware"—thus Doane said—"that to admit the authority of Duke Ma Ch'un at this sorrowful time is to submit both yourself and your lovely daughter to a fate that is wholly undeserved, one that I— if I may term myself the friend of both—can not bring myself to consider without indulging the wish to offer strong resistance. It has been said, 'The truly great man will always frame his actions with careful regard to the exigencies of the moment and trim his sail to the favoring breeze.' Your Excellency must forgive me if I suggest that, whatever value you may place upon your own life, we can not thus abandon your daughter, Hui Fei."

The viceroy's voice, when he spoke, had lost much of its timbre. It was, indeed, the voice of a weary old man. Yet the words came forth with the old kindly dignity.

"I asked you, Griggsby Doane, to make with me this painful journey to my home. We did not know then that we were moving from one scene of tragedy to another more terrible. But motive must not wait on circumstance. It need not be a hardship for my other children to live on in Asia as Asiatics. As such they were born. They know no other life. They will experience as much happiness as most. But with Hui Fei it is different. She must not be held away from contact with the white civilization. I did not give her this modern education for such an end as that. Hui Fei is an experiment that is not yet completed. She must have her chance. That is why I brought you here, Griggsby Doane. My daughter must be got to Shanghai. There she has friends. I have ventured to count on your experience and good will to convey her safely there. Will you take her—now? To-night? I had meant to send with her the jewels and the paintings of Ming, Sung and Tang. Both collections are priceless. But the gems are gone—to-night. The paintings, however, remain. Will you take those and my daughter, and two servants— there are hardly more that I can trust—and slip out by the upper gate, and in some way escort her safely to Shanghai?"

"She would not go," said Doane. "Not while you, Your Excellency, live, or while your body lies above ground."

The viceroy, hesitating, glanced up at the vigorous man who spoke so firmly, then down at the scattered papers on the *kang*. In the very calm of that shadowed face he felt the bewildering strength of the white race; and he knew in his heart that the man was not to be gainsaid. His mind wavered. For perhaps the first time in his shrewd, patiently subtle life, he felt the heavy burden of his years.

"I will send for her," he said now, slowly. "I will give her into your keeping. At my command she will *go*."

"No, Your Excellency, I have already sent word to her to prepare herself for the journey. Again you must forgive me. Time presses. It remains only to collect the paintings. You must have those, at the least. We start now in a very few moments. I have found here, a prisoner in your palace, the master of a junk that lies at the river bank, and have taken it upon myself to detain him further. He will convey us to Shanghai. It is now but a few hours before dawn. Hostile soldiers stand impatient at the outermost gate, eager to heap shame upon you and all that is yours. You must change your clothing—the dress of a servant would be best."

He waited, standing very still.

"You will forgive indecision in a man of my years," began the viceroy. After a moment he began again: "The world has turned upside down, Griggsby Doane."

"You will come?"

The viceroy sighed. Trembling fingers reached out to gather the papers.

"I will come." he said.

Adrift in unreality, fighting off from moment to moment the drowsy sense that these strange events were but a blur of dreams in which nothing could be true, nothing could matter, Rocky found himself at work in a dim room, taking down in great handfuls from shelves scrolls of silk wound on rods of ivory and putting them in lacquered boxes. Mr. Doane was there, and the servant, and a second servant of lower class, in ragged trousers and with his queue tied about his head. Still another Chinese appeared, shortly, in blue gown and sleeveless short jacket; an older man who looked, in the flickering faint light of the single lantern, curiously like the viceroy himself. The first servant disappeared and returned with the short poles of bamboo used everywhere in China in carrying burdens over the shoulder, and with cords and squares of heavy cotton cloth.

Every bit of woodwork that his hands touched in moving about, Rocky found to be intricately carved and gilded and inlaid with smooth lacquer. And dimly, crowded about the walls, he half saw, half sensed, innumerable vases, small and large, with rounding surfaces of cream-colored crackle and blood-red and blue-and-white and green which threw back the moving light like a softly changing kaleidoscope. And there were screens that gave out, from their profound shadows, the glint of gold.

They packed the boxes together, wrapped the large and heavy cubes in the squares of cloth and lashed them to hang from the bamboo poles. Four of them, then, Mr. Doane, Rocky himself and the servants, each balanced a pole over his shoulders and lifted the bulky cubes. The old man, who surely, now, was the viceroy, carried a European hand-bag. There were other parcels.... They made their way along a nearly dark corridor and out into the moonlight. Here, in a porch, stood four silent figures—Dixie Carmichael he distinguished first; then Hui Fei, wearing a short coat and women's trousers and a loose cloak. Her hair was parted and lay smoothly on her pretty head, glistening in the moonlight.... And the little princess was there, clinging to the hand of her sister and rubbing her eyes. They moved silently on, all together, following a path that wound among shrubbery, over an arching bridge to a gate.

Rocky could dimly see the timbers studded with spikes and the long hinges of bronze. The servant, with a great key, unlocked the gate, which closed softly behind them.

The pole weighed heavily on Rocky's unaccustomed shoulder. There was a trick of timing the step to the swing of the bales, that, stumbling a little, he caught. He was to remember this—the little file of men and women gathered from the two ends of the earth and walking without a spoken sound down through a twisting, sunken Chinese road to the Yangtze. And sensing the gathering drama of his own life, brooding over it with slowly increasing nervous intensity, he found himself coming awake. If this kept on he would soon be excitedly beyond sleep. But it didn't matter. They were saving Hui Fei. Not a word of explanation had been offered; but it was coming clear. As for the rest of it, he asked himself how it could matter. The presence of Miss Carmichael, a dangerous girl, an adventuress—he was thinking quite youthfully about her—who might easily be capable of anything, who could in a moment destroy the hope that was the only foundation, thus far, of his new life, and perhaps would choose to destroy it—even this, he tried to tell himself, couldn't possibly matter. Over and over, stumbling and shuffling along, he told himself that; almost convinced himself that he believed it.

He was to remember most vividly of all the first glimpse, through a notch in the hills, of the river. The viceroy paused at that point, and turning back from the shining picture before him, where the moonlight silvered the unruffled surface of the water, toward the home of his ancestors over the hill, spoke in a low but again musical voice a few lines in which even the American youth could detect the elusive vowel rhymes of a Chinese poem. And he saw that Mr. Doane stood by with the slightly bowed head of one who attends a religious ceremony. It was a moving scene. But could he have understood the words the boy would have been puzzled. For the poem—

the *Surrendering* of Po Chu-I. breathed resignation, humility, the negative philosophy so dear to Chinese tradition, but nothing of religion in the sense that he a Westerner, understood the word, nothing of mysticism or romantic illusion or childlike faith; rather a gentle recognition of the fact that life must go as it had come, unexplained, without tangible evidence of a personal hereafter; that, too, the individual is as nothing in the vast scheme of nature.

They were ferried out, shortly after this, to the great junk they had twice seen within the twenty-four hours, her smooth sides curving yellow in the moonlight, her decks now scraped and scrubbed clean, flowers blooming in porcelain pots about a charming gallery that extended high over the river astern. The crew, roused from slumber, came swarming out from under the low-spread mattings. The *laopan* stepped nimbly to his post amidships on the poop. The heavy tracking ropes were hauled aboard, and the craft swung slowly off down the current.

Doane, with a lantern, escorted his excellency and Hui Fei, and the whimpering little princess, to the rooms below; then returned and with the same impersonal courtesy conducted Miss Carmichael down the steps. But at the door he indicated she stopped short; wavered a moment, lightly, on the balls of her feet. Then she accepted the lantern from him, bit her lip, and let fall the curtain without replying to his suggestion that she had better sleep if she could.

Alone there, she held up the lantern. The floor had been lately scrubbed; but, even so, she made out a faint broad stain in the wood. And a bed of clean matting was spread where she had left a grisly heap.

For a time Dixie stood by the square small window, looking out over the shining river toward the dim northern bank with its hills that seemed to drift at a snail's pace off astern. Her quick mind had never been farther from sleep. Her thin hands felt through her blouse the twisted ropes of pearls that were wound about her waist. Her lips were pressed tightly together. These pearls represented a fortune beyond even Dixie's calculating dreams. To keep them successfully hidden during the days, perhaps weeks to come of floating down the river in close companionship with these two strong observant men, and a half crazy American boy, and clever Oriental women, would test her resourcefulness and her nerve. Though she felt, ever, now, no doubt of the latter....

The thing was tremendous. Now that the confusion of the day and night were over with, she found a thrill in considering the problem, while her sensitive fingers pressed and pressed again the hard little globes. There were so many of them; such beauties, she knew, in form and size and color.... Never again would such an opportunity come to her. It was, precisely, if on the grandest scale imaginable, her sort of achievement. Tex was gone. The Kid was gone. No one could claim a share or a voice: it was all hers—wealth, power, even, perhaps, at the last, something near respectability. For money, enough of it, she knew, will accomplish even that. While on the other, hand, to fail now, might, would, spell a life of drab adventure along the coast, without even a goal, without a decent hope; with, always, the pitiless years gaining on her.

She searched, tiptoeing, about the room, lantern in hand, for a place to hide her treasure; then reconsidered. In some way she must keep the pearls about her person; though not, as now, looped around her waist. An accidental touch there might start the fateful questioning.

She put down the lantern; stood for a long time by the curtained door, listening. From up and down the passage came only the heavy breathing of exhausted folk. She slipped out cautiously; made her way to the sloping deck above—how vividly familiar it was!—tiptoed lightly aft, past the uncurious helmsman, around the huge coils of rope and the piled-up fenders of interwoven matting, out to the pleasant gallery where the flowers were.

And then, as she stepped down and paused to breathe slowly, deeply, again the heavy-sweet perfume of the tuberoses, a boyish figure sprang up, with a nervous little gasp of surprise, from the steamer chair of Hong Kong grass.

She said, in her quiet way, "Oh, hello!" And then, with a quick sidelong glance at him, accepted the chair he offered. He seemed uncertain as to whether he would go or stay. Lowering her lids, she studied him. He was standing the excitement well, even improving. His carriage was better; he stood up well on his strong young legs. And he was quieter, better in hand, though of course the never-governed, long overstimulated emotions would not be lying very deep beneath this new, more manly surface. He was very good-looking, really a typical American boy.

He stood now, fingering the petals of a dahlia and gazing out astern into the luminous night. She pondered the question of exerting herself again to win him. The money was there, plenty of it. He would be as helpless as ever in her experienced hands. And the mere use of her skill in trapping and stripping him would be enjoyable.... He was lingering.

She decided in the negative. He would surely become tempestuous. And as surely, if she permitted that, he would discover the pearls. And—again the thrill of mastery swept through her finely strung nerves—she had those. They were enough. But they must be better hidden. There was her problem still, a problem that aught at any instant become delicately acute. She considered it, lying comfortably back in the chair, luxuriating in the richly blended scent of the crowded blossoms, while her nearly closed eyes studied the restless boy.

Abruptly he turned. What now? Was he about to become tempestuous all on his own? It would be anything but out of character. Her slight muscles tightened, but her face betrayed no emotion, would have betrayed none in a more searching light than this soft flood from the moon. He was sentimental over the Manchu princess, now, of course. She hadn't missed that. But in the case of an ungoverned boy, she well knew, the emotion itself could be vastly more important than its immediate object But now she was to meet with a small surprise.

"Look here!" he began, crude, naive, as always, "there's something— perhaps—I ought to tell you. I tried to carry on with you. You've got a right to think anything about me—"

At least he was keeping his voice down. She lay still; let him talk.

"—But I've changed. Smile at that, if you want to!"

She did smile faintly, but only at his clear, clean ignorance of the insult that underlay his words.

"—I *was* on the loose. It's different now. I'm going to try to do something with my life. Whatever happens—I mean however my luck may seem to turn—"

He could hardly go on with this. The next few words were swallowed down. It was plain enough that he couldn't think clearly. And he couldn't possibly know that he was giving her an opening through which, within a very few moments, she was to see the outline of the policy she must pursue during these difficult days to come on the junk.

She lifted her head; leaned on an elbow. "Do you know," she said, in a voice that seemed, now, to have a note of friendliness, "I'm sorry for you."

"Sorry for me!"

"Don't think I can't see how it is. And you mustn't misunderstand me. I'm older than you. I'm pretty experienced. My life has been hard. There couldn't be anything serious between you and me. You've wakened up to that."

The new note in her voice puzzled him, but caught his interest. He stood looking straight down at her.

"I know you're in love," she went on.

"But—"

"Don't be silly. It's plain enough. She's very attractive. Nobody could blame you."

"She's wonderful!"

"It's nice to see you feeling that way. It—it's no good our talking about it, you and me. All I've got to say is—please don't think I'd bother you. I may have led a rough life at times—a girl alone, who has to live by her wits—but—oh, well, never mind that! Every man has had his foolish moments. I understand you better than you will ever know—and—well, here's good luck!" And she offered her hand.

He took it, breathless, eager. He seemed, then, on the point of pouring out his story to this new surprising friend. But a slight sound caught his attention. He looked up, and slowly let fall the hand that was gripped in his; for at the break of the deck, just above them, hesitating, very slim and wan, stood Miss Hui Fei.

The situation was, of course, in no way so dramatic as it seemed to the boy. He, indeed, drew back, overcome; the habit of guilty thought was not to be thrown off in a moment. Miss Carmichael, sensing that he would begin erecting the incident into a situation the moment he could clumsily speak, took the matter in hand; rising, and quietly addressing herself to the Manchu girl. Breeding, of course, was not hers, could not be; but her calm manner and her instinct for reticence could seem, as now, not unlike the finer quality.

"Do have this chair," she said. "I was going down."

Miss Hui Fei smiled faintly. "I coul'n' sleep," she murmured.

"There's one little article I suppose none of us thought to bring—" thus Miss Carmichael, balancing in her light way on the balls of her feet—"needle and thread." She even indulged in a little passing laugh. "I think my maid—" began Miss Hui Fei.

"Oh, no! I wouldn't bother you!"

"Yes! Please—I don' min'."

She turned; and the boy started impulsively toward her. Miss Carmichael moved away, over the deck, but heard him saying, in a broken voice:

"You'll come back? I've got to tell you something!"

To which Miss Hui Fei replied, in a voice that was meant to be at once pleasant and impersonal: "Why—yes. I think I'll come back. It's so close down there." The two young women went below. Quietly Miss Carmichael waited in the passage.

The needle and thread were shortly forthcoming. The white girl smiled; seeming really friendly there in the dim ray of light that slanted in through a window.

"It's good of you," she said.

"Oh, no—it's nothing."

"We're in for a rather uncomfortable trip of it. I hope you'll let me do anything I can to help you. I'm more used to knocking about, of course."

"We'll all make the best of it," said the Manchu girl, and turned, with an effort at a smile, toward the stairs.

Miss Carmichael entered her own room. The lantern still burned, but the candle-end was low. She saw now an iron lamp, an open dish full of oil with a floating wick. This she lighted with the candle. Next, moving about almost without a sound, she fastened the swaying door-curtain with pins. Then she slipped out of her blouse and skirt; untied the pearl cape; and seated on the bed of matting, with her back to the door, began patiently sewing the pearls into her undergarments. It was to be a long task. Before dawn the lamp burned out, and fearful of being caught asleep with the amazing treasure about her she stood at the window and let the wind blow into her face until the faintly spreading light of dawn made the work again possible. The drowsiness that nearly overcame her now she fought off with an iron will. Nothing mattered—nothing but success. Her thin deft fingers worked in a tireless rhythm. Only once, very briefly, did she yield to the impulse to weigh the exquisite lustrous globes in her hands; to hold them close to the light. Her tireless reason told her that this wouldn't do. It brought an excited throbbing to her weary head.... She settled again to her task; time enough to gloat later. By way of a healthy mental occupation she counted the pearls as she threaded them—up to a thousand—on up to two thousand—then (the sun was redly up now; and folk were stirring about the deck) three thousand. In all, a few more than thirty-seven hundred pearls she threaded about her person; and then slipped back into blouse and skirt before permitting herself a few hours of sleep. The diamond-studded clasps she wrapped in a bit of cloth and stuffed into her hand-bag.

The Chinese maid woke her then, bringing food that had been cooked, she knew, in the brick stove up forward, where the crew slept. She could bring herself to eat but a few mouthfuls.... This didn't matter, either. No hardship was of consequence in such a battle as hers; she would have submitted coolly to torture rather than surrender her prize. But it suggested fresh tactics. She had a knack at cooking. Quietly, later in the day—she knew better than to try effusive friendliness; to play herself to the last would be best—she spoke to Mr. Doane of that small gift. A kitchen was improvised in the *laopan's* cramped quarters, aft; and Miss Carmichael, quite intent about her business, coolly cheerful about it, indeed, began to prove her capacity. And she knew, then, that she was winning. They would soon be respecting her, even liking her.

Even so she would keep her distance; then they would have to keep theirs. That was all she needed.

To Rocky, the most elusive memory of all this eventful night was the conversation with Miss Hui Fei. For she returned in a moment—so he remembered it—and sank wearily into the steamer chair. The picture of that scene was to vary bafflingly in his mind. At times he saw himself, torn with an emotion now so great that it seemed the end of life, standing over her, saying, passionately:

"I know how it looked—you're finding us here like that! And you'd have reason. I did flirt with her. I'm ashamed now. I hadn't seen you—felt you—like this. But that's all over. I was telling her—Please! You've got to know!—that I love you. Or telling her enough. She understood. And she was awfully decent. She took my hand, wished me luck."

There must have been a brief time then when the poor girl was endeavoring pleasantly to turn aside this torrent of heavily freighted words. Certainly he was talking feverishly on. He could remember pulling down a coil of rope from the steersman's deck and sitting moodily beside her; and there was a sensation in their minds, his and hers, of being at cross-purposes. There was something about her, back of the weary smile—a smile that was long to haunt him, dim in the moonlight, exquisite in its sensitive beauty—that eluded his pressing desire until it seemed near to driving him mad. Kipling's *East is East, and West is West*, slipped in among his thoughts; kept coming and coming until it became a nerve-wracking singsong in his brain.

There was one period, fortunately very short, when he seemed to be almost forcing a quarrel. Why, he couldn't afterward imagine. That part of it was dreadful in the retrospect. He had reached the point, apparently, when he couldn't longer endure the failure to reach her. There was simply no response. It was almost as if he were frightening her away. Perhaps it was just that.

But the most vivid memory was of the unaccountable force that suddenly rose in him, seizing on his tongue, his brain, his very nerves. The power of the Kanes was abruptly his, and it brought its own skill with it. It was, distinctly, a possession. It simply came, at this very top of his emotional pitch. There must have been preliminaries. He must have said things that she must have answered. But these lesser moments dropped out. Even a day later, he could see, could almost feel, himself on one knee beside the steamer chair, saying those amazing things, without a shred of memory as to how he got there. Never had he so spoken, to girl or woman; for in the escapades of the younger Rocky there had always been a reticence if seldom a restraint. It was precocity; the blood that was in him.

"You beautiful, wonderful girl!" he was breathing, close to her ear. (He was never to forget this.) "How can you hide your feelings from me? Can't you see it's just driving me mad?.... You're adorable! You're exquisite! You thrill me so—just your voice; the way you walk—your hands—your hair!.... Can't you understand, dear, it isn't what they call 'love.'" (This with a divine contempt.) "It's the cry of my whole being. I want to give you my life. I want to know *your* life—study it—come to understand the wonderful people that has made you possible! I'm going to study it—history, art, everything!.... I worship you! I dream so of you—all the time—daytimes! I just half-close my eyes and then, right away, I can see you, walking. And I see you as you were at the dance on the boat." He choked a little; then rushed on. "And in those dreams I always take you in my arms—No, let me say it! The angels are singing it, the wonderful truth!—I take you in my arms and kiss your hair and your eyes. You always close your eyes—oh, so slowly—and I press my lips on the lids. And your arms are around my neck. I can feel your hands. But I never kiss your lips—not in those dreams. Because that will mean that you have given me your soul, and I always know I must wait for that....

"Please! You must listen! Can't you see I'm just tearing my heart out and putting it in your hands—under your feet? There isn't any other life for me. I can't live without you. I could give up my friends, my home, my country, and be happy just serving you."

He had captured her hand; had it tight in his two hands and was kissing it tenderly. The thrill was unbelievable now. It was ecstasy. He could hear himself murmuring over and over, "You're so exquisite! So thrilling! I love the way your hair lies over your forehead. I love your eyes, especially when you smile".... On and on.

The tired sad girl in the steamer chair could not fail to respond in some measure, in every sensitive nerve, to so ardent a wooing. Even when she rose, and struggled a little to withdraw her hand, she couldn't be angry. He was surprising; in his very boyishness, compelling.

Then, a little later, he was sitting moodily on the extension front of the chair, face in hands, plunged into a wordless abyss; she sat on the edge of the steersman's deck, leaning against the rail, her face close to a lotus plant, with one flower that looked a ghostly blue in the fading moonlight, and just later, shaded through pink to deep red with the first quick-spreading color of the dawn. His emotional outburst had passed, for the moment, like a gust. He seemed to himself, already, to have failed. His thoughts were turned, behind the gray half-covered face, on death. For so swung the pendulum. He couldn't, in these depths, draw significance from the remarkable fact that she had risen only to drop down again and carry forward the talk that he let fall, and that he had, for the time at least, swept away those mental obstacles. Certainly Miss Hui Fei was not elusive now.

The things she was saying, in a deliberate, matter-of-fact way, bewildered him.

"I don' want you to make love to me like tha'."

"But how can I help it? You're so wonderful. You thrill me so. I tell you it's my whole life. I can never live on without you—not any more. It's got to be with you, or—or nothing."

It was strange. This impulsive affection had grown very, very rapidly within him; yet, even a day earlier he couldn't have pictured this scene. Not a phrase of these burning sentences he was so fervently uttering had been consciously framed in his mind. A part of the thrill of the situation lay in the very fact that he was so wildly committing himself. Now that it was being said, he felt no desire to take a word back. He meant it all; and more—more.

But she—still, even in the telltale morning light, quaint, charming, adorable—was growing so practical about it.

"You're a ver' romantic boy."

"I'm not! This is real! Can't you understand that it's love—forever?"

"Please!.... I don' want you to think I don' un'erstan'. It's ver' sweet an' generous of you—"

"I'm not generous! I want you!"

"I do apprecia' all it woul' mean. You offer me so much—"

"You dear girl, I offer you everything—everything I have or am! I don't want to live at all unless it's with you always at my side."

"But I don't think—Please! I woui'n' hurt you for anything. You've helped so—helped saving my father's life an' mine. It's won'erful—but I don' think life is like that. People mus' have so much in common to marry in the Western way. They mus' love each other, yes. But in their min's an' feelings they mus' share so much—their backgroun's...."

He was out of the chair now; was beside her on the deck.

"Listen!" he was huskily saying. "We'll get married right away in Shanghai. We've got to! I won't let you say no! And then we won't go back.

Well stay out here. There'll be money enough, in spite of the pater. We'll study this East together. I'm going to devote all the rest of my life to it. We'll build our common interest. I shall never want anything else!"

"How do you knew that?"

"Can you doubt me?" He had both her hands now. He seemed so young, so eager. He would fight for what he greatly desired, as his father had fought before him. However crudely, boyishly, he would fight.

"No"—her own voice was, surprisingly, a little unsteady—"of course I don' doubt you. But how can you know what you're going to wan'—years from now. I don' un'erstan' that. It does seem pretty romantic to me. I don't know for myself. I coul'n' tell."

This, or perhaps it was her failure to rise to his ecstasy, plunged him again into the depths.

"It's you or nothing now," he repeated. "You or nothing."

"Wha' do you mean by that?"

"I've got to have you. If I can't, I'll—oh, I guess I'll just drop quietly overboard. What's the use?"

"Do you think it's fair to talk li' that?"

"Perhaps not, but—I guess I'm beside myself."

"Listen!" said she now: with a friendly, even sympathetic pressure of his trembling hands, "I'll tell you what I think. I think the thing for you to do is to go back to college."

This stung him. "How can you talk like that," he cried, "when—"

"I don' wan' to hurt you. But please try to think this as I wan' you to."

"Haven't you *any* feeling for me?"

"Of course, an' I'm ver' grateful."

"For God's sake, don't talk like that."

There was a pause. He withdrew his hands; plunged his feverish face into them.

She rose, wearily. Said: "I'm going to try to sleep."

"And you could go? Leaving it like this?"

"Please! I can't help—"

"Oh, I understand—" he was on his feet before her; caught her arms in his hands that now were firm and young—"I haven't moved you yet, that's all. But I will. We Kanes aren't quitters. We don't give up. And I'm not going to give you up. I'm going to win you. Can't you see that I've got to? That I can't live.... Listen! You're the loveliest, daintiest little girl in the world. You're exquisite. Your voice is music to me. I've got to live my life to that music. It'll be beautiful! Can't you see that? I don't care how much time it takes. I'll settle down to it. But I'll win you. And we'll be married at Shanghai?"

He was very nearly irresistible now. The power in him was real. She broke away; then, a surprise to herself, lingered. Strangely to her, this ardent, still somewhat impossible boy, with his vital, Western force, had actually created an atmosphere of romance in which she was, for the moment, and in a degree, unveloped. She knew, clearly enough, that she must exert herself to escape from it: but lingered.

He caught her hands again; covered them with kisses; held them firmly while his eyes, suddenly radiant, sought hers and, during a moving instant, held them. She went below then. And Rocky dropped into the steamer chair and smiled exultantly as he drifted into slumber.

When they met again, away from the others, after an excellent luncheon of fowl and vegetables prepared by the surprising Miss Carmichael, his mood was wholly changed. He had charm; consciously or unconsciously, he made it felt.

"I wasn't fair to you," he began.

"If you don' min'," said she, "we jus' won' talk abou' that."

"Can't help it." He smiled a little. "There's no use pretending I can think about another thing. I'm madly in love with you—hopelessly gone. It'll probably simplify things if you'll just accept that as a fact. But last night— this morning—whenever it was!—after all we'd been through—you know, it wasn't so unnatural that I got all fired up that way."

As this half-smiling, half-serious youth was plainly going to be even more difficult to manage than the ardent boy of the glowing dawn, she was silent.

"Here's the thing," he went on. "I was too worn out myself to be considerate of you. I meant every word, of course. You'll never know how wonderful you seem to me." This rather wistfully. They were leaning on the rail, gazing at the rocky hills along the southern bank. "It's all wrong for me to be so impatient. I know I've got to make good. I've got to earn you. That won't come all at once. But I am going to try not to get stirred up like that again. God knows you've got enough to bother you."

"I'm ver' uncertain abou' my father," said she. "How do you mean?"

"Oh—he stays in his room. He doesn' come out with us. An' he's always working."

"Well—does that mean anything? Wouldn't he naturally be busy?"

"I don' think so. No, like this."

"But I don't understand what—"

"It isn' easy to say. When a man like father—what you call a mandarin—feels that he mus'"—her voice wavered—"that he mus' go, there is a grea' deal that he must wri' to his frien's an' to the governmen'. He doesn' wan' to be disturb'. I can' tell wha' he's doing. It worries me."

Doane, during the sunny dreamy afternoon, heard them, now and again. They were quite monopolizing the pleasant after gallery. And they were drifting on into their love story. He could not restrain himself from watching and listening. Despite the fact that his own dream was over, Doane felt about it, in his heart, like a boy. The sight of her quickened his pulse. Thoughts of her—mental pictures—came irresistibly. And these, at times, puzzled his heart if never his reason; the moment on the top deck of the steamer, when she climbed the after ladder and first confided her tragic difficulty; the dance she "sat out" with him.

.... He called himself, often enough, a fool. But his spirit refused to accept the words that formed in his mind. He was simply at war with himself.... The sort of thing happened often enough in life, of course. Every man lived through such periods. Men of middle age in particular.... Thus he fell back, over and again, on reason. It was all he could do. Plainly the experience would take a lot of living through.

To hope that her quick youth could altogether resist Rocky's ardent youth was asking too much, of course. The young people were almost certain to find themselves helpless—their emotions stirred by what they had been living through; thrown together here, romantically, on the junk. Whatever small difficulties they might encounter in exploring each other's nascent feelings would be softened by the very air they were breathing. The young are often, usually, helpless when nature so works upon them.... But Doane wasn't bitter. At times he nearly convinced himself that he felt only concern lest they rush along too fast; surrender their hearts, only to find too late that the necessary affinity was not growing into flower. The boy must have some proving, of course. That lovely girl mustn't be sacrificed.

Late in the afternoon they were singing, softly, even humorously. Doane caught snatches of *Mandalay*, and the college songs. That would seem to them a fine bond, of course—the mere casual fact that both knew the songs. For youth is quite as simple as that.... So they were rushing on with it, while an older man pondered. Rocky hung unashamed on her every word, every movement; waited forlornly about whenever she went below; starting at sounds, sinking into moods, and shining with radiance when she reappeared. He even had gentle moments.... What girl could be insensible to all that? He himself was avoiding them, of course. There was no helping that; certainly in this stage of the romance.

His excellency appeared on deck during the second afternoon; greeted Doane in friendly fashion—looking oddly simple in his servant costume; blue gown, plain cloth slippers, skull-cap with a knot of vermilion silk. They walked the deck together; later, they sat on a coil of rope. In manner he was very nearly his old self; smiling a thought less, perhaps, but as humanly direct in his talk as a Chinese.

"We shall soon be parting, Grigsby Doane," he remarked, "and I shall think much of you. Do you know yet where you shall go and what you shall do?"

"No," Doane replied. "All I can do now is the next thing, whatever that may prove to be."

"You will help China?"

"I shall hope for an opportunity."

"You are, first and last, a Westerner."

"I suppose that is true."

"I did think you a philosopher, Griggsby Doane. So you seemed to me. Like our humble great, almost like Chuang Tzü himself. But in the moment of crisis your nature found expression wholly in action. At such times we of the East are likely to be negative. We are a static people. But you, like your own, are dynamic."

This shrewd bit of observation struck Doane sharply. Come to think, it was true.

"At the critical moment you wasted not one thought in reflection. You weighed none of the difficulties; you ignored consequences. You took command. You acted. As a result—here we are.... I suppose you were right. At any rate, I yielded to your active judgment. It has saved my daughter."

"And you, as well, Your Excellency, if I may say so."

"Very well—myself too.... I shall always think of you now as I have twice seen you—once in that curious boxing match on the steamer; and again as you took command of me and my own house. I regret that in my position as a Manchu, however progressive, I can not be of any considerable service to you with the republicans. It is in their camp that your advice will help. Only there. Shall you go to them?"

Doane found it impossible to mention the invitation of Sun-Shi-pi. That would be a sacred confidence. So he replied in merely general terms:

"I should like to sit in their councils. They seem to represent, at this time, China's only material hope. Though I am not strongly an optimist regarding the revolution. China is so vast, so sunken in tradition, that the real revolution must be distressingly slow. Still, I have some familiarity with the constitutional history of my own country, and, I think, some acquaintance with yours. And I love China. Yes, I should like to help."

"You are a great man, Griggsby Doane. You have known sorrow and poverty. To the merely successful American I do not look for much real guidance. But China needs you. I hope she will find you out in time."

They talked on, of many things. His excellency was gently, at times even whimsically, reflective. At length he touched, lightly at first, on the subject of Rocky Kane. A little later, more openly, he asked what the boy's standing would be in New York.

Doane thought this over very carefully. It was curious how that confusing element of mere feeling reappeared promptly in his mind. But he explained, finally, that while the boy was young, and had been passing through a phase of rather adventurous wildness, still his father was a man of enormous prestige in society as in the financial world. The boy had nice qualities. Given the right influences he might, with the wealth that would one day be his, become like his father, a powerful factor in American life.

"I find myself somewhat puzzled," remarked his excellency then. "He seems devoted to my daughter. I can not easily read her mind. And I would not attempt to direct her life as would be necessary had she been merely a Manchu girl reared in a Manchu environment. Is she, do you think, and as your people understand the term, in love with him? I find their present relationship somewhat alarming."

"It would be difficult to say, Your Excellency—" thus Doane, simply and gravely. "The young man is, of course, in love with her."

"Ah," breathed his excellency. "You are sure of that?"

"Yes. She is undoubtedly accustomed to play about pleasantly with young men as do the young women of America." Sudden, poignant memories came of his own lovely daughter, as she had been; and of the puzzling romance that had seemed for a time to injure her young life—a romance in which he, her father, had played a strange part. But that was, after all, but an echo from another life; a closed book.

"Your daughter, I am sure," Doane continued, "can be trusted to form her own attachments. She is a noble as well as a beautiful girl."

"Indeed—you find her so, Griggsby Doane? That is pleasant to my ears. For into the directing of her life have gone my dreams of the new China and the new world. I would not have her choose wrongly now. But I do not understand her. It is difficult for me to talk freely with her."

"I am sure," said Doane slowly, "that if you could bring yourself to do so"—as once or twice before, in moments of deep feeling, he forgot to use the indirect Oriental form of address—"it would make her very happy."

"You think that, Griggsby Doane?" His excellency considered this. Then added: "I will make the effort."

"If I may suggest—talk with her not as father with daughter, but on an equality, as friend with friend."

His excellency slowly rose; and Doane, also rising, felt for the first time that the fine old statesman fully looked his age. He was, standing there, smiling a thought wistfully, an old man, little short of a broken man. And then his dry thin hand found Doane's huge one and gripped it in the Western manner. This was a surprise, evidently as moving to Kang as to Doane himself; for they stood thus a moment in silence.

"My dearest hope, of late," said the great Manchu—the smoothest of etiquette giving way, for once, before the pressure of emotion—"has been that my daughter's heart might be entrusted to you, Griggsby Doane."

Again a silence. Then Doane:

"That was my hope, as well."

"Then—"

"No. It is plainly impossible. All life is before her. The thought has not come to her. It never will. I see now that she could not be happy with me. And I think she ought to be happy. I must ask you not to speak of this again. Let youth call unto youth. And let me be her friend."

His excellency went below after this. Miss Hui Fei was also below, sleeping. Rocky Kane had been playing with the little princess, out on the gallery; but now, evidently watching his chance, he came forward to the informal seat the mandarin had vacated.

It was to be difficult—always difficult. The boy, plainly, couldn't live through these tense days without a confidant. Doane steeled himself to bear it, and to respond as a friend. There was no way out; would be none short of Shanghai; just an exquisite torture. It was even to grow, with each fresh contact, harder to bear. The boy was so curiously unsophisticated, so earnest and honest an egotist.

"—I've asked her," he said now.

Doane could only wait.

"She hasn't said yes. That would be absurd, of course—so soon." He was so pitifully putting up a brave front. "But she does like me. And it's something that she hasn't said no. Isn't it something?"

That was hardly a question; it was nearer assertion—what he had to think. Doane managed to incline his head.

"But never mind that. God knows why I should bother you with it. You've been so kind—such a friend. We—are friends, aren't we?"

Doane felt himself obliged to turn and meet his eyes. And such eyes! Ablaze with nervous light. And then he had to grip another hand—this one young, moist, strong. But he managed that, too.

"Listen! I do bother you awfully, but—I've been thinking—here we are, you know. God knows when I'll find a man who could help me as you can. And we brought all those wonderful old paintings aboard here. I've been thinking—well, since I've got so much to learn of Chinese culture, why not begin? Couldn't I—would they mind if I looked at some of the pictures? And—if it isn't asking too much—you could tell me why they're good. Just begin to give me something to go by. Isn't it as good a way to make the break as any?"

It was a most acceptable diversion. Doane, though several boxes of the paintings were in his own rooms, sent a servant to ask a permission that was cordially granted. And as there was a wind blowing, they went below, and talked there in low voices in order not to disturb the sleeping girl, while the elder man carefully opened a box and got out a number of the long scrolls that were wound on rods of ivory, handling them with reverent fingers.

He chose one from the brush of that Chao Meng-fu who flourished under the earliest Mongol or Yuan rulers, a roll perhaps fourteen or fifteen inches in width, and in length, judging from the thickness, as many feet, tied around with silk cords and fastened with tags of carven jade. The painting itself, naturally, was on silk, which in turn was pasted on thick, dark-toned paper, made of bamboo pulp, with borders of brocade. The projecting ends of the ivory rollers, like the tags, were carved.

At the edge of the scroll were, besides the seal signature of the artist, and the date—in our chronology, A. D. 1308—many other signatures in the conventional square seal characters of royal and other collectors who had possessed the painting, with also, a few pithy, appreciative epigrams from eminent critics of various periods. On that one margin was stamped the authentic history of the particular bit of silk, paper and pigment during its life of six full centuries; for no hand could have forged those seals.

There was no likelihood that the boy—lacking, as he was, in cultural background—would exhibit any sensitive responsiveness to the exquisite brush-work of the fine old painter or to his consciously subjective attitude toward his art. But there is a way in which the simple Western mind that is not preoccupied with fixed concepts of art may be led into enjoyment of such a landscape scroll; this is to exhibit it as do the Chinese themselves, unrolling it, very slowly, a little at a time, deliberately absorbing the detail and the finely suggested atmosphere, until a sensation is experienced not unlike that of making a journey through a strange and delightful country. Doane employed this method—it was surely what that old painter intended—and led the boy slowly from a pastoral home, so small beneath its towering overhanging mountain crags, that lost themselves finally in soft cloud-masses, as to appear insignificant, out along a river where lines of reeds swayed in the winds and boats moved patiently, across a lake that was dotted with pavilions and pleasure craft—on and on, through varied scenes that yet were blended with amazing craftsmanship into a continuous, harmonious whole.

The time crept by and by. When Doane finally explained the seal characters at the end and retied the old silk cords with their hanging rectangles of unclouded green jade, the sun was low over the western hills.

Rocky's face was flushed, his eyes nervously bright. "I don't get it all, of course," he said; "but it makes you feel somehow as if you'd been reading *The Pilgrim's Progress!*"

Doane gravely nodded.

"Shall we look at another?" said Rocky.

"No. That is enough. The Chinese knew better than to crowd the mind with confused impressions of many paintings. A good picture is an experience to be lived through, not a trophy to be glanced at."

"I wonder," said the boy, "if that's why I used to hate it so when my tutor dragged me through the Metropolitan Museum?"

"Doubtless."

"And this picture has a great value, I suppose?"

"It is virtually priceless—in East as well as West," replied Doane as he replaced it among its fellows in the box.

Thus began, late but perhaps not too late, what may be regarded as the education of young Rockingham Kane.

CHAPTER XII
AT THE HOUR OF THE TIGER

THEY passed, that evening, the region of Peng-tze where Tao Yuanming, after a scant three months as district magistrate, surrendered his honors and retired to his humble farm near Kiu Kiang, there to write in peace the verse and prose that have endured during sixteen crowded centuries; and on, then, moving slowly through the precipitous Gateway of Anking and, later, around the bend that bounds that city on the west, south and east. Those on deck could see, indistinctly in the deepening twilight, the vast area of houses and ruins—for Anking had not yet recovered from the devastations of the T'ai-ping rebels in the eighteen-sixties—where half a million yellow folk swarm like ants; and very indistinctly indeed, farther to the north, they could see: the blue mountains. Slowly, quietly, then, Anking, with its ruins and its memories fell away astern.

Half an hour later the sweeps were lashed along the rail. The great dark sails, with their scalloped edges between the battens of bamboo, seeming more than ever, in the dusk, like the wings of an enormous bat, were lowered; and with many shouts and rhythmic cries the tracking ropes were run out to mooring poles on the bank. Forward the mattings were adjusted for the night. The smells of tobacco and frying fish drifted aft. A youth, sipping tea by the rail, put down his cup and sang softly in falsetto a long narrative of friendship and the mighty river and (incidentally) the love of a maiden who slipped away from her mother's side at night to meet a handsome student only to be slain, as was just, by the hand of an elder brother.... From the cabin aft drifted a faint odor of incense. A flageolet mingled its plaintive oboe-like note with the song of the youth by the rail.... From a near-by village came soft evening sounds, and the occasional barking of dogs, and the beat of a watchman's gong.... The greatest of rivers—greatest in traffic and in rich memories of the endless human drama—was settling quietly for the night.

At the first rays of dawn the forward deck would be again astir. Sails would be hoisted, ropes hauled aboard and coiled; and the shining yellow craft would resume her journey down-stream, with carven and brightly painted eyes peering fixedly out at the bow, with carefully tended flowers perfuming the air about the after gallery, a thing of rich and lovely color even on the rich and lovely river; slipping by busy ports, each with its vast tangle of small shipping and its innumerable families of beggars in slipper-boats or tubs awaiting miserably the steamers and their strangely prodigal white passengers. T'ai-ping itself, of bloody memory, lay still ahead; and farther yet Nanking the glorious, and Chin-kiang, and the great estuary. Slowly the huge craft would drift and sail and tie, moving patiently on toward the Shanghai of the ever-prospering white merchants, the Shanghai that somewhat vaingloriously had dubbed itself "the Paris of the East." And no one of the thousands, here and there, that idly watched the golden junk as it moved, not without a degree of magnificence, down the tireless current, was to know that a Manchu viceroy, a prince hunted to the death by his own blood, a statesman known to the courts of great new lands, was in hiding within those timbers of polished cypress. Nor would they know that a princess, his daughter yet strangely of the new order, voyaged with him clad in the simple costume of a young Chinese woman. Nor would they dream of certain inexplicable whites. Nor would they have cared; for the voyage of the yellow junk was but a tiny incident in the crowded endless drama of the river; to the millions of struggling, breeding, dying souls along the banks and on the water, merely living was and would be burden enough. So China merely lives—dreaming a little but hoping hardly at all—with every eye on the furrow or the till; lives, and dies, and—lives again and on.

Late in the third afternoon, Rocky Kane, sitting, head forlornly in hands, in his narrow room, heard a light step—heard it with every sensitive nerve-tip—and, springing up, softly drew his curtain. But the quick eagerness faded from his eyes; for it was Dixie Carmichael.

Her thin lips curved in the faintest of smiles as she moved along the corridor toward her own curtained door. But then, as she passed and glanced back, her skirt, in swinging about, caught on a nail; caught firmly; and as she stooped to release it, a string of pearls swung down, broke, and rolled, a score of little opalescent spheres, along the deck, a few of them nearly to Rocky's feet. He stooped—without a thought at first—picked them up and turned them over in his fingers; then, stepping forward to return them, observed with an odd thrill of somewhat unpleasant excitement, that the girl had gone an ashen color and was staring at him with something the look of a wild and hostile animal. She turned then; glanced with furtive eyes up and down the corridor; and swiftly gathering up the remaining pearls clutched them tightly in one hand, extending the other and saying, in a quick half-whisper: "Give me those."

He hesitated, confused, unequal to the quick clear thinking he felt, even then, was demanded of him.

"What are you doing with them?" he asked.

"Not so loud! Come here!" She was indicating her own doorway; even drawing the curtain; while her head moved just perceptibly toward the room immediately beyond her own where Miss Hui Fei, he knew, would be resting at this time.

"Where did you get them?" he asked, huskily, doggedly.

There was a long pause. Again her subtle gaze swept the corridor. "You'd better step in here," said she, very quiet. "I've something to say to you."

Sensing, still confusedly, that he ought to see the thing through, struggling to think, he yielded to her stronger will.

She followed him into the room and let the curtain fall. "Give me those pearls," she commanded again.

He shook his head.

During a tense moment she studied him. She moved over by the translucent window of ground oyster shells, itself, in the mellow afternoon light, as opalescent as the pearls in her hand and his. Her gaze, for an instant, sought the wide stain on the floor where the Manila Kid had, so recently, wretchedly died; and her instant imagination considered the incomprehensible mental attitude of these quiet Chinese who had, without a word, disposed of the body and painstakingly cleansed the spot. No one, observing them day by day, now, as they calmly pursued their tasks, could suspect that the slanting quiet eyes had so lately seen murder.... As for the youth before her she was, now that her moment of fright had passed, supremely confident in her skill and mental strength. He was, still, little more than an undeveloped boy. And his position, now that he had set up his flag of reform, would be absurdly vulnerable.

"Once more"—her low voice was cool and soft as river ice—"give them to me."

He shook his head. "Tell me first where you got them."

"If you're determined to make a scene," said she, "I advise you to be quiet about it. You wouldn't want—her—to know you're in here."

"I—I"—this was the merest boyishness—"I've told her about—well, that I tried to make love to you. I'm not afraid of that."

"Still—you wouldn't want her to hear you now." This was awkwardly true. And his hesitation as he tried to consider it, to work out an attitude, ran a second too long.

"The pearls are mine," she pressed calmly on. "The best advice I can give you is to return them and go."

"But—"

"Do you think I want the people aboard this junk—anybody—to know that I have them?"

"I believe you stole them from the viceroy's place."

"That, of course—Well, never mind! What you may believe is nothing to me."

"Will you tell Mr. Doane about them?"

"Certainly not. And you won't."

"Why shouldn't I?"

"It's none of your business."

"Perhaps it's my duty."

"Listen"—he felt himself wholly in the right, yet found difficulty in meeting her cold pale eyes—"it's my impression that I've been acting rather decently toward you. Of course, I could have—"

"What could you have done?"

"For you own good, keep your voice down. I will tell you just this—you were pretty wild in Shanghai for a week or two."

"Well?" This was hurting him; but he met it. "And there's no likelihood that you've told her all of it. Were you such a fool as to think you could keep it all secret? Out here on the coast—and from a woman with as many underground connections as I have?"

"There's nothing that!—"

"Listen! I'm not through with you. You've been a very, very rough proposition. I know all about it. No—wait! There's something else. I knew all about you when you were making up to me on the steamer. I could have trapped you then—tangled your life so with mine that you could never have got away from me, never in the world. But I didn't. I liked you, and I didn't want to hurt you—then."

"You do want to hurt me now?"

"It may be necessary."

"Since you're taking this position"—he was finding difficulty in making his voice heard; there seemed to be danger of explosive sounds—"probably I'd better just go to Mr. Doane myself with these things."

"If you do that I'll wreck your life."

"You don't mean that you'd—"

"You seem to be forgetting a good deal."

"But you—"

"I will defend myself to the limit. I've really been easy with you. You see, you don't know anything about me. Least of all what harm I can do. You'd be a child in my hands. Turn against me and I'll get you if it takes me ten years. You'll never be safe from me. Never for a minute."

He looked irresolutely down at the lustrous jewels in his hand.

"You had these sewed in your skirt. There must be more there."

"Are you proposing to search me?"

"No—but".... His black youth was stabbing now, viciously, at his boyishly sensitive heart; but still, in a degree, he met it. "I'm going to Mr. Doane. I don't care what happens to me."

He even moved a soft step toward the door; but paused, lingered, watching her. For she was rummaging among the covers of her bed. He caught a brief glimpse of a hand-bag that she meant him not to see. She took from a bottle two green tablets. Then she faced him.

To the startled question of his eyes she replied: "They're corrosive sub mate. I shall take them now unless you—give me the pearls. If you want to have my death on your hands, take them to Mr. Doane. But it's only fair to tell you that if you do it—if you mix in this business—your own life won't be worth a nickel. They'll get you, and they'll get the pearls. You're caught in a bigger game than you can play.

"Get out, while you can"—as the low swift words came she reached out and took the pearls from his nerveless hand—"and I'll protect you. You can have your pretty Manchu girl. You can ride around in a rickshaw and look at old temples and buy embroideries. Just don't mix in affairs that don't concern you."

"I"—he was pressing a hand to a white forehead—"I've got to think it over."

"Remember this, too"—she laid a hand on his arm—"you could never fasten anything on me. The proof doesn't exist. Nobody can identify unmounted pearls. As a matter of fact I got these"... during a brief but to her perverse imagination an intensely pleasing moment she closed her eyes and lived again through that strange scene on the steps of the pavilion; again in vivid fancy rolled over the inert body that had been Tex Connor, took the amazing cape of pearls from his shirt and rolled the body heavily back...."I got these from a man I knew—an old friend. Just mind your own business and no one will harm you. But remember, you're walking among dangers. Step carefully. Keep quiet. Better go now."

He found himself in the corridor; walked slowly, uncertainly, up to the deck; sat by the rail and, head on hand, moodily watched the river and the hills. He asked himself if he had, by his very silence, struck a bargain with the girl; but could find no answer to the question, only bewilderment. Could it be that she was only a daring thief? It could, of course, but how to get at the truth? Abruptly, then his thoughts turned inward. His wild days had seemed, since his change of heart, of the remote past; but they were not, they had still been the stuff of his life within about a week. It was unnerving. He thought, something morbidly, as the sensitive young will, about habits.... The day had gone awry, too, in the matter of his love. A reaction had set in. Hui Fei was keeping much to herself. It had become difficult to talk with her at all. And that had bewildered him.... He was all adrift, with neither sound training nor a mature philosophy to steady him, life had turned unreal on his hands; nothing was real—not Hui or her father, certainly not himself, not even Mr. Doane. His background, even, was slipping away, and with it his sense of the white race. This, it seemed, was a yellow world—swarming, heedless, queerly tragic. His soul was adrift, and nobody cared. Toward his father and mother he felt only bitterness. There were, it appeared, no friends.

He thought, it seemed, confusedly, excitedly, of everything; of everything except the important fact that he was very young.

Early on the following morning Doane found the little princess playing about the deck, and with a smile seated himself beside her. She settled at once on his knee, chattering brightly in the Mandarin tongue of her play world.

He responded with a note of good-humored whimsy not out of key with her alert clear imagination. It was pleasant to fall again into the little intimacies of the language that had become, during these twenty years and more, almost his own. He pointed out to her the trained cormorants diving for fish, and the irrigating wheels along the banks; and then told quaint stories—of the first water buffalo, and of the magic rice-field.

Soon she, too, was telling stories—of the simpleton who bought herons for ducks, of the toad in the lotus pool, of the child that was born in a conch shell and finally crawled with it into the sea, of the youngest daughter who to save the life of her father married a snake, of the magic melon that grew full of gold and the other melon that contained hungry beggars, of the two small boys and the moon cake, and of the curious beginning of the ant species.

She scolded him for his failure, at the first, to laugh with her. Her happy child quality stirred memories of old-time days in T'ainan-fu, when his own daughter had been a child of six, playing happily about the mission compound. They were poignant memories. His eyes were misty even as he smiled over the bright merriment of this child, and in his heart was a growing wistful tenderness. To be again a father would be a great privilege. He was ripe for it now, tempered by poverty and sorrow, yet strong, with a great emotional capacity on which the world about him had, apparently, no claim to make. He was simply cast aside, left carelessly in an eddy with the great stream of life flowing, bankful, by. The experience was common enough, of course. In the great scheme of life the fate of an individual here and there could hardly matter. He could tell himself that, very simply, quite honestly; and yet the strength within him would rise and rise again to assert the opposite. The end, for himself, lay beyond the range of conscious thought; but at least, he felt, it could not be bitterness. He seemed to have passed that danger.... The little princess was soberly telling the old story of the father-in-law, the father, and the crabs that were eaten by the pig. At the conclusion she laughed merrily; and then Ending his response somewhat unsatisfactory, scowled fiercely and with her plump fingers bent up the corers of his mouth.

He laughed then; and rolled her up in his arms and tossed her high in the air.

When Hui Fei came upon them they were gazing out over the rail. Mr. Doane seemed to be telling a long story, to which the child listened intently. She moved quietly near, smiling; and after listening for a few moments seated herself on the deck behind them.

The story puzzled her. She leaned forward, a charming picture in her simple costume, black hair parted smoothly, oval face untouched with powder or paint. She smiled again, then, for his story was nothing other than a free rendering into Chinese of Stevenson's:=

"In Winter I get up at night

And dress by yellow candle-light..."=

He went on, when that was finished, with a version of:=

"Dark brown is the river,

Golden is the sand...."=

—and other poems from *The Child's Garden of Verses*.

Hui Fei's eyes lighted, as she listened. Mr. Doane, it appeared, knew nearly all of these exquisite verse-stories of happy childhood and exhibited surprising skill in finding the Chinese equivalents for certain elusive words. What a mind he had.... rich in reading as in experience, ripe in wisdom, yet curiously fresh and elastic! It seemed to her a young mind.

The little princess was especially pleased with *My Bed Is a Boat*, and made him repeat it. At the conclusion she clapped her hands. And then Hui Fei joined in the applause, and laughed softly when they turned in surprise.

"Won't you do *The Land of Counterpane?*" she asked.

It was later, when the child had run off to play among the flowers, that he and she fell to talking as they had not talked during these recent crowded days. There were silences, at first. Despite his effort to seem merely friendly and kind, he felt a restraint that had to be fought through. In this time, so difficult for her at every point, he felt deeply that he must not fail her. Her greatest need, surely, was for friendship. The excited youth who dogged her steps and hung on her most trivial glance could not offer that. And melancholy had touched her bright spirit; he sensitively felt that when the little princess ran away and her smile faded. Sorrow dwelt not far behind those dark thoughtful eyes.

Early in the conversation she spoke of her father. Her thoughts, clearly, were always with him.

"I wan' to ask you," said she simply and gravely, "if you know what he is doing."

Doane moved his head in the negative.

"He has been in his room for more than a day. When I go to his door he is kin' but he doesn' ask me to come in. And he doesn' tell me anything."

"He is not confiding in me," said Doane.

"I don' like that, either, Mis'er Doane. For I know he thinks of you now as his closes' frien'. There is no other frien' who knows what you know. An' you have save' his life an' mine. My father is not a man to fail in frien'ship or in gratitu'."

Doane's eyes, despite his nearly successful inner struggles, grew misty again. Impulsively he took her hand gently in his. At once, simply, her slender fingers closed about his own. It seemed not unlike the trusting affection of a child; he sensed this as a new pain. Yet there was strong emotional quality in her; he felt it in her dark beauty, in the curve of her cheek and the lustrous troubled splendor in her eyes, in the slender curves of her strong young body. She was, after all, a woman grown; aroused, doubtless, to the puzzling facts of life; a woman, with an ardent lover close at hand, who was—this as his wholly adult mind now saw her—already at her mating time. And feeling this he gripped her hand more tightly than he knew. But even so, he was not unaware of his own danger. It wouldn't do; once to release his own tightly chained emotions would be to render himself of no greater value to her in her bewilderment than any merely pursuing male. He set his teeth on that thought, and abruptly withdrew his hand.

She did not look up—her gaze was fixed on the surface of the river. The only indication she gave that she was so much as aware of this odd little act of his was that she started to speak, then paused for a brief instant before going on.

"I ask—ask myself all the time if there is anything we coul' be doing."

Doane's head moved again in the negative.

"If not even his gratitu'—"

"Gratitude," said Doane gently, "becomes less than nothing when it is demanded."

"True, it can no' be ask', but it can be given."

"Sometimes"—he was thinking aloud, dangerously—"I wonder if any healthy human act is free from the motive of self-interest. Generosity is so often self-indulgence. Self-sacrifice, even in cases where it may be regarded as wholly sane, may be only a culmination or a confusion of little understood desires."

She looked up at this; considered it.

"Certainly," he went on, "your father owes me nothing."

Her hand moved a little way toward his, only to hesitate and draw back. She looked away, saying in a clouded voice: "He—and I—owe you everything." It wouldn't do. Doane waited a long moment, then spoke in what seemed more nearly his own proper character—quietly, kindly, with hardly an outward sign of the intensely personal feeling of which his heart was so full.

"Your father has spoken to me of you as an experiment."

"You mean my life—my education."

"Yes. He feels, too, that the experiment has not yet been fully worked out. I often think of that—your future. It is interesting, you know. You have responded amazingly to the spirit of the West. And of course you'll have to do something about it."

"Oh, yes," said she, musing, "of course."

"Whatever personal interests may for a time—or at times—absorb your life".... this was as close as he dared trust himself to the topic of marriage_"I feel about you that your life will seek and find some strong outward expression."

"Yes—I have often fel' that too. Of course, at college I like' to speak. I went in a good 'eal for the debates, an' for class politics."

"You have an active mind. And you have a fine heritage. Knowing—even feeling—both East and West as you do, your life is bound to find some public outlet. Something."

"I know." She seemed moody now, in a gentle way. Her fingers picked at a rope. "But I don' know what. I don' think I woul' like teaching. Writing, perhaps. Even speaking. That is so easy for me."

"There is a service that you are peculiarly fitted to perform." She glanced up quickly, waited. "It is a thought that keeps coming to my mind. Perhaps because it will probably become the final expression of my own life. For my life is curiously like yours in one way. You remember, that—that night when we first talked—on the steamer—"

"I climb' the ladder," she murmured, picking again at the rope.

"—And we agreed that we were both, you and I"—his voice grew momentarily unsteady—"between the worlds."

"Yes. I remember." He could barely hear her, "It is true, of course."

"It is true. And for myself, I feel more and more strongly every day that I must pitch into the tremendous task of helping to make the East known to the West."

"Tha' woul' be won'erful!" she breathed.

"I have come to feel that it is the one great want in Western civilization, that the philosophy, the art, the culture, indeed, of China has never been woven into our heritage. It is strange, in a way—we derived our religion from certain primitive tribes in Syria. But they had little culture. The Christian religion teaches conduct but very nearly ignores beauty. And then there is our insistent pushing forth of the Individual. I have come to believe that our West will seem less crass, less materialistic, when the individual is somewhat subdued." He smiled. "We need patience—sheer quality of thought—the fine art of reflection. We shall not find these qualities at their best, even in Europe. They exist, in full flower, only in China. And America doesn't know that. Not now."

A little later he said: "That work has been begun, of course, in a small way. A slight sense of Chinese culture is creeping into our colleges, here and there. Some of the poetry is bring translated. The art museums are reaching out for the old paintings. The Freer collection of paintings will some day be thrown open to the public. But traditions grow very slowly. It will take a hundred years to make America aware of China as it is now aware of Italy, Egypt, Greece, even old Assyria.... and the thing must be freed from Japanese influence—we can't much longer afford to look at wonderful, rich old China through the Japanese lens."

"An' you're going to make tha' your work," observed Hui Fei.

"I must. I begin to feel that it is to be the only final explanation of my life."

There was a silence. Then, abruptly, in a tone he did not understand, she asked: "Are you going to work for the Revolution?"

"That is the immediate thing—yes. I shall offer my services."

"Coul' I do anything, you think? At Shanghai, I mean? Of course, I'm a Manchu girl, but I can no' stand with the Manchu Gover'ment. I am not even with my—my father there."

"It is possible. I don't know. We shall soon be there."

"Will you tell me then—at Shanghai?"

He inclined his head. Suddenly he couldn't speak. She was holding to him, as if it were a matter of course; yet he dared not read into her attitude a personal meaning of the only sort that could satisfy his hungry heart. The difficulty lay in his active imagination. Like that of an eager boy it kept racing ahead of any possible set of facts. All he could do, of course, was to go on curbing it, from hour to hour. It would be harder seeing her at Shanghai than running away, as he had half-consciously been planning. But it was something that she clung to him as a friend. He mustn't, couldn't, really, fail her there.

All of the last day they sailed the wide and steadily widening estuary. The lead-colored water was roughened by the following wind that drove the junk rapidly on toward her journey's end. But toward sunset wind and sea died down, and under sweeps, late in the evening-, the craft moved into the Wusung River and moored for the night within sight of a line of warships.

A feeling of companionship grew strongly among those fugitives, yellow and white, as the evening advanced. They had passed together through dangerous and dramatic scenes. Now that danger and drama were alike, it seemed, over, with the peaceable shipping of all the world lying just ahead up the narrow channel, with, in the morning to come, a fresh view of the bund at Shanghai, where hotels, banks and European clubs elbowed the great trading hongs, with motor-cars and Sikh police and the bright flags of the home land so soon to be spread before their weary eyes, they gathered on the after gallery to chat and watch the flashing signal lights of the cruisers and the trains on the river bank, and dream each his separate dream. Even Dixie Carmichael, though herself untouched by sentiment, joined, for reasons of policy, the little party. Hui Fei was there, between Doane and the moodily silent Rocky Kane. The Chinese servants smilingly grouped themselves on the deck just above. And finally—though it is custom among these Easterners to sleep during the dark hours and rise with the morning light—his excellency appeared, walking alone over the deck, smiling in the friendliest fashion and greeting them with hands clasped before his breast.

Doane felt a little hand steal for a moment into his with a nervous pressure. His own relief was great.

For this smiling gentleman could hardly be regarded as one about to die. They placed him in the steamer chair of woven rushes from Canton. And pleasantly, then, their last evening together passed in quiet talk.

His excellency was in reminiscent mood. He had been a young officer, it transpired, in the T'aiping Rebellion, and had fought during the last three years of that frightful thirteen-year struggle up and down the great river, taking part in the final assault on Su-chau as a captain in the "Ever Victorious" army of General Gordon. Regarding that brilliant English officer he spoke freely; Doane translating a sentence, here and there, for young Kane.

"Gordon never forgave Li Hung Chang," he said, "for the murder of the T'ai-ping Wangs, during the peace banquet. It was on Prince Li's own barge, in the canal by the Eastern Gate of the city. Gordon claimed that Li procured the murder. He was a hot-blooded man, Gordon, often too quick and rough in speech. Li told me, years later, that the attack was directed as much against himself as against the Wangs, and regarded himself as fortunate to escape. He never forgave Gordon for his insulting speech. But Gordon was a vigorous brave man. It was a privilege to observe him tirelessly at work, planning by night, fighting by day—organizing, demanding money, money, money—with great energy moving troops and supplies. He could not be beaten. He was indeed the 'Ever Victorious.'"

It was, later, his excellency who asked Hui Fei and young Kane to sing the American songs that had floated on one or two occasions through his window below. They complied; and Dixie Carmichael, in an agreeable light voice, joined in. At the last Duane was singing bass.

The party was breaking up—his excellency had already gone below—when Rocky, moved to the point of exquisite pain, caught the hand of Hui Fei.

"Please!" he whispered. "Just a word!"

"Not now. I mus' go."

"But—it's our last evening—I've tried to be patient—it'll be all different at Shanghai—I can't let you."

But she slipped away, leaving the youth whispering brokenly after her. He leaned for a long time on the rail then, looking heavily at the winking lights of the cruisers. It was a relief to see Mr. Doane coming over the deck. Certainly he couldn't sleep. Not now. His heart was full to breaking.... The fighting impulse rose. During this past day or so he had seemed to be losing ground in his struggle with self. The startling incident in Miss Carmichael's room had turned out, he felt, still confusedly, as a defeat. It had left him unhappy. This night, out there in the blossom-scented gallery, he had sensed the strange girl, close at hand, cool as a child, singing the old college songs with apparent quiet enjoyment, as an uncanny thing, a sinister force. Even when speaking to Hui Fei, her influence had enveloped him.... This would be just one more little battle. And it must be won.

Accordingly he told Mr. Doane the story. The older man considered it, slowly nodding.

"It is probably the fact," he said, at length, "that she stole the pearls at Huang Chau. She was with Connor and Watson. But it is also a fact that she might have pearls of her own. And in traveling alone through a revolution it would be her right to conceal them as she chose. It is true, too, that unset pearls couldn't be identified easily, if at all. And she is clever—she wouldn't weaken under charges.... No, I don't see what we can do, beyond watching the thing closely. As for her threats against you, they are partly rubbish."

But Rocky cared little, now, what they might be. Once again he had cleaned the black slate of his youth. His head was high again. He could speak to Hui Fei convincingly in the morning.

His excellency, alone in his cabin, took from his hand-bag the book of precepts of Chuang Tzü; and seated on his pallet, by the small table on which burned a floating wick in its vessel of oil, read thoughtfully as follows:

"Chuang Tzü one day saw an empty skull, bleached but intact, lying on the ground. Striking it with his riding whip, he cried, 'Wert thou once some ambitious citizen whose inordinate yearnings brought him to this pass?—some statesman who plunged his country into ruin and perished in the fray?—some wretch who left behind him a legacy of shame?—some beggar who died in the pangs of hunger and cold? Or didst thou reach this state by the natural course of old age?'

"When he had finished speaking, he took the skull and, placing it under his head as a pillow, went to sleep. In the night he dreamt that the skull appeared to him and said: 'You speak well, sir; but all you say has reference to the life of mortals and to mortal troubles. In death there are none of these.... In death there is no sovereign above, and no subject below. The workings of the four seasons are unknown. Our existences are bounded only by eternity. The happiness of a king among men can not exceed that which we enjoy.'

"Chuang Tzü, however, was not convinced, and said: 'Were I to prevail upon God to allow your body to be born again, and your bones and flesh to be renewed, so that you could return to your parents, to your wife and to the friends of your youth, would you be willing?'

"At this the skull opened its eyes wide and knitted its brows and said: 'How should I cast aside happiness greater than that of a king, and mingle once again in the toils and troubles of mortality?'"

He closed the book; laid on the table his European watch; and sat for a long time in meditation. As the hands of the watch neared the hour of three in the morning, he took from the bag a box of writing materials, a small red book and a bottle of white pills.

The leaves of the book were the thinnest gold. On one of these he inscribed, with delicate brush, the Chinese characters meaning "Everlasting happiness." Tearing out the leaf, then, he wrapped loosely in it one of the pills—these were morphine, of the familiar sort manufactured in Japan and sold extensively in China since the decline of the opium traffic—and swallowed them together. He inscribed and took another, and another, and another.

Gradually a sense of drowsy comfort, of utter physical well-being, came over him. The pupils of his eyes shrunk down to the merest pin-points. His head drooped forward. His frail old body fell on the bed and lay peacefully there as his spirit sought its destiny in the unchanging, everlasting Tao.

CHAPTER XIII
HIS EXCELLENCY SPEAKS

IT was daybreak. Doane, standing in his cabin by the opened window, looked out with melancholy in his deep-set eyes over the muddy low reaches that border the Wusung. It was a familiar scene; indeed he knew it better than any spot in his native land—the railroad along the bank, the brick warehouses, the native village of Wusung, the inevitable humble families in the fields gathering in the last crops of the season.

Overhead the *laopan* was shouting, tackle creaked, the crew half sang, half grunted their chanties. From the cruisers, one after another, floating musically on the still air, came the call of bugles—the *reveille* of the American navy. So these were ships from home. The stars and stripes would soon, at "colors," be rippling from each gray stem.... There was an ache in his heart.

Then other noises came—a little confusion of them, somewhere here on the junk—excited whispers, a sound that might have been sobbing, and then—yes!—the low wailing of women.

He turned; listened closely. Light feet came running along the corridor. A familiar, lovely voice called his name, brokenly. Then Hui Fei drew aside his curtain. Her cheeks were stained with tears.

Quickly, his arm about her shoulders as she swayed unsteadily, but without a word, he walked beside her along the corridor to the cabin of his excellency.... There were the few servants, kneeling by the inert body and bowing their heads to the floor as they mourned. Doane straightened the body and closed the eyes.... It was Hui Fei who found the roll of documents on the table and placed them in Doane's hands. He saw then, through the mist that clouded his own eyes, that they were addressed to himself: "To my dear friend, Griggsby Doane, I entrust these my last papers." The name alone was in English; written in a clear hand, not unlike that of a painstaking schoolboy, each letter carefully and roundly formed.

Hui Fei sent the servants to another cabin, but remained herself, seated on the floor by the side of the huge strong man who was now without question the head of the strangely assorted family. She was calmer. Doane did not again hear her sob; he did not even see tears. During that difficult moment when Rocky Kane appeared in the doorway and asked huskily, sadly, if he could help, she even smiled, very faintly, very gently, as she moved her head in the negative. And the youth, after a hesitant moment, left them.

Doane spread out the documents on the floor. The first, addressed directly to himself, he laid aside for the moment. To the second, addressed to the throne—"by the hand of His Imperial Highness, Prince Ch'un, Regent, as soon as it may be possible to convey to him in this hour of China's sorrow this inadequate expression of my last thoughts"—was attached a paper requesting that "my closest friend, Griggsby Doane" read it thoughtfully, "in order that he may understand fully the circumstances in which I find myself at this the end of my long life.

"I, your unworthy servant,"—it read—"have learned with sorrow and tears of the decree permitting me to withdraw from this troubled life in solitude and peace without the painful consequences of a death by the headsman's sword. And in bowing humbly to your will I, your unworthy servant, recognize that my life lies wholly in your hands to be disposed of as seems best to the imperial wisdom. But in thus proving my never weakening loyalty to the imperial will I also must express the sober thoughts of one who has pondered long over the evils that beset our land and who has ventured at times, weakly, to hope that China might pay heed to certain lessons of recent history and find a way to oppose successfully the pressure of other powerful nations upon us. For it has been my privilege, as a long-time servant of the throne, to observe certain of these other nations at first hand and to learn a little of their power, which is very great.

"On another occasion I, your unworthy servant, wittingly incurred danger of death or imprisonment, because, in the eagerness of my convictions, I dared to suggest certain reforms to the throne. There is a saying that the tree which bends before the gale will never be broken off but will grow to a ripe old age, and my hope has always been for a great and growing China. At that time princes and ministers about the throne asked permission to subject me to a criminal investigation, but his late majesty was pleased to spare me. Therefore my last years have been a boon at the hand of his late majesty."

There followed a clear, dignified statement of the urgent need for vast reforms. His excellency recalled in detail his long years of service and his decorations and honors. Quietly he called attention to the fact that all, or nearly all, China was in revolt, that the throne tottered, that to permit the government longer to be dominated by corrupt eunuchs was an affront to modern as to ancient thought and morality. It was clear to himself, he stated, that without a skilfully organized system of gradual, perhaps rapid, modernization, China would soon crumble to pieces under the heel of the greedy foreigners. And there was profound pathos in the passing remark that perhaps his suicide, far from home, his vast estate seized by government agents or despoiled by robbers, his person, alone, beyond the reach of harm—safe, in fact, with the hated foreigners—might stand as a final proof of his loyalty to the throne in serving which his long life had been spent.

"But at the moment of leaving this world I feel that my mind is not so clear as I could wish. The text of this my memorial is ill-written and lacking in clarity of thought. I am no such scholar as the men of olden times; how, then, could I face the end with the calm which they showed? But there is a saying, 'The words of a dying man are good.' Though I am about to die, it is possible that my words are not good. I can only hope that the empress and the emperor will pity my last sad utterance, regarding it neither as wanton babbling nor the careless complaint of a trifling mind. Thus shall I die without regret. I wish, indeed, that my words may prove overwrought, in order that those who come after, perhaps more happily, may laugh at my foolishness.

"I pray the empress and the emperor to remember the example of our great rulers of the past in tempering peace with mercy; that they may choose only the worthy for public service; that they may refrain from striving for those things desired by the foreigners, which would only plunge China into deeper woe, but that by a careful study of what is good in foreign lands they may help China to hold up her head among the nations and bring us finally to prosperity and happiness. This is my last prayer, the end and crown of my life."

The junk was moving up the river as Doane finished reading, passing one of the war-ships. The bugles were blowing again. A beam of warm sunlight slanted in through the window of stained glass and threw a kaleidoscope of color on the wall.

Hui Fei sat motionless, her hands folded humbly in her lap, gazing at the floor. Her face was expressionless. She seemed wholly Oriental.

With a sigh, Deane rolled the memorial and tied it with the ribbon. The one beneath it, he saw now, was addressed to Hui Fei. Without a word he handed it to her and then settled to read his own. Hers was the shorter. When she had finished she lowered it to her lap and sat motionless, as before.

Doane now took up the paper addressed to himself and read as follows:

"My friend, Griggsby Doane, grieve not for me, and be sure that in the manner of my end I have had no wish to bring evil upon you. It is in a measure sad that this end should come upon a hired junk instead of on a plot of hallowed ground, as I would have chosen. But there was no choice. I have waited until assured of my daughter's safety.

"Inform the magistrate at Shanghai of my death, and see that my Memorial to the Throne is forwarded promptly. Give to my daughter Hui Fei the letter addressed to her. It my wish that you also should read that letter, and I have so instructed her. It is also my wish that she should read this letter to you. Buy for me a cheap coffin, and have it painted black inside. The poor clothes I wear must serve, but I wish that the soiled soles of my shoes be cut off. Twenty or thirty taels will be ample for the coffin.

"I do not believe it will be necessary for the magistrate to hold an inquest. Please have a coating of lacquer put on the coffin, to fill up any cracks, and have the cover nailed down pending the throne's decision as to my remains. Then buy a small plot of ground near the Taoist temple outside of Shanghai and have me buried as soon as possible. There is no need to consider waiting for an opportunity to bury me at my ancestral home; any place is good enough for a loyal and honest man.

"You will find about a thousand taels in my bag, also the few jewels we found at my home. Sell the jewels and keep for yourself the balance that will remain after my burial expenses are paid. The *laopan* of this junk has his money. This he will deny, and will cry for more; but do not heed him.

"Remember there is nothing strange or abnormal in my passing; death has become my duty. It may be true that the historic throne of the Manchus is rocking, is falling, but despite the understanding that has been given to me of what is good in Western civilization I have never swayed in my heart from loyalty to that throne and steadfast devotion to its best interests as I can see them, and I do no less than obey the mandate of my empress and my emperor.

"Do not grieve unduly for me. It is my wish that all of you, my friends and family, should live happily in the life that lies before you. To you, Griggsby Doane, out of the gratitude and admiration of my proud heart, I give and bequeath all the little that may be left of my worldly goods, including the money, the pitiful handful of jewels, the historic paintings and my daughter Hui Fei. It is my wish that you will marry her at once, and that in your best judgment you sell any or all of the paintings to provide what money you and she may need, and also that you and she care lovingly for the younger child. It may be better to educate her in the Western manner, but that will be as you may decide. In the matter of this marriage with my daughter, Hui Fei, I have sought the opinion of each of you regarding the other. I have your assurance that it has been your own wish. And Hui Fei informs me that she respects and admires no man more than yourself. You will see, therefore, that I have approached this matter in the Western spirit, and as a result I see no reason why the marriage should be delayed or that my beloved daughter should be left alone at the mercy of an unscrupulous world. I have informed her, also, of my decision. My gifts to you make a most inadequate dowry, but they are all I have. I wish for you both great happiness and many descendants.

"And now, Griggsby Doane, my dear friend, I take my leave of you. I, at seventy-four years of age, can claim an unsulliod record. My faiuilly tree goes back more than seven hundred years; for three centuries there have been members of my clan in the Imperial Household or in the Government Bureaus, and for four hundred years we have devoted ourselves to husbandry and scholarship. For twenty-four generations my family has borne a good name. I die now in order that a lifetime of devotion to duty and loyalty to the throne may be consummated."

Slowly Doane lowered the document. He could not speak; he could hardly think. There beside him, still motionless, sat the young woman who was now, by all the traditions of her people, abruptly his.

Dutifully, observing that he had finished reading, she gave him her own letter; and he, in exchange, handed her his. Thus they read on. And then, again quietly exchanging the documents, they sat without a word by the peaceful body.

Little by little Doane's brain cleared. It was a time, he felt—*the* time, indeed—when all his experience, all his character and skill, must come into use. Now, it ever, he must be wise and steady and kind. Very gently he took her hand; it lay softly in his; she did not lift her eyes.

"We will not think of this matter now," he said. "Our only thought must be to carry out his plans regarding the funeral. If it shouldn't seem best, later, to fulfill quite all his last wishes, perhaps he, from the other side of the barrier, will understand what he couldn't wholly understand while on this earth. But this I must say now—-whatever direction your life may take, try to think of me as filling, the best I can, your father's place. I shall hope to be your dearest friend. Lean on me. Use me. And be sure I will understand."

Her slim fingers tightened once again about his.

"He was a won'erful father," she began, and choked a little.

He left her there; sent in her maid to her; himself mounted to the deck.

The sun was well up. Other junks sailed up and down the tide. A bluff-bowed freighter, flying the Dutch flag, lay at anchor near one of the Chinese torpedo boats that had gone over to the chaotic new republic. The American steamers were far astern, but a motor launch flying an officer's flag and with blue uniforms visible under the awning, plowed by on her way up to the city. In the distance, up ahead, beyond the crowding masts and funnels of the steamers that came from all the world, could be seen the buildings and spires and the smoke-haze of European Shanghai.... The bund there, within a few hours now, would be crowded with pony-carriages and motor-cars and over-fed tourists riding in rickshaws drawn by ragged coolies. The hotels would be thronging with talkative young women and drink-flushed men, all eagerly retailing confused and inaccurate news of "the revolution"; out at the British country club on Bubbling Well Road blond men would be playing tennis in flannels: and the gambling houses would be brightly illuminated until late at night, and the Chinese shopkeepers in Nanking Road would be selling their souvenir trinkets, their useless little boxes of coinsilver and cloisonne and damascene work and their painted snuff-bottles and green soapstone necklaces and blue-and-white pottery quite as if no troubles could ever arise to disturb the destiny of nations.

Doane sighed again. The last letter of his excellency was in his hand, held tightly; though he was not at this time aware of it. He glanced aft, and saw Rocky Kane standing on the gallery, among the flowers, gazing not forward toward the jangling, money-seeking, pleasure-mad city that is the principal point of contact between the culture of the West and that of the East, but off astern, as if endeavoring to see again the lost Yangtze Kiang of his glowing romance.

Doane went to him; aware, then, of the paper rolled so tightly in his hand, said—a huge figure, towering over the boy, his face sad and more than ever deeply lined, but with a grave kindliness about the eyes:

"My boy, it is important that you and I have a talk. Suppose we sit down." He indicated the steamer chair; but Rocky insisted that he take it, himself dropping heavily down on the step of the deck.

"How—how is she standing it?" he asked, his troubled eyes searching that strong face before him.

"As well as we could ask. It is bound to be very hard for her—especially during these next few days. But she has courage. And she knows he would wish her not to mourn.... A matter has come up that concerns you, Rocky" — it was the first time he had used that familiar name; the boy's moody eyes brightened momentarily, and a touch of color rose in his cheeks—"and I don't feel I can delay telling you about it. First, you had better let me read you this."

He had not thought, before this moment, of the necessity that he himself make the translation for the boy. It had to be difficult; he would have given much if the thing could have been managed in some less directly personal way; but for that matter, difficulties lay so thickly about him now that there was no good in so much as giving them a thought. And so—deliberately, with great care to find the nearly precise English equivalent of every obscure phrase—he read the letter through.

He dared not look at the boy's face, but could not but become aware of the hands that twitched, clasping and unclasping, in his lap, and of the feet that at times nervously tapped the deck. When the task was done he quietly folded the paper and slipped it into a pocket.

The silence grew long and trying. Doane searched and searched his own still confused mind for the right, the clear word; but could not, during these earlier moments, find it. The boy, plainly, was crushed; but behind the clouded eyes and the knit brows an emotional storm was gathering. Doane felt that. It had to come, of course. And it would have to be handled.

But the first words were almost calm.

"So that"—thus the brooding youth—"so that's how it is!"

Doane waited. After a little the boy sprang up. "But in God's name, why didn't you tell me!" he cried. "You've let me come and talk to you! You—This isn't fair! You've made a fool of me! You—" Doane rose too. They stood side by side among the heavily scented blossoms. Doane felt moved to put a kindly hand on the slender shoulder beside him; but a following thought cautioned him that even a touch would be resented at this moment.

"I didn't tell you," he said, "because until I read this paper I didn't know."

"But you must have known! You told—him. Told him you loved her! Probably you've been telling her, too—here under my eyes. Oh, God, what a fool I've been.... If you'd only been square with me!"

"This is not fair," said Doane, still very quiet. "We must talk this out, but not now—not while you are angry."

"Angry! What in heaven's name is the sense of talking it out! It's settled, isn't it?"

"I'm not sure."

"That's not so!" The boy seemed to be recovering somewhat now from the first shock of unreason. He turned away to hide the tears in his eyes. "You've admitted to her father, if not to her, that you love her.... Oh, why didn't I see it! Why did I have to be such an awful fool!... She knows it now. And you know as well as I what she'll do. She'll never go against her father's last wish—never. You know that!"

"I recognize that she must be seeing it in that light now, but—"

"Oh, what's the use of talk. You *know!* For God''s sake, let me alone, can''t you!"

Doane's brows drew slowly together; but this and a note of something near command in his voice, were the only outward indications of the storm within his breast.

"This is not a time for either you or me to be thinking of ourselves. You may be sure that Hui Fei will not be thinking so. And it may help you to realize that this situation is difficult for me, as it is for you. It is true that Hui Fei's only thought, now, under the stress of this sorrow, will be to submit to her father's every wish. But this stress will pass. There is only one course to take—"

"But—"

"Listen to me! And try to meet the thing like a man. We will wait until this sad business is over. We will at least try to give up thinking of ourselves. I will see that Hui Fei and her sister are cared for by friends."

"But all the time you'll be seeing her, and—"

"I must still ask you to listen and try to think clearly. As soon as it seems wise I will lay the situation before Hui Fei. I will try to persuade her that her own life is, in the last analysis, more important than even her father's dying wish. I believe that she—would—be happier with a young man like yourself than with an—older man. It is possible that she can be led to see that her own happiness must be a factor in her choice. Have you the patience and the courage to wait for that?"

He extended his hand. The boy looked at it, then up at the stern, but still kindly face; hesitated; then, with a quivering of the lip and an explosive— "Oh God!"—rushed away; walked very fast, almost ran, the length of the deck; made his way through the crowded waist and around the cook's well; and stood, his bare head thrown proudly back, in the prow, beside the quietly wondering *tai-kung,* staring toward the long curving sweep of the tree-shaded bund of Shanghai as it came gradually into view around the bend just below the city.

CHAPTER XIV
THE WORLD OF FACT

THE yellow junk was now abreast the landing hulks of the great international shipping companies just below the city. Rocky left the bow and made his way to the after cabins without once lifting his somber gaze to the silent figures on the poop. Slowly—his eyes wild, his thoughts beyond control, bitterness in his heart—he moved along the dim corridor.

A puff of wind found its way through an open window; a blue curtain swung out, discovering, through a doorway, Miss Carmichael, seated in a chair beneath the window. It was lighter in her cabin. She had laid aside the familiar middy blouse and skirt, and appeared to be sewing something on her petticoat. For an instant she looked up, her eyes meeting those of the pale youth who stood motionless in the corridor. The curtain swung back then; but as it swung the youth stepped through the doorway and stood within the room.

"I don't know that I asked you in," said she coolly.

His eyes were intent on the amazing, glistening strings of pearls that were looped everywhere about her clothing.

Through narrowed lids she watched him, sitting very still, needle poised just as she had drawn it through. On his young face was an expression of firm decision that she had not before seen there. He looked oddly, now, like his father. There was, apparently, a trace of the Kane iron in him. The situation was of wholly accidental origin; he couldn't have planned it; his first expression, out in the corridor, had been of startled surprise; the decision to step within must have been instant; yet now, suddenly, he meant business. She caught all that.... Here, after all, was a young man who presented difficulties.

"Take off those pearls," said he quietly.

"You are in my room," said she as quietly.

"I shall take the pearls when I go."

"You'll have my life to answer for."

"Your life is nothing to me."

"Your own life is."

"Never mind about that."

"I've warned you fairly."

"Stand up."

"You propose to take them from me by force?"

"Yes. Unless you choose to give them to me."

"And you expect me to trust you with them."

"Yes."

There was a silence.

"Of course you are stronger than I," she observed musingly.

He offered no reply to this.

Her thin mouth curved into the faint smile that was as cold as her calculating brain. "So"—said she "we're enemies, then?"

This evidently did not interest him.

"I think," she went on, quietly desperate, "that I'll try crying and screaming. I'm something of an actress."

"Scream your head off," said he, the slang phrase sounding almost courteous in this new quiet voice of his.

"There's not a person—alive—that could prove these pearls aren't my own." Her voice dwelt on that one telling word, "alive," with an almost caressing note of satisfaction.

He shook his head with a touch of impatience. And she was studying him, her quick thoughts darting sharply about—-darting in every conceivable direction—for an avenue of escape. She knew, however, as the moments passed and the pale youth stood his ground that there was only one. She had supposed him weak. It hardly seemed that her judgment could have gone so far wrong.

"You're cruel to me," she said softly.

"Stand up."

Now she obeyed. He drew near.

"I didn't think you'd turn out this sort, Rocky. You liked me at first." She moved a hand, hesitatingly, within reach of his own. But he ignored it. "Aren't we going to see each other at Shanghai? Are you just going to be brutal with me—like this?.... I'd like to see you."

"Will you take them off," said he, "or must I?"

She turned to him, with curiously mixed passions coming to life in her face.

"Oh, my God, Rocky!" she cried very low, "haven't you any human feelings? Can you just come in here—into my own room—and rob me, without a decent word?.... Haven't I played fair with you? Haven't I kept out of your way? Haven't I?...." She moved close against him, slid her sensitively thin hands over his shoulders; looked straight up into his eyes, almost honestly. "Rocky, don't tell me you're this kind!".... She was clinging to him now.

He caught her hands, and, without roughness but with his young strength, removed them. She let them fall at her side.

"I'm not going to wait much longer on you," he said.

"You're hard as nails, Rocky." Her underlip was quivering; her pale eyes were a little darker, and seemed full of feeling. She turned suddenly to the rough bed, and reached under the cover for her shopping bag. Hiding it from him with her body, she opened it and took out the triangular bottle; then lingered an instant to look at the clasps of the pearl cape that were set with large, perfectly cut diamonds. There were five of the clasps, and perhaps fifty of the sparkling, glittering stones. In value they would vary somewhat-: but in themselves, even without the pearls, they represented a fortune. She quietly closed the bag and replaced it under the covers.

With the rough-edged little bottle in her hand she faced him.

"I knew a girl," she said, with a far-away look in her eyes, "who took five of these tablets and then lived two days. She suffered terribly, of...."

He caught the bottle from her hand and threw it against the wall, where it broke. The green pills rolled about the floor.

"Oh, well," she remarked—"I can take them after you've gone."

"After I've gone you can do as you think best."

"But something will have to be done about me. Rocky. You'll have to get me ashore. And see about burying me.... And you'll have to explain me."

This moved him not at all. Apparently he *was* to be one of the Kanes—strong, pitiless, destined for success and power. There would be weak moments; but all that her uncannily shrewd eyes saw in him. For that matter, Miss Carmichael had known many men of the sort that in America are termed "big"—certain of them with an unpleasant secret intimacy—and each had possessed and (at moments) been possessed by strong passions.

It had never been wholly a matter of what is called brain; always there had been emotional force, with a dark side as well as a bright.

Overhead the great clumsy sails creaked. Soft feet pattered about the deck. The nasal voices of the crew broke into a chantey. A chain rattled.

"We must be there," said she. "We're anchoring, I think." And she glanced out the window at one of the roofed-over opium hulks that lay in those days directly opposite the bund. Finally she looked again at him.

"Very well," she said then; and raised her arms above her head. Swiftly, at once, he began stripping off the festoons of pearls. The only other thing said was her remark, in a casual tone: "It's understood that you're using force. And you'll hear from it, of course."

As soon as he had gone she slipped into her blouse and skirt. Once again she looked thoughtfully at the radiant gems that were left to her; then went, coolly swinging the little bag, up on deck, where certain of the crew were already drawing around to the ladder at the side the sampan that had been towing astern.

Rocky had gone directly, on tiptoe, to Doane's cabin. The huge sad-faced man was there; quick, however, with a kindly smile.

Rocky said—"I beg your pardon, sir?"—stiffly, not unlike a proud young Briton—and from a tied-up handkerchief and bulging pockets—even from his shirt above his tightly drawn belt—produced enormous quantities of perfectly matched large pearls; laid them on the bed in a heap; helped Mr. Doane make a bundle of them in a square of blue cloth.

"They are yours, sir," he explained.

He withdrew then, with a coldness of manner that to the older man was moving; and went out on deck to await his turn in the sampan.

Doane found a temporary home for Hui Fei and her sister at the mission compound of his friend, Doctor Henry Withery, in the Chinese city; himself lodging with other friends. Rocky went to the Astor House, across Soochow Creek, which was still, in 1911, a famous stopping place for the tourists, diplomats, military and commercial men, and all the other more prosperous among the white travelers that pour into Shanghai from everywhere else in the world by the great ships that plow unceasingly the Pacific and Indian Oceans and the Yellow and China Seas; to pour out again (in peaceful times) from Shanghai by rail and by lesser craft of the river and the coast to Hong Kong and Manila to Hankow, to Tientsin and Peking, to Nagasaki, Kobe, Yokohoma and Tokio.... and Shanghai had never been so crowded as now, with its thousands of travelers detained, awaiting news from this or that revolutionary center; with the American Marines and the British and German sailors; with Manchu refugees swarming into the foreign settlements; with revolutionists, queueless, wearing unaccustomed European dress, parading everywhere.

Doane found time to call at the hotel and leave word regarding the burial of his excellency; but was not to know that Rocky, himself, immured in his room, gave the word that he was out and there awaited the friendly chit that Doane sent up by the blue-robed servant. Nor was he to know that the boy dressed carefully for the ceremony, only to find the ordeal too great for his overstrung emotions. It was as an afterthought, a day or two later that Doane sent him Hui Fei's address.

It was after this sad experience that Doane, in accordance with his promise to the late Sun Shi-pi, called on Doctor Wu Ting Fang and offered his services to the revolutionary party. Another day and he was hard at work, bending his strong, finely trained and experienced mind to the great task of presenting the dreams and the activities of Young China fairly and sympathetically to the press and the governments of the Western World.... And so Griggsbv Doane, concealing—at moments almost from his own inner eye—the ache in his heart, the unutterable loneliness of his solitary existence, found himself once more fitting into the scheme of organized human life. A grave man, with sad eyes but with a slow kindly smile, always courteously attentive to the person and problem of the moment, thinking always clearly and objectively out of a comprehensively tolerant background that seemed to include all nations and all men; a gently tactful man; a tireless, powerful figure of a man, who could work twenty hours on end without a trace of fatigue, going through masses of minor detail without for a moment losing his broad view of the major problems—such was the Griggsby Doane one saw at revolutionary headquarters during that late autumn of 1911.... Life had caught him up. Whatever his private sorrow, the world needed him now. Rapidly, in all that confusion, he was formulating policies, helping to direct the current of one stream of destiny. In past years Griggsby Doane had been discussed and forgotten. He had even been laughed at as an unfrocked missionary by ribald, dominant, not infrequently drunken whites along the coast. It occurred to no one to laugh at him now.

These were the days when in half the provincial capitals of China the Manchus that had ruled during nearly three centuries were hunted to their death, men and women alike, like vermin. Bloody heads decorated the lamp posts that had been erected in the Western fashion beside freshly macadamized streets. Slaughter, as in other dramatic moments in Oriental history, had become a pastime. Palaces and wealthy homes in a hundred cities were looted and burned, and a vast new traffic started up in the silks and paintings and pottery and objects of art suddenly thrown into the market.... Hankow had been taken by the imperial troops, but was to be recaptured as a charred, gutted ruin. General Li Yuan-hung was now "president of the Republic of China," up at Wu Chang, by right of military organization and popular acclaim. Admiral Sah, of the Imperial Navy, was about to witness the unanimous mutiny of his fleet. The great Yuan Shi-K'ai, himself a Chinese born, was in command of the imperial troops while negotiating on either hand with the frantic throne and the upsurging revolutionists. At Peking heads were falling and great princes were fleeing or hiding pitifully within the walls of the legations.... Within a few weeks Sun Yat Sen was to leave London on his long journey eastward by way of Suez and Singapore, but without the enormous golden treasure so confidently expected by the revolutionists. Before his arrival, even, he was to be elected president of the new China, in the recently captured Nanking—where a National Assembly in cropped heads and frock coats already would be grinding out fresh tangles of legislation.... The event was outrunning the mental capacity of man. What was now tragic confusion would grow through the swift-following years into tragic chaos, as the most numerous and most nearly inert of peoples struggled out of the sluggish habit of centuries toward the dubious light of modernity.

But through the chaos Griggsby Doane was never for a moment to lose the new vision that had finally cleared his long troubled mind. Behind the crumbling of the empire, underlying the torn and bleeding surface of Chinese life, lay a tradition finer, he was to believe until his dying day, than any so far developed in the truculent West—a delicate responsiveness to beauty in nature and art, a reflective quality, an instinct for peace—it was all these at once, and more; a blend of art in living and living in art; a finish that was exquisite in concept, a sensitiveness that lifted the soul of man above the ugly fact. Even the brittle perfection of Chinese etiquette—regulating every passing human contact, clothing in silken manner the naked thought—was like a fine lacquer over the knotted wood of life... America, he felt, with all its earnestly insistent young virtues, worshiped the fact. To the Americans must be preached the gospel of sensitive thought, of reflective enjoyment of the beautiful. Those old master painters of Tang and Sung breathed beauty; it was sweet air in their lungs; whereas in America beauty was too often like a garment to be bought in a shop and worn for show.... Yes, this revolutionary work was a gratifying opportunity for service, of great momentary importance because the Chinese people must be rescued from Manchu conquerors and their eunuchs, from disease and famine, and from ignorance of the new world that had come amazingly, brutally, into being while the old Middle Kingdom slumbered; but it was not the main work. The aggressively greedy West, now, with its merchants and warships and armies, was destroying the soul of China even while teaching her a smattering of the materialistic new faith. There must be a counter-influence; as the East now so strongly felt the West, so must be the West made sensitively aware of the East. It was fair give and take. It might yet help the world to find a stable balance.... This was what the difficult life of Griggsby Doane was coming to mean. The East had crept into his heart. So he must turn back to the West.

For three days Mr. Doane's brief chit—with the address of Hui Fei in the native city—burned in Rocky Kane's pocket; then, early in the third afternoon, he went down to the Japanese steamship offices (for the keen little brown people had already captured the Pacific traffic from the Americans) and bought the second officer's room on a crowded liner leaving at the end of the week for San Francisco.... On the fourth afternoon he called a rickshaw and rode out beyond the American post-office to the address the older man had given him.

But Mr. Doane, it appeared, was not in; already he was established at Doctor Wu's revolutionary headquarters. Rocky considered driving there; even took the address and rode part of the way: but reconsidered, returned to the hotel, and sent a messenger to Hui Fei with this chit:

"I'm sailing Saturday. Do you feel that you could see me for a few moments?"

The reply, within the hour, bade him come. He found her in Western dress—-a tailored suit, very simple; her glistening black hair parted smoothly—as he would always most vividly remember it—gently sad in manner, yet able to smile. She would be like that, come to think of it; not crushed by the tragedy, not sunken in the grief that, among Westerners, is so often a sort of histrionic egotism.... They sat in a tiled courtyard among dahlias. More than ever like a proud young Briton was Rocky.

"It is good of you to see me." Thus he began.... "I couldn't go without a word."

She murmured then: "Of course not."

"I want you to know, too, that I am coming to see"—he had to pause; in this new phase of sober young manhood he had not yet achieved steady self-control.

She broke the silence with a question about the revolution. It is to his credit that he talked, stumbling only at first, clearly. And as the strain of the meeting gradually relaxed, he became aware of her sobered but still intense absorption in the struggle; aware, too, increasingly, of her strong gift of what is called personality. Her mind was quick, bright, eager—better, it seemed (he had to fight bitterness here) than his own. And she was impersonal to a degree that he couldn't yet attain—couldn't, in fact, quite understand. He had to speak slowly and carefully; feeling his way with a dogged determination among uprushing emotions, moved as never before by the charm of appearance and manner and speech of which she was so prettily unconscious.... He had come—perhaps with more than a touch in him of (again) that Western histrionism, the intense overstressing of the individual and his feelings—as a man who was effacing himself that the woman he loved might be happy with another man. Confused with this wholly unconscious call upon the sympathies, undoubtedly, was an unphrased incredulity that she—so strongly a person, fine and courageous and outstanding as he knew her to be—could accept this being almost casually left as part of a legacy to that other man. It was incredible. Unless she loved the other man.... So he came around again to the personal; unaware, of course, that he was feeling inevitably with his strongly individualistic race. Even when she dwelt on race, a little later in their talk, he found no light. He couldn't have; for the American seldom can see what lies outside himself.

"I don' know yet what I can do," she was saying, very honestly and simply (they hadn't yet mentioned Mr. Doane). "Of course I'm a Manchu, after all. An' blood does coun'. I feel that. A good many people to-day talk differen'ly, I know. We saw a good 'eal of Socialism at college. The idealists to-day—the Jews an' Russians an' even some of our Chinese students—the younger men—talk as if race doesn' matter. But of course it does. It will ta' thousan's of years, I suppose, to bring the races together. An' maybe it's impossible. Maybe it can' be done at all. I think tha's the tragedy of so much of this beautiful dreaming.... An' here you see I'm a Manchu, an' yet I wan' the Manchus put out of China. Because they won' let China grow. An' China mus' grow, or die."

He was moodily watching her; head bowed a little, gazing out under knit brows. "Do you know," he said, "it's a queer thing to say, of course, but sometimes you make me feel terribly young."

She smiled faintly. "You are—rather young, Rocky."

He closed his eyes and compressed his lips; his name, on her lips, was dangerously thrilling music to him. After a moment he went doggedly on.

"The crowds I've gone with at home haven't talked about these things. They wouldn't think it good form."

"I know," said she. "They woul'n'."

"I'm beginning to wonder if we're—well, intelligent, exactly. You know—just motors and horses and girls and bridge and 'killings' in Wall Street."

"Killings?" Her brows were lifted.

"Oh—picking up a lot of money, quick."

"That," she mused, "is what I sometimes worry about. You know, I love America. I have foun' happiness there. I love the books an' the colleges and the freedom an' all the goo' times. But it is true, I think—money is God in America. Pipple don' like to have you say it, of course. But I'm afraid it is true. Ever'-thing has to come to money—the gover'men', the churches, ever'thing. I have seen that. That is the hard side of America. I don' like that so well." Finally—coming down, helplessly, on the personal, yet with a courageous light in his eyes—he said: "I do want you to know this—Hui. You won't mind my speaking of my love for you—"

Her hand moved a very little way upward. "Please! I can't help that. It's my life now. I'm full of you. And it has changed me. I'm—I'm going back.... I'm going at things differently. I want you to know that. Because if I hadn't met you it couldn't possibly have happened. And if I hadn't—well, learned what it means to love a wonderful girl like you. I want you to know how big the change is that you've made."

"Rocky," she said gently—"will you do something for me?" He waited...."I wan' you to go back to college."

"I've already made up my mind to that," he replied, more quietly. "It's the job for me now. It's the next thing."

"I'm glad," said she. "An' I'd love it if you'd write to me sometimes."

He inclined his head.

Then, for a moment, his old turbulent inner self unexpectedly (even to himself), lifted its head.

"I tried to see Mr. Doane—that is, I thought perhaps I ought to tell him that I was coming out here."

She seemed slightly puzzled at this. Her lips framed questioningly the words: "Tell him?"

"I—I perhaps can't say much—but I'm sure you and he will be happy. I—oh, he's a big man. He's terribly busy now, of course—you know what he's doing—at Wu Ting Fang's headquarters?"

She inclined her head rather wearily, saying: "He wrote me a ver' kin note—jus' to say that he was busy."

"They talk about him some at the hotel. All of a sudden he seems to be a power here."

She went without a further word into the house, returning with a slip of paper. Into her manner had crept at the mention of Doane's name, a gentler, more wistful quality that she seemed not to think of concealing; it was even a confiding quality, intimately friendly.

"I don' quite un'erstand it," she said. "A gen'leman called from the Hong Kong Bank an' lef' this."

Rocky read the paper; a receipt for a sealed parcel of pearls and for other separate jewels and a sum of money.

"Oh—he put it all there in your name," said he, while a sudden new hope rose into his drying throat and throbbed in his temples.

"Yes. It puzzle' me—a little."

He turned the paper over and over in his fingers, once again struggling to think.... She sat motionless, gazing at the dahlias.

Blindly then he groped for her hands, found them and impulsively gripped them.

"Hui"—he whispered huskily—"tell me—if it's like this—if you—if he.... All this time I've supposed you and he were.... I want you to come with me to America. We both do love it there. I'll give up my life to making you happy. I'll slave for you. I'll make of my life what you say. just let us try it together...."

She silently heard him out—through this and much more, leaving her hands quietly in his. Finally then, when the emotional gust seemed in some measure to have spent itself, she said, gently:

"Rocky, I wan' you to listen to what I'm going to tell you. You said I make you feel young. Well—can' you see why? Can' you see that I'm quite an ol' lady?"

"But that's nonsense! You—" His eyes were feasting on her soft skin and on the exquisite curve of her cheek.

"No—you mus' listen! First tel me how old you are."

Unexpectedly on the defensive, Rocky had to compose himself, arrange his dignity, before he could reply. "I was twenty-one in the summer."

"Ver' good. An' I was twenty-five in the spring."

"But—"

"Please! I don' know what you coul' have thought—how young you thought I was when I wen' to college. But tha's the way it is. I'm an ol' lady. I have learn' to like you ver' much. I'm fond of you. I wan' to feel always tha' we're frien's. But we coul'n' be happy together. Our interes' aren' the same—they coul'n' be. Can' you see, Rocky? If there is something abou' me tha' stirs you—that is ver' won'erful. But we mus'n' let it hurt you. An' that isn' the same as marriage. Marriage is differen'—there mus' be so much in common—if a man an' woman are to live together an' work together, they mus' think an' hope an'...."

Her voice died out. She was gazing again, mournfully at the dahlias. When he released her hands they lay limp in her lap.

With a great effort of will he wished her every happiness, promised to write, and got himself away.

This was on Thursday. Rocky walked at a feverish pace from the native city to the European settlement that was so quaintly not Chinese—more, with its Western-style buildings that were decorated with ornamental iron balconies and richly colored Chinese signs, like a "China-town" in an American city—and wandered for a time along Nanking Road; then out to Bubbling Well Road; away out, past the Country Club to the almost absurdly suburban quarter with its comfortably British villas; seeing, however, little of the busy life that moved about him, threading his way over cross-streets without a conscious glance at the motorcars and pony-drawn victorias (with turbanned mafoos cracking their whips) and bicycles and the creaking passenger wheelbarrow's on which fat native women with tiny stumps of feet rode precariously. For those few hours were to be recalled in later years as the quietly darkest in the young man's life. There was no question now of dissipation; he knew with the decisiveness of the Kanes that he had turned definitely away from the morbid oblivion of alcohol and opium, as from the unhealthy if exciting diversion of loveless women. But the bitterness would not down all at once. Indeed it was savagely powerful, still, to cloud his reason. The only evidence of victory over self of which he was aware was the fact that he could now look almost objectively at himself, and could fight.

He was back at the hotel between seven and eight, but couldn't eat. For an hour he walked his room, locked in. Then, in sheer loneliness, a little afraid of himself, he went down to the spacious lounge and sat in a corner, behind a palm, staring at a copy of the *China Press* and listening, all overstrung nerves, to the cackle and laughter of the self-centered tourists and the curiously bold and loud commercial men from across the Pacific. He heard this, in his younger way, as Doane would have heard it, even as Hui;

it was all heedless, light-brained; careless.... Confused with the bitterness (in a bewildering degree) was a sense of the finely reflective atmosphere that had lately enveloped him and that he was not to lose easily. He felt—sitting, all nerves, in this babel—the fine old Chinese gentleman who had gone serenely to the death that was his destiny. He felt—constantly, intensely— the princess who had brought to her American college an instinct for culture the like of which neither he nor any of his friends at home had brought or found there. And he felt Mr. Doane—felt a spaciousness of mind in the man, a patience, a tolerance—felt him as a gentleman—felt him while still, in his heart, he was bitterly fighting him.... The thing had closed over his head—the sheer quality of these remarkable folk. He was simply out of a cruder world. He hadn't the right to stand with them—the simple right of character and breeding. And no amount of determination, no amount of storming at it could alter the fact. It would take years of patient work. Ever, then he might miss it; for his environment soon again would be that of the cackling tourists he now hated. Even at college it would be all the dominant athletics, the parties and the motors and girls and drinking, the association with those sons of prosperous families who were all consciously cementing alliances with the financial upper class that quietly ruled America while hired politicians prated and performed without in the smallest measure controlling or even altering the blatant facts.... He and his kind, at college, despised the "grind." And you had to be a grind if you weren't the other thing. Yet Hui Pei had managed it differently. She was neither and both. It seemed to be a difference of mental texture....

A slim girl, richly dressed, with a sable wrap about her shoulders and a pretty little hat, was threading her way among the crowding chairs and tables and the talkative groups in the lounge. He glanced up: then looked closely. It was Dixie Carmichael. She stood before him, wearing her icy, faintly mocking smile. He rose.

"How are you?" said she.

He could only incline his head with a sort of courtesy, and contrive an artificial smile. He seemed to have been dreaming, outrageously. Life had begun now'.

"I'm running down to Singapore," said she. "Friends there. And a look-see?"

"Oh," he murmured, "indeed." She looked out-and-out rich; and she was surprisingly pretty, without a sign that she had ever known danger or even care.

"Staying here?" she asked.

"No. I start back home Saturday."

"So?.... Well, that'll be pleasant." With a final glance of what seemed almost like triumph she sailed away. And he knew that in taking the pearls he had not taken all from her. Apparently, too, she meant him to know it. That would be her moment of triumph. And that was all; not a word was spoken regarding his violence or her threats.... He saw the yellow porters carrying out her luggage of bright new leather.

He resumed his seat; twitched for a time with increasing nervousness; got up and went aimlessly over to the desk; asked the Malay clerk for mail.

A smiling little Japanese appeared, rather officious about a great lot of bags and a trunk or two that were coming in. He had a familiar look; even raised his hat and stepped forward with outstretched hand. It was Kato.... And then Dawley Kane came in—tall, quiet, neatly dressed, his nearly white mustache newly cropped.

To his pale son Dawley Kane said merely—"Well!"—as he took his hand; and then was busy registering. That done, he asked: "Had dinner?" Rocky shook his head. "I don't care for any." Daw ley Kane's quietly keen eyes surveyed his son. "What's the matter? Not well."

"I'm well enough."

"Sit down with me, can't you?" And turning to the attending Japanese he said: "You'll excuse me Kato. I'll be dining with my son. And tell Mr. Braker, please.... Just a minute Rocky, till I wash my hands."

They were shown to a table in the great diningroom, where the cackling was louder than in the lounge (they dine late on the coast)—where blue-gowned waiters moved softly about as if there had never been a revolution and wine glasses glistened and prettily bared shoulders gleamed roundly under the electric lights.

And Rocky, seated gloomily opposite this powerful quiet man—who took him unerringly in of course; dishearteningly, Rocky felt—found himself in a depression deeper than any he had known before. His father was so strong and he brought back with him the enveloping atmosphere of the mighty, splendidly successful white world in which they both belonged—a world that crushed the heart out of weaker peoples while it blandly talked the moralities. He felt it as a Juggernaut. It had the amazingly successful racial blend of character and plausibility. That would be the British quality; and, more roughly and confusedly, the American.

"Getting rather interesting up the river." remarked Dawley Kane, over his soup. "How'd you get down?"

"On a junk."

"Any trouble?"

"Oh—some."

"Been here long?"

"Several days. I'm sailing Saturday."

"Sailing?" Mr. Kane raised his eyebrows. "Where?"

"Home."

"You decided not to consult me?"

"Oh.... Don't ride me, father! It's the next thing. I'm going back to college."

"Oh—I see." Mr. Kane looked over the menu, ordered his roast, and selected a red wine, cautioning the waiter to set it near the stove for five minutes. "It's wicked to heat Burgundy," he said, when the waiter had gone, "but it's the only way you can get it served at the right temperature. I discovered that when we were here before.... I gather, my boy, that you've come to your senses in the matter of that little yellow girl."

Rocky did not wince outwardly; he merely sat still. But his mind, at last, was active. And he knew—saw it in a flash—that no explanation he could possibly make, would be intelligible. You can not—yet—talk across the gulf between the worlds. It was his first intelligent glimpse of the tremendous fact that Doane had so long and so clearly felt and seen. So he merely— at last, when his father looked closely at him—inclined his head and said, huskily:

"I'm going to work out this college business'. That's my job clear enough."

This new attitude was to bring, later in the evening, confidences from the father.

"It's been an interesting journey for me, Rocky." Thoughtfully Dawley Kane smoked his Manila cigar.

"It's enabled me to understand somewhat the delicate international situation out here. I couldn't see why our agents weren't accomplishing more. The trouble is, of course, that every square foot of China's staked out by the European nations. If you don't believe that, just get a concession from the Chinese Government—for a big job—water power development, mining, railway building, or an industrial monopoly—that part of it isn't so hard—and then try to carry it through. You'd find out fast enough who are the real owners of China. And those owners would never let you start.

Great Britain controls this great empire of the Yangtze Valley as completely as she controls India. France owns the south—Russia the northwest and the north—Japan, from Korea and Lower Manchuria is penetrating the northwest, too; they're bound, the Japanese, to tip Russia out one of these days, and they're very clever and patient about slipping into the British regions. They've got the Germans to contend with, too, in the Kiochow region. But someday—either in the event of the final break-up of China or in the event of the European nations coming to an out-and-out squabble (which is almost a certainty, at that) Japan will be found to have pulled off most of the big prizes for herself. We'll have to fight Japan someday, I suppose—over the control of the Pacific—but in the meantime, those little people are the best bet. They know the East as the rest of us don't, they're clever, and their diplomats aren't hampered by the sort of half-enlightened public opinion that's always tripping us up in the West—sentimental idealism, that sort of thing—and they control their press infinitely better than we do. They've got everything, the Japanese, except money. And we've got the money. It'll be just a question of security, that's all; and watching them pretty closely. I've made up my mind to play it that way.... A survey of the actual conditions out here makes our American diplomacy look pretty naive. We talk idealism—open door and all—while all the rest of them are moving in and setting up shop and getting the money."

Later, in Dawley Kane's spacious suite overlooking the park-like street where the colored lanterns of the rickshaws glowed pleasantly under the trees, the father said, laying a hand affectionately on the boy's shoulder:

"I can't tell you how happy you've made me, Rocky. It looks as if you'd turned your corner. Just don't go in for too much thinking about what you've been through. There's nothing in remorse. As a matter of fact, a little rough experience is a good thing for a boy. After you get your balance you'll be all the closer to life for it.... Go ahead with your college plans, get your degree, and then after a year or two in the New York office I'll bring you out here. We shall be playing for big stakes. And we shall need good men.... That's the whole problem, really—the men. I had my eyes on this man Doane, but he turned out to be only a sentimentalist after all."

It was the hopelessness of it that drove Rocky out—after a respectful good night—and over to the revolutionary headquarters. He knew that Mr. Doane worked most of the night; and took what sleep he got on a cot there.

CHAPTER XV
IN A COURTYARD

HE sent in his name, and waited for an hour in an outer office. For even at this late hour in the evening headquarters was a busy place. Chinese gentlemen crowded in and out, dressed, to a man, in the frock coats and the flapping black trousers they didn't know how to wear. High officers slipped quietly in and out—in khaki, with the white brassard of the Revolution on their left arms; sometimes with merely a handkerchief tied there Orderlies and messengers came and went. And clerks of untiring patience sat at desks.

It was a difficult hour. Rocky had only his confused emotions to guide him, and his hurt heart. There were moments, even, when he didn't know why he had come. But he never thought of giving up. Whatever their curious relations, he had to see Mr. Doane, who was now the only stable figure in the rocking world about him. The man had been fine—square. That he knew now. And his nervous young imagination was veering toward hero-worship. He was utterly humble.

Naturally he was boyish about it, when they finally led him into that inner office. He said, flushing a little:

"I know you're busy, Mr. Doane—"

"Not too busy for you. I kept you waiting to clear up a lot of things." The man's great size and calmness of manner—the question rose; had he ever in his life known weariness?—were comforting.

"I'm—sailing Saturday."

This, for a brief moment, brought the kindly though strong and sober face to immobility.

"You see, sir, I've come to feel that the best thing for me is to go back and—-start clean."

A slight mist came over Doane's eyes. What a struggle the boy had had of it! And how splendidly he was working through!.... Thought came about the children of the rich in America... the problem of it....

"I—couldn't go without seeing you. You see, sir, it's you, I guess, that've put me on my feet. I sort of—well, I want you to know that I *am* on them. It''s been a strange experience, all round. A terrible experience, of course. It shakes you...."

"It has shaken me, too," Doane observed simply.

"I know. That is, I see all that more clearly now. I was going to speak of it—it's one of the things, but first.... Mr. Doane, will you write to me? Once in a while? I mean, will you—could you find time to answer if I write to you? You see, it isn't going to be easy, over there. I've got to go clean outside my own crowd. And outside my family. They won't one of them understand what I'm up to. Not one. And—when you come right down to it, I suppose it's a question whether the thing licks me or not. But"— his shoulders squared; he looked directly into that kind, deeply shadowed face—"I don't believe it will lick me!"

"No," said Doane, "it won't lick you."

"I shall never be able to shake China off now. It's got me. And I don't know a thing about it yet. Of course I shall be reading and studying it up."

"I'll send you a book once in a while."

"And I know I'm coming back out here someday. But it won't be as my father wants me to come. You see, I'll have money."

"A great responsibility, Rocky."

"I know. I'm beginning to see that. But—I know all this must sound pretty young to you!—but I'm afraid I shall be leaning on you sometimes—"

"Write to me at those times."

"All right. I will."

"There is an amazing health in the American people."

"Yes—that's so, of course."

"It's a curiously blundering people, of course. And there's a hard, really a Teutonic strain—that blend of practical hard-headedness, even of cruelty, with sentimentality—"

Rocky's brows came together. Mr. Doane and his father plainly didn't use that word "sentimental" in the same sense, "—it comes down to a strain of—well, something between the old Anglo-Saxonism and the modern Prussianism. It's in us—in our driving business tactics, our narrow moral intolerance, our insistence on standardizing vulgar ideas—forcing every individual into a mold—in our extraordinary glorification of the salesman. We seem to have a good deal both of the British complacency and the rough aggressiveness of the German. But the health is there—wonderfully. What America needs is beauty—not the self-conscious swarming after it of earnest and misguided suburban ladies—but a quiet sense of the thing itself. Beauty—and simplicity—and patience—and tolerance—and faith. Prosperity has for the moment wrecked faith there. Simply too much money. But you'll find health growing up everywhere. Just let yourself grow with it. You've been deeply impressed by China. But if I were you, I'd let all that take care of itself. Never mind what you may come to feel next year or ten years from now. It may be mainly China or mainly America. Just work, and let yourself grow."

At the door they clasped hands warmly. And then, finally, Rocky got to the point:

"Mr. Doane—this is what I wanted to say—I saw Hui Fei this afternoon, and—"

Doane was silent; but still gripped his hand, "—and we talked things all out. She knows I'm—knows I'm going back. And—this is it.... You don't mind my.... I think you ought to find time to go over there and see her. She seems puzzled about—I don't know quite how to say all this. You know how I've felt—feel.... Of course, the thing is to look the facts in the face. I hope I'm man enough to do that." His voice was unsteady now. "I'm not the one. I never was. She was clear about it, to-day, but... I think you ought to see her. Oh, I'm sure it isn't just her father's will...."

Rocky found himself, without the slightest sense of ungentleness on the part of Mr. Doane, through the door and confusedly saying his good-by before the patient clerks and the waiting crowd in the anteroom. He walked back to the hotel with a warm glow of admiration and friendship in his heart. There would be—he knew, even then—sad hours, probably bitter hours, in the long struggle to come. But this talk was going to help.

On Doane the boy's announcement had an almost crushing effect. His spirit was not adjusted to happiness. The terrific strain of the work was a blessing. He framed, that night and during the following day, innumerable little chits to Hui Fei—pretexts, all, for a visit that needed no pretext. And the day passed. Self-consciousness was upon him; and a constant mental difficulty in making the situation credible. And there was the pressure of time; an awareness that to Hui Fei—perhaps even to the Witherys—his silence would soon demand a stronger explanation than the mere pressure of business. He had to keep reminding himself that the girl was helpless, that he himself was the only guardian whose authority she could recognize; his reason whispering from moment to moment that she would not touch the money he had so promptly put at her disposal. No, she would wait.

It was his old friend Henry Withery who brought him to it; appearing late on the Saturday afternoon, determined to drag him off for dinner.... Withery, looking every one of his forty-eight years, patient resignation in the dusty blue eyes, and a fine net of wrinkles about them. His slight limp was the only reminder of tortures inflicted by the Boxers in 1900, out in Kansuh. He had taken over the T'ainan-fu mission for a year after Doane left the church in 1907; and during two years now had been here in Shanghai.

"There's no good killing yourself here, Grig," he said. "We've not had ten minutes with you yet, remember. And we must talk over that girl's affairs. She's very sweet about it, but it's plain that she's waiting on you."

His tone was genial; quite the tone of their earlier friendship, with nothing left of the constraint that had come into their relationship during Doane's difficult years on the river—the years that couldn't be explained, even to old friends.... And Withery knew nothing of the curious personal problem of his and Hui Fei's lives. His manner made that clear.... It remained to be seen whether Mrs. Withery knew.

.... Doane, it will be noted, was still struggling, as of settled habit, with the thought of freeing the girl from the obligation laid upon her.

But Mrs. Withery didn't know, didn't dream. She was quite her whole-souled self. He might have been Hui Fei's father, from anything in her manner. He felt a conspirator.

Her father's tragic end accounted altogether for the girl's silence. She met him naturally, though, with a frank grip of the hand.

It was a pleasant enough family dinner. They talked the revolution, of course. No one in Shanghai at the beginning of that November talked anything else. Hui Fei quietly listened; her face very sober in repose. She seemed—she had always seemed—more delicately feminine in Western costume. She was more slender now; her face a perfect oval under the smooth, deep-shadowed hair. Her dark eyes, deep with stoically controlled feeling, rested on this or that speaker. Doane found them once or twice resting thoughtfully on himself.

After dinner Mrs. Withery, with a glance at her husband, laid a sympathetic hand on Hui's shoulder.

"My dear," she said, all friendly sympathy, "Mr. Doane's time is precious, these days and nights. I know that you should take this opportunity to talk over your problems with him. I shall be bustling about here—suppose you take him out into the courtyard."

Without a word they walked out there; stood by a gnarled tree whose twisted limbs extended over the low tiled roofs. There was a little light from the windows. The long silence that followed was the most difficult moment yet. Doane found himself breathing rather hard. In Hui Fei he felt the calm Oriental patience that underlay all her Western experiences. She simply waited for him to speak.

He looked down at her, quite holding his breath. She seemed almost frail out here, in the half light. He was fighting, with all his strength and experience, the warm sweet feelings that drugged his brain.

"My dear—" he began; then, when she looked frankly up at him, hesitated. He hadn't known he was going to begin with any such phrase as that. He got on with it...."I'm wondering how I can best help you. If I were a younger man there would be no question as to what I would have to say to you." Utterly clumsy, of course; with little light ahead; just a dogged determination to serve her without hurting her.

"I think a good 'eal of wha' they tell me you're doing"—thus Hui Fei, in a low but clear voice; not looking up now. "I've almos' envied you. Helping li' that."

"It must be hard for you—with all your mental interests—to sit quietly here."

"My min' goes on, of course," she said. "Yes, it isn' ver' easy."

This was getting them nowhere. Doane, after a deep breath, took command of the situation. Sooner or later he would have to do that.

"Hui, dear," he said now—very quietly, but directly, "this is a difficult situation for both of us. The only thing, of course, is to meet it as frankly as we can. I learned to love your father—"

She glanced up at this; her eyes glistened as the light caught them.

"—but we can not blindly follow his wishes. He had seen and felt the West, but he died a Manchu."

Her soft lips framed the one word, "Yes." The softness of her whole face, indeed, was disconcerting; it was all sober emotion, that she plainly didn't think of trying to hide.

"And I'm sure you'll understand me when I tell you that I can not accept his legacy."

She startled him now with the low but direct question: "Why not?"

"My dear...." He found difficulty in going on.

"I don' know what I ought 'o say." He barely heard this; stopped a little. "I don' know wha' to do."

"Can't you, dear—isn't there some clear vision in your heart—don't you see your way ahead? Remember, you will always have me to help—if I can help. It will mean everything to me to be your dearest friend."

"I want 'o work with you," she murmured.

"I haven't dared believe that possible," he said thoughtfully.

"Do you wan' me to?"

"Yes. But it has to be clearer than that." He was stupid again; he sensed it himself. "There is so much of life ahead of you. It's got to be clear that wherever your heart may lead you, child—that you shall have my steady friendship. The rest of it can grow as it may."

"I wan'...." He couldn't make out the words; he bent down close to her lovely face. "I want 'o marry you."

They both stood breathless then. Timidly her hand crept into his and nestled there.

"Tha's the trouble"—her voice was a very little stronger—"there isn' anything else. It's ever'thing you think an' do—ever'thing you believe. We're both between the worl's, so...."

The noise in his brain was like the pealing of cathedral bells at Christmas time. Yet in this rush of ecstatic feeling he suddenly saw clearly. The fabric of their companionship had hardly begun weaving. All his experience, his delicacy, his fine human skill, must be employed here. Ahead lay happiness! It was still nearly incredible.... And there lay—extending before them in a long vista—their intense common interest. The thing was to make a fine success of it. Build through the years.

And happiness was greatly important. He had so nearly missed it.... Looking up through the branches of the old tree, he smiled.

Then he led her into the house.

"Have you had your talk already?" asked Mrs. Withery pleasantly.

"We've settled everything," said Doane. "We're going to be married."

"Very soon," said Hui Fei.